D0102700

THE LAST CUENTISTA

THE LAST CUENTISTA

Donna Barba Higuera

LQ

LEVINE QUERIDO

MONTCLAIR · AMSTERDAM · HOBOKEN

This is an Arthur A. Levine book
Published by Levine Querido

www.levinequerido.com • info@levinequerido.com
Levine Querido is distributed by Chronicle Books LLC

Library of Congress Control Number: 2021932056

ISBN 978-1-64614-089-3

Printed and bound in China

MIX
Paper from responsible sources
FSC™ C144853

Published August 2021

FOURTH PRINTING

For Dad:

From the very first bedtime stories to our daily chats,

thank you for a lifetime of stories.

THE LAST CUENTISTA

I

LITA TOSSES ANOTHER PIÑON LOG ONTO THE FIRE. Sweet smoke drifts past us into the starry sky. Her knees crack as she sits back down on the blanket next to me. The cup of hot chocolate with cinnamon she's made me sits untouched this time.

"I have something I want you to take with you on your trip, Petra." Lita reaches into her sweater pocket. "Since I won't be there for your thirteenth birthday . . ." She holds out a silver pendant in the shape of a sun. Its center is filled with a flat black stone. "If you hold it up to the sun, its light glows through the obsidian."

I take it from her hand and hold it up, but there's no sun. Only the moon. Sometimes I try to imagine I can see things I really can't. But I'm sure a faint glow filters through the middle of the stone. I move the pendant back and forth. It disappears completely when I move it too far from the center of my vision.

When I look back, Lita is motioning to an identical pendant around her neck. "You know," she says, "Yucatecos believe obsidian holds magic. A doorway to bring lost ones together." She purses her lips. Her brown skin wrinkles toward her nose like cracked bark on a tree.

"They shouldn't force me to go," I say.

"You have to, Petra." Lita looks away for a long time before speaking again. "Children are not meant to be separated from their parents."

"You're Dad's parent. He should stay with you then. We all should." Even as I say it, I know I sound like a little kid.

She laughs a deep, soft chuckle. "I'm too old to travel so far. But for you . . . Dios mío, a new planet! How exciting."

My chin trembles and I bury my head into her side, squeezing her around the waist.

"I don't want to leave you."

Her stomach lowers with a deep sigh. Somewhere off in the desert behind Lita's house, a coyote howls, calling for its friends.

As if on cue, the chickens cluck, and one of her fainting goats bleats.

"You need a cuento," she says, referring to one of her tall tales.

We lie back looking up at the night sky. The warm desert wind blows over us as Lita pulls me into the tightest hug ever. I never want to leave this spot.

She points up at Halley's Comet. From here, it doesn't look so dangerous.

"Había una vez," she begins her story, "a young fire snake nagual. His mother was Earth, his father the sun."

"A nagual snake?" I ask. "But how can the sun and Earth be parents to something part human, part animal—"

"*Sssh.* This is my story." She clears her throat and takes one of my hands in hers. "Fire Snake was angry. His mother, Earth, fed and nurtured him, but his father, the sun, stayed away. His father would bring crops, but he also brought great drought and death. One very hot day as Sun loomed over the nagual," Lita waves her arm toward the heavens, "he challenged his father. Even though his mother begged him to stay with her forever, the young Fire Snake sped off toward his father."

Lita remains silent for a moment. I know the stall is part of her strategy to keep me in suspense. It works.

"Then what?"

She smiles and continues. "With his tail flaming behind him, Fire Snake gained speed until he could not slow himself.

But as he approached his father, Sun, he realized his mistake. His father's flames were far more powerful and stronger than anything else in this universe. The nagual looped around his father, speeding back toward his home, but it was all too late. His father's fire had burned his eyes, so he could no longer see." Lita clicks her tongue. "Pobrecito, blinded and moving so fast he could never slow down. Never able to find his mother." She sighs. Now comes the part in all her stories where her voice becomes lighter, like she's casually giving directions to the corner panadería. "So, every seventy-five years, he retraces the journey, hoping to reunite with her." She points again at the fire snake. "Close enough to sense his mother, but never to embrace."

"Except this time," I say, heat running up my back.

"Yes," she answers, pulling me closer. "In a few days, the fire snake will finally find his mother. Y colorín Colorado, este cuento se ha acabado," she says, ending her cuento.

I rub her hand over and over, memorizing her wrinkles. "Who told you that story? Your grandma?"

Lita shrugs. "She told me bits. I might have made most of it up."

"I'm scared, Lita," I whisper.

She pats my arm. "But for a moment, did you forget your troubles?"

I don't answer out of shame. Her story *had* made me forget. Forget about what could happen to her and everyone else.

"Don't you be afraid," she says. "I'm not. It's only the nagual coming home."

I glance up at Fire Snake in silence. "I'm going to be just like you, Lita. A storyteller."

She sits up, legs crossed, facing me. "A storyteller, yes. It's in your blood." She leans in. "But just like me? No, mija. You need to discover who you are and be that."

"What if I ruin your stories?" I ask.

Lita cups my chin in her soft, brown hand. "You can't ruin them. They've traveled hundreds of years, and through many people to find you. Now, go make them your own."

I think of Lita and her mother, and her mother's mother. How much they knew. Who am I to follow them?

I clutch the pendant in my hand. "I'll never lose your stories, Lita."

"You know, the planet you are going to will have a sun or two also." She taps her pendant with her fingernail. "Look for me when you arrive?"

My lower lip quivers, and tears fall down my face. "I can't believe we're leaving you."

She wipes a tear from my cheek. "It's impossible for you to leave me. I'm part of you. You're taking me and my stories to a new planet and hundreds of years into the future. How lucky I am."

I kiss her cheek. "I promise to make you proud."

Gripping my obsidian pendant, I wonder if Lita will watch the fire snake through the smoky glass, when he finally reunites with his mother.

2

THE SHUTTLE FROM SANTA FE TO THE LAUNCH SITE IN the San Juan National Forest near Durango takes less than two hours. A half hour of that time was filled with a speech from Dad, explaining to Javier and me how we needed to stop squabbling, be kind, and work hard.

It seemed weird to me that the government specifically chose the Colorado forest instead of a military base. But when I see the secluded roads and kilometers of dense forest, I understand. Even three massive interstellar colonization ships meant for the exodus off Earth could get lost out here.

Pleiades Corp designed these luxury vessels to take rich people across the galaxy in comfort. I'd seen their megascreen advertisements along hoverways showing a ship's five-star hotel interior. Chandeliers with Pleiades Corp's signature color, royal purple, illuminating the faces of actors in fancy clothes, holding martini glasses and smiling as they stared out at a fake nebula. A man with a voice like he gargled avocado oil each morning speaking over tinkling piano music: "Pleiades Corporation. Reimagining what you thought interstellar travel would be. Luxury living among the stars, reserved for the adventurous elite."

I think of what the ships are now. Those people on the megascreen with the bleach-toothed smiles were nothing like us: scientists, terra-formers, and leaders the government thought deserved to live more than others. And how did my family make the cutoff? How did those government politicians choose? What if Mom and Dad had been older? How many of those politicians got a fast pass?

It feels wrong to be sneaking off Earth while so many are left behind. They don't even inform my parents of our destination until the day before. Dad says Pleiades had been storing their ships in a massive underground facility at the old Denver airport—they weren't supposed to leave Earth on their first official trip for another two years. The maiden test flights into nearby space a few months earlier had been successful, but because we're now leaving so suddenly, this will be the first interstellar journey.

If a solar flare hadn't shifted the comet off course a week earlier, we'd be watching Fire Snake harmlessly pass Earth in a few days like it had since the beginning of time.

The departure facility isn't more than an old, converted ranger station beyond some gates to the National Park. I try not to think about what I saw at the front entrance. From the station we're instructed to take a trail into the forest with other passengers. More families gather just behind ours, waiting for their turn to hike to the ship. The grove of aspen and pine trees filter the sunlight like the *Jonah and the Whale* stained glass panel at church. I jump at the outburst of baby bird chirps above our heads. I look up to see a mama barn swallow skitter off from her nest for more food. The babies' cheeps go quiet as soon as she leaves. The mama bird doesn't know all her work is a waste of time. I train my narrow vision on the tiny heads peeking over the edge of the nest. At first, I feel sorry for them, so small and defenseless. But then I realize, in a way, the birds are the lucky ones. They'll never know what hit them.

We continue to the ship along the path that could be any hiking trail. It's the least official final exodus off Earth you could imagine. My parents told me that chatter tracking showed too many fringe and conspiracy groups suspecting something was up out here. Turns out they were right. My little brother, Javier, skids to a stop when we emerge from the camouflage of the cedar canopy to an open field of green. A monstrous ship resembling a stainless-steel-and-crystal praying mantis comes into view.

"Petra . . . ?" He clenches my wrist.

At the opposite end of the field sits an exact replica of our ship. So far away, it looks half the size of the behemoth in front of us. With only two ships left, I know one is already gone. Dad said they lost contact when the final ping came as they approached Alpha Centauri.

"It's okay." I urge Javier on, even though I want to run back into the forest too.

I think of Lita and my teachers and my classmates, and I wonder what they're doing right now. I don't want to imagine them being so afraid they'd try to hide from something they can't hide from.

Instead, I picture Lita and Tía Berta lying under the red-and-black fringed blanket, drinking coffee with "secret sauce" as they watch the nagual snake come home.

"Berta! This isn't the time to be stingy." Lita would tip the brown glass bottle, pouring rich liquid of the same color into her coffee cup.

"I suppose you're right," Tía Berta replies. "We won't have another Christmas to keep this for." Lita will make an even bigger pour into Tía Berta's cup. They'll clink their clay mugs, take a long drink, and lean back shoulder to shoulder against Tía Berta's one-hundred-year-old pecan tree.

This is the story my mind will keep of them.

Before my parents were chosen, lots of people had already

started looting. When I asked Mom why they bothered, when all that stuff would be gone soon, her eyes filled with tears.

"People are afraid. Some will do things they never thought they were capable of. We're in no position to judge anyone."

I still don't understand how some people are so calm and others are rioting. I'm supposed to feel happy my parents were chosen to go to the new planet, Sagan. But I feel like I've been given the last glass of water on Earth and I'm just gulping it down while everyone watches.

I look up at the comet and wince. I *hate you.*

Like ants on an orderly march to our hole, my family and I walk quietly across the grass field with several scientists and one other family with a blond teenager. As we get closer, instead of the cement commercial launch pad I expect, there's just freshly cut grass.

Mom speaks quietly. "You won't even know any time has passed when we're up there. There's nothing to be nervous about." But when I look over, I catch her scrunching her eyes tight and shaking her head like that will somehow make this all go away. "And when we arrive to Sagan," she continues, "we'll start over, like on a farm. There will be others around your age."

She can't make this better. I don't want *any* new friends ever again. I even had to set Rápido loose behind Lita's house. Maybe my tortoise will somehow survive the comet's hit deep within his burrow, and live out his life without me.

"This is stupid," I mumble. "Maybe I should just tell them about my eyes so they won't let us on the ship."

Mom and Dad exchange a glance. Mom takes me by the elbow and pulls me aside. She smiles at the other family as they pass.

"What are you doing, Petra?"

I feel tears rising up. "What about Lita? It's like you don't even care."

Mom closes her eyes. "I can't tell you how hard this is for all of us." She lets out a breath and then looks at me. "I'm sorry for how this is hurting you, but this is not the time."

"When will be the time?" I say too loudly. "Hundreds of years from now when she's already gone?"

The blond boy now ahead of us glances back. His dad elbows him, and he turns back around.

"Petra, we can't know exactly what will happen." Mom glances furtively at the other family. She grabs her braid and twists its end in her hand.

"I think you're lying."

Mom glances at Dad and lays her hand on my arm. "In this moment, Petra, the world does not revolve around you. Have you thought of how others might be feeling?"

I *almost* say the world might not revolve at all anymore, but my arm vibrates. I look over and see Mom is trembling.

She points back in the direction we came. "Did you notice the people waiting outside the gates?"

I look away. I don't want to remember the woman pulling off her wedding ring and pushing her baby forward, toward the armed guard. "Please, please," she mouthed over and over as we drove right through the gates. Just like the tracking had predicted, that young family and hundreds of others had somehow figured out the government was hiding something out here.

"They'd give anything to be onboard with us." Mom leans down, her eyes boring into mine. "Do you want to leave?"

I think of the mom with her baby, and if I never saw Dad or Mom or Javier again.

"No," I answer.

A woman and a young girl approach holding hands. The girl has a silver spiraled horn jutting out the top of her head from her hoodie. As they pass, she makes an obvious head turn and stares at me suspiciously.

"Suma, *tttccch*," her mom whispers, and the girl looks away.

Mom glances in their direction, and I know she's seen them watching us too. "So, can you please keep your opinions to yourself for now?"

Mom walks ahead and marches right past Dad and Javier. Dad raises his eyebrows at me and motions with his head. And with that, I know even he's had enough. Javier runs back to me, nearly tripping on a rock on the path. He falls into me and I pull him to a stand. He takes my hand. "It's okay," he says, just like I had to him moments earlier. This time, he urges me along.

I take a deep breath as we approach the entrance ramp of the praying mantis ship. Its front end, the size of a soccer field, looms over us. Windows around the front section look like its mouth is cracked open, baring long teeth between the top of its head and bottom of its jaw. Two hind legs hinge onto the field anchoring it in place.

In the distance, tiny specks enter the belly of the other bug ship, set to leave shortly after us.

Javier points to two oval wing-like compartments at the back of our ship. "Is that where we'll be?" he asks.

Dad nods.

"It's bigger than my school," Javier whispers.

"Yep." Mom fake-smiles like she's trying to convince him we're going to Disneyland again. "Very few ships can carry so many people so far away."

"And we'll be asleep?" he asks.

"Just like a nap," Mom says.

The "nap," and what it will give us, is the only bright spot. But unlike Javier's thirty-minute catnaps, this sleep will last three hundred and eighty years.

3

I DON'T KNOW HOW I HADN'T PUT TOGETHER WHAT WAS really happening in the week before we left, when I *accidentally* overheard my parents talking.

They lowered their voices in the living room—I knew the technique. It meant that while they knew we were asleep, they weren't taking any chances at us overhearing something. I yanked off my Josefina American Girl Doll's head and splayed her dark hair over my pillow. I hadn't even played with Josefina for five years, but I kept her within arm's reach for these exact occasions.

I tiptoed out of my room and passed Javier's door. The glow from his aquarium cast enough light into the hall for me to see.

A whisper loud enough to shock Josefina to life came from his room. "Where are you going, Petra?"

His door squeaked as I hurried inside. "Nowhere. Just getting a glass of water."

He scooted over in his bed to make room. Instead of his jammies, he wore his Gen-Gyro-Gang hoodie he hadn't changed out of for three days. Ever since the Chinese geneticists recreated Wally the Wooly, and the tiny, cloned mammoth clomped out onto a world stage, every kid under the age of eight had a GGG hoodie with Wally front and center, a baby Hypacrosauras on one side, and a dodo bird on the other. Javier reached up and handed me his *Dreamers* book, a real paper version that had been my dad's when he was little. It was so old, it was written long before librex and story generators even came along.

"Not now, Javier." I slid his favorite book back in the shelf over his bed.

"Awww," he whined.

For a second, Mom and Dad's voices stopped, and I put my finger to my mouth. "We're supposed to be asleep." I leaned over to give him a goodnight kiss and cracked my pinky toe on the side of his bed. I slapped my hand over my mouth and fell into the bed next to him.

"Sorry," he whispered.

I grunted. "It's not your fault. I didn't see it." I massaged my toe. "Stupid eyes."

Javier reached out to hold my hand. "Don't worry, Petra. I will be your eyes for you."

A knot formed in my throat, and I spooned around him. I took his hand in mine and rubbed my finger over his constellation birthmark, a smattering of freckles in the crook of his thumb, our silent message only he and I know. I settled into his pillow, my head next to his, and we watched his African dwarf frog swim back and forth from the bottom to the top of the tank. With his lanky legs and webbed feet, he looked like a tomatillo with toothpicks jutting out of it. "You're feeding that frog too much."

"I named him Gordo, so it's fine," he said.

I giggled and rubbed his birthmark until his breathing deepened. From the outer spine of his *Dreamers* book, the mother's watchful gaze looked down on us—her eyes and lips kind, like Lita's.

I slid out from behind Javier and onto the floor. The hall was dim, so I decided it was safer to crawl to the living room to eavesdrop. I felt my way there, so I didn't bump into something, and crept to the backside of the sectional.

"It's sort of morbid," Mom said. "One hundred and forty-six people, exactly the number of Monitors on each ship, is all it takes for humans to continue with enough genetic diversity in case the rest of us die."

They were always posing some scientific hypothetical with

each other for fun. I thought this must've been just one of those nerd date-night conversations.

Mom continued. "It feels like the Monitors are making such a sacrifice for the rest of us."

"They were chosen for this mission for a reason, just like us," Dad said.

"But we get to travel the entire way."

"They're still passengers," Dad said. "And we don't know exactly what awaits us. Who's to say if their lives will be any better or worse than ours?"

It was starting to sound like it wasn't a hypothetical conversation. The ten o'clock chime rang out from the clock in the kitchen.

"Screen on," Dad said, turning on the ten o'clock news programmed specifically for them.

I peeked through the upper part of the couch cushion.

"Tonight, we join the Global Peace Forum, where an international movement is growing." The newscaster raised her eyebrows, but not a single wrinkle lined her forehead. "This . . . interesting new movement has received both great praise and even greater criticism."

A man with his hair cut sharply at his temples and a pointed nose spoke. His soft voice didn't match his sharp features. "This century has seen many trials. Soon, there will be more. Imagine a world where humans could reach a consensus. With collective unity, we can avoid conflict. With no conflict, no war. Without the cost of wars, no starvation. Without differences in culture, in appearance, knowledge . . ."

I poked my head farther through the cushions for a better look. Behind him, men and women with bleached, slicked-back hair and matching uniforms stood in a stiff row, hands folded over each other at their waist. Identical smiles and not a single hint of makeup.

"Inconsistency and inequality are what have led us to such unrest and unhappiness. This collective effort ensures survival," the man said.

"Yeah," Dad said to the guy who couldn't hear him. "At what cost?"

"Isn't that what we're doing too though?" Mom asked. "Surviving?"

Dad sighed.

The man took a step back so he was in line with the others. "Join us. Our Collective is stronger as a single unit. With your trust, we can erase the hurt and pain of the past. We will . . ."

They all spoke in unison. "Create a new history."

Dad muted the speakers. "I think they're talking an entirely different kind of survival. Tell me *that* isn't frightening," he said, pointing.

I sat back on my feet. The world those randos proposed didn't sound so bad to me. No war. No starvation. No figuring out what you'd have to wear to school the next day.

As if Dad was reading my mind, he continued: "What they want isn't so much the scary part, it's how they propose doing it."

I normally couldn't stay up late enough to watch the news, so

I knew I must've been missing out on some good stuff this whole time. What exactly was this guy proposing that was so scary?

I saw Dad shaking his head. "Equality's good. But equality and sameness are two different things. Sometimes those who say things without really contemplating what it truly means . . . That dogma runs a thin line."

I told myself I'd look up *dogma* the next day.

"You don't think a few will make it through." Mom pointed toward the screen.

"We can't worry about that. We have bigger problems, competing with other countries for ships."

"I guarantee at least Japan and New Zealand have a few leaving in the next few days. The question is whether or not they have a secret viable settlement too." Mom sighed. "Maybe this Collective is right. So much for international peace and cooperation."

I heard a thump-thump and knew Dad was patting her knee. "It'll be our job to remember the parts we got wrong and make it better for our children and grandchildren. Embrace our differences, and still find a way to make peace."

I crawled back to my room and pushed Josefina onto the floor. I wondered if one of those Monitors they mentioned would help me clean my new room. What part of the U.S. was this ship taking us to, for Mom and Dad's new project? How could I get Javier to stop overfeeding his frog?

It wasn't until later I learned that, on that night, unlike me and the people on the news, my parents already knew what was going to happen. We weren't even going to be awake to interact with the Monitors, or make a mess in our rooms. We weren't going to somewhere else on Earth. My parent's "mission" is on a planet outside our entire solar system, called Sagan. The Monitors, chosen to watch over us while we sleep, won't even be alive to see it. But hopefully, their great-great-great-grandkids will be there when we wake up.

And Javier's overweight frog is in a pond eating as much as he wants.

4

APPARENTLY, THE GUY WHO INVENTED EN COGNITO (aka Downloadable Cognizance) bought his way onto the third ship by giving access to every passenger leaving Earth. So, while we're unconscious on the journey, I'll be getting the botany and geology lessons my parents chose for me. But because I'm nearly thirteen, I get to choose an elective too. My En Cognito elective alone is probably worth more than our house and Lita's combined. Hundreds of years . . . and lifetimes and lifetimes of folklore and mythology lessons, will be deep in my mind by the time we arrive on Sagan. I can't even imagine all the stories I'll know.

I'm so busy thinking of how proud Lita would've been, I barely notice my mom motioning to my dad as we walk up to the ship. Dad grabs Javier's hand, and Mom grips my elbow at the same time. "I gotcha," she whispers.

Suddenly, I know what they're doing, and I want to cry. I know what they aren't saying out loud—they can't risk me screwing this up for us. The organizers don't want someone with a "genetic defect" like my eyes for the new planet.

Waiting at the entrance ramp are at least seven people, all young, all dressed in identical dark-gray jumpsuits. Only their heads show rainbow tones of neutral skin colors from white to dark brown. They search the crowd and one by one approach someone in the group we've walked in with.

A young man with round wire glasses walks toward us quickly from the ship's ramp. He looks down at his tablet and smiles at my mom. "Dr. Pena?"

"Yes," Mom answers. "But, it's Peña with an *ñ*," she corrects. "Like, *lasagna*."

He smiles. "Sorry. Peña." He pushes something on his tablet, and it beeps. He turns to my Dad. "And . . . Dr. Peña?"

Dad nods.

The man taps his holotack and speaks into its tip. "Peña: two adults, two minors. Nice to meet you. I'm Ben, the children's Monitor for the ship." He motions for us to follow him in. "Sorry to rush, but we're a bit pressed for time." He glances nervously in the direction of the perimeter gate behind the trees. I look back too but see nothing other than the forest we just came from.

The other Monitors are already disappearing into the gaping entrance of the ship with the rest of the passengers.

"Here we go," Mom says almost to herself—but also the cue that she's leading me in.

Purple strip lighting encircles the entrance, just like on the Pleiades Corp commercial, but beyond that it is dark except for a faint blue glow. Every other company emblem indicating the ship was meant to be a luxury liner has been erased. I scan with my eyes from side to side at the surroundings to get a bigger picture like the eye doctor told me I should. My vision is still okay with lots of light, but by twilight I have to shuffle my way around even at home, or trip and die on one of Javier's toys. It's called retinitis pigmentosa and it's like watching the world through a toilet paper roll. It's supposed to worsen as I age.

I turn back for one final glimpse at the sky and bump into something. "Sorry," I say, before noticing it's just a door jamb. Javier and I snicker.

Mom puts a finger to her lips and shakes her head in warning.

I close my eyes and inhale, taking my last ever breath under Earth's open sky.

We continue up the ramp until we are standing in the hold of the ship. A shiny dark shuttle squats in the shadows like a carpet beetle, waiting for when it will go into duty in four hundred years.

Rows and rows of metal bins line the hold like a warehouse. Ben leads us toward the elevator where the door has just closed with the two families we walked in with. While we wait, Ben motions to a steel door with a flashing blue light, its latch encased within a clear locked box. "Food stores and water filtration, treated and sealed for arrival on Sagan." Then he points to an empty dark corner of the hold and looks at Mom and Dad. "That's where your labs will be."

Dad raises his eyebrows.

Ben smiles. "I know it doesn't look like much now, but don't worry. It will be assembled and waiting for you upon your arrival." He motions toward the entrance ramp we just walked in on. "And that will be converted to the shuttle dock."

The elevator chimes softly, and the door opens. Its outer walls are made entirely of rounded glass, but a circular tube of dark metal encapsulates the glass walls. Ben presses 6 and the glass doors slide shut.

We rise up and up inside a suffocating dark tube. Javier grips on to Dad's leg.

Ben smiles at Javier. "The worst is over," he says. "The distance from the hold to the main floor is half the height of the ship."

As soon as he says it, the elevator chimes for the first floor. The metal enclosure disappears. Windows on one side of the elevator stare down into the cavernous body of the ship.

I have the same dizzy sense I had when I walked out of the tunnel into the Olympic stadium in Dallas on our class field trip.

Javier releases Dad's leg and runs to peek out into the ship's belly. "Whoa!" he says, hands splayed flat on the windows.

I realize even I am gasping. I'm staring out at an atrium as cavernous as six football fields.

Bing. The elevator chimes for the second floor.

On the opposite side, just like a football stadium, hundreds of private suites overlook a field of green several stories below. A massive park covers nearly the entire lower floor. Walking paths, like veins in a leaf, weave through the green below. Scattered benches and tables along the trails look miniature from where we stand at least fifteen meters above. Lanterns glitter like fireflies lighting the paths.

On the second level just above the park, the entire perimeter is lined with eight lanes separated by white stripes just like a running track. Along the wall behind the lanes, I catch sight of exercise equipment and the rectangles of turquoise blue from individual lap pools.

Human dots in the distance travel up and down glass elevators on each corner. The elevator chimes for the third floor.

"My room is right there." Ben points to a door directly across from us by the window suites overlooking the park. He shifts his finger two floors below his room. "Just above the theater," he says, motioning to the main floor. There's an outdoor amphitheater with a stage and holoscreen way larger than the ones at Cinetrak 8. For a second I wonder who decides what movies they'll watch.

"Cafeteria," Ben continues, pointing to the main floor.

A large open room that could be a food court at any mall lies directly behind the park. Tables and chairs meld directly into the walls to be part of the ship. Cubbies hold food rations from floor to ceiling, enough for all of the Monitors for hundreds of years. I gag thinking about where they'll get the liquid to hydrate the meals. There's no way the ship has a compartment big enough to hold enough water for three hundred and eighty years. A wall of magnawaves is the only sign of anything resembling a normal kitchen.

Bing. The elevator chimes for the fourth floor.

Any awe I'm feeling for the ship suddenly disappears when I remind myself why we're here. I'll only get to use it all just before we land anyway. The feeling in my stomach is replaced by a boulder thinking of the things I'm trading for this. Like Lita's kitchen and the earthy smell of soaking husks and green chile.

I stare down at the ship's cafeteria, which I'm positive has no masa or chile verde. Lita would have never fit in here anyway. I see her dark wrinkled hands spooning masa onto a corn husk.

I blink over and over trying to make the tears evaporate before they trickle over. I can't be the only one feeling like this is all a big mistake. God will figure it out and nudge Halley's comet . . . or the nagual . . . or whatever it is back on track.

Bing. The elevator chimes for the fifth floor.

I look up, hoping no one will notice my watery eyes. The domed ceiling, at least another thirty meters above our heads, is lined with two giant screens. Billowing clouds drift across what looks like the real sky. Massive banks of LEDs throw out full-spectrum lighting just like Mom's greenhouse.

Ben stands next to me and looks up too. "It will shift to the night sky in two hours, so it'll feel just like home for us."

I follow his finger as he points down again at the park. "Real plants even," he says.

"It's beautiful," I whisper.

Mom kisses my cheek and I know our fight is over. She speaks softly in my ear. "Look carefully in the middle."

I slowly scan to the center of the park. A circle wall of cobblestone sits like a medieval centerpiece. In the middle of the ring of stone stands a small tree.

"A Christmas tree?" Javier asks.

Mom snickers. "It's Hyperion."

I turn toward her, and we bonk noses. I chuckle. She must be delirious. My depth perception can't be *that* off. There's no way that sprig is the tallest tree in the world. Even though Hyperion's true location is protected, anyone with a botanist for a parent would know about the famous tree. My mom even saw it in person once. She said she hugged it and cried.

I glance over at her. She stares at the tiny tree adoringly, with the first genuine smile on her face I've seen in the past few days. "Well, not Hyperion exactly, but I was able to acquire her sapling." Her voice quivers. "We're leaving behind so many beautiful things. Bringing the offspring of something with such strength and resilience was the one thing that made the most sense to me." She sighs. "It will still be a baby compared to its mother when we arrive. They're using the time-released nutrients to control its growth and keep it and other plants alive." Mom casually refers to her revolutionary soil additive. She laughs nervously. "No pressure."

Bing. The elevator chimes for the sixth floor.

"Congratulations, by the way," Ben smiles. "Truly remarkable."

Mom gives him a small nod. The door slides open, and we step out.

The rest of the passengers have already disappeared through one of the mazes of corridors. We follow Ben into a tunnel closest to the ship's outer edge. It slopes upward and the lights are dim, so I hold onto the railing. We near the top of the tunnel, which means we are nearing the front tip of the mantis's right wing.

"You know," Ben continues, "I know Dr. Nguyen, who's in charge of the seed vault and plant starts during the first leg of our journey."

Mom's smile falters a bit as Dad pats her back. "She's a friend," Mom says. "When you see her, please tell her thank you. And . . ." It grows uncomfortably quiet.

"Of course," Ben says. "I will pass along your message."

I peek in open doorways on either side. People wearing gray jumpsuits like Ben's stand at panels, gliding their fingers over holoscreens.

"Teen stasis room," Ben says, motioning to an open door to our right.

An empty row down the middle of the room is lined on each side with what looks like at least thirty white coffins with glass-domed tops. Most of the lids are already shut, fluorescent fluid glinting inside.

I ease my hand out of Mom's and hesitate at the door.

A woman with a tight bun and a tablet stands in front of one of the pods. The family with the older blond kid is in front of her. She glances up at me, her forehead scrunching like I'm a fly who just landed on her control panel. She pokes her tablet with her holotack, and the door slides shut with a thunk.

Ben leans toward me. "Lead Monitor. Takes her job pretty seriously."

I'm just grateful we have Ben instead of that lady.

"Dr. and Dr. Peña, you'll be on the fore-starboard of the ship. Your children will be housed on the aft-port. Just ahead—"

Dad stops. "Wait, no one told us we were going to be separated."

Ben turns back toward Dad, stumbling over his words. "It's . . . it's protocol." He lowers his voice. "I'm really sorry, Dr. Peña. You'll just be across the ship." He glances toward the room with the Lead Monitor. "We have orders to sort and store by age for efficient observation."

Sort and store? Like we're eggs in a carton. Over-sanitized air burns my nostrils and eyes.

My parents exchange a glance. Mom looks just as concerned as Dad, but she clenches my dad's forearm. "It'll be okay, sweetheart," she says.

Dad gives her a quick kiss on her forehead. I look down at Javier, who has the same half-frown as Dad. I grip his arm and kiss his forehead. "It'll be okay, sweet-fart," I whisper, mimicking Mom's voice.

Javier smiles and leans into me.

Ben looks relieved as Dad motions for him to continue.

He walks through the open door, then turns to face me and Javier. "Here we are. Youth. Ages six to twelve."

5

THE LIGHT IN THE "YOUTH" ROOM IS EVEN DIMMER than the rest of the ship. Three rows of six stasis pods line the room and sort of look exactly like . . . eggs in a carton. All but seven of the pods are already occupied. Dark shapes float in the center of the glowing liquid. It reminds me of the green water of the mangrove canals near Lita's childhood home in Tulum, the most peaceful place on Earth. But I've always wondered if the looming dark shadows gliding just under the surface might munch off a toe or two.

Javier grabs me around the waist.

Ben bends down to Javier's eye level. "I know it looks a little scary. But I'll be taking care of both of you as long as I'm around."

Ben twists a latch on one of the empty pods. With a suctioned pop, the lid springs open. "See, just like a well-check scanner at the doctor's office."

"Who'll put you guys in?" Javier asks Ben, pointing to the pod.

Mom throws an arm around Javier's head, wrapping her hand over his mouth. "Sorry," she says. "He doesn't understand."

Ben bends back down in front of Javier. "We have the coolest job ever. We get to live our whole lives on this ship." Ben waves his arm. "Traveling through space. Did you see how awesome my new home is?"

Javier nods.

He's right. I guess it is better than dying on Earth. But Ben's park still won't have the smell of the desert flowers after the rain. The massive screen overhead might simulate the day and night sky, but it won't have the crack of a lightning strike or rumble of thunder. His view into the darkness of space is empty compared to the orange and reds of the Sangre de Cristo Mountains back home.

Ben continues. "I even got to help the people on the first ship fall asleep before they took off. Builders, farmers . . . lots of kids. And when your ship lands on Sagan, they'll be ready for"—he taps Javier's forehead—"the science our ship brings."

I think of the other ship we'd seen on the way in, and wonder how many kids are traveling with their parents like us.

Ben hands my mom a plastic bag and pulls out a changing partition. While Mom helps Javier change, Ben motions for Dad to step closer to the pod. He lowers his voice, and his tone shifts like he's already said the exact words a hundred times that day: "En Cognito's downloadable cognizance puts the organs and brain to sleep immediately. The gel preserves tissue indefinitely, removing senescent cells and waste. It not only provides nutrients and oxygen the body will need for such a long stay in stasis, but lidocaine in the gel numbs nerve endings, making the gel's colder temperature comfortable upon awakening."

Dad takes a deep breath. "I understand. Thank you."

Ben quickly changes the subject, and his voice shifts back to a normal level. "And"—he looks at his tablet—"I have both Javier's and Petra's En Cognito programs. Standard core, with an emphasis on botany and geology in the sciences."

"Yep," Dad says, giving me a thumbs-up.

I roll my eyes. At least I won't have to actually "listen" to the lectures, since the En Cognito device that puts us to sleep is also programmed to embed those topics directly into our brains. By the time we arrive to Sagan, I'll be as much of an expert as Mom is in botany and Dad in geology. Obviously, though, that isn't the good part. With all the folklore and mythology, along with

Lita's stories, I have at least a chance to try and convince Mom and Dad I should be a storyteller instead. But like Lita said, I'll have to make the stories my own.

Javier walks out wearing small black shorts, like he's going to the beach. As Mom hands Ben the plastic bag with Javier's clothes and favorite book, Dad picks Javier up and grips him into a hug.

Mom rubs Javier's back, while he stares at the open pod.

"I wanna go home," Javier whimpers. "Please, can we go home?"

Mom eases Javier from Dad's arms. "It's just a nap."

Javier's breath catches over and over as he tries to hold in his cries. Mom sets him gently in the pod, her arms still wrapped around him.

I want my brother's last memory going into centuries of sleep to be something good. I kneel over him and set my cheek on his. I close my eyes, imagining my hand in Lita's, piñon smoke drifting into the New Mexico sky. I hold his hand just like Lita held mine. I rub the freckled constellation birthmark on his left thumb. He makes the smallest smile. I decide to tell him the story Lita told me my last night with her, the one that calmed me most. Softly and patiently just like her, I speak. "You know, the stars are the prayers of abuelas and mothers and sisters . . ."

Javier sniffs in my ear. I continue.

". . . for the children they love. Each star, filled with hope." I sit back and point up. "¿Y cuántas estrellas hay en el cielo?"

"How many stars in the sky?" he repeats, cracking open an eye to stare at the ceiling like he's imagining the night sky. "I don't know," he answers.

I lean in close and whisper in his ear. "¿Cincuenta?"

"Only fifty?" He smiles, probably imagining a gazillion stars.

"Or *sin* . . . cuenta?" I smile, and rub his head just like Lita had.

"Countless," he whispers, understanding Lita's riddle.

I wonder if I've told it as well as she had, if my hand in his is as calming as Lita's was in mine. I can't remember the rest. She ended it in a way that felt . . . comforting. What did she say? "All those estrellas that will surround us out there, those are our dead ancestors. They will whisper messages in our ears."

Javier sits up. His eyes go wide. "Stars are dead relatives?"

"No, Javier. I meant like—"

"Like ghosts? In space?" Javier grips the side of the pod and tries to get up. "Mom. Please. I don't want to go."

This is not going the way I'd hoped. "That's not what I meant," I try to correct. But it's too late. Javier is on the verge of ugly cry.

Ben interrupts. "Dr. Peña, please. We really need to get going."

Mom rubs Javier's head to calm him down like she does when he has a nightmare. "Yes, yes. I know." She lays him back down. She turns to me. Wrinkles angle outward from the narrowed corners of her eyes. "Really, Petra, this isn't the right time for a story."

Her words are a sledgehammer to my stomach.

Javier's chin shakes. "I want to go home."

Maybe my parents are right, and I should just study plants and rocks like them. Maybe wanting to tell stories is "living in a fantasy world" or me with my "head in the clouds."

"We *are* going home, Javier," I try to recover, sticking to what I hope will be true. "We'll run and play on Sagan just like we always have." Javier nods, but his attempt at a smile looks more pained than convincing.

Dad pats my back.

I force a smile back, but I think I've already done too much damage. What's Lita's secret? I will never be as good as her.

"Ready?" Ben whispers to my mom.

My mom nods stiffly, but her eyes are filling with tears.

He presses a button and straps slither out, holding Javier in place.

I feel the heaviness of Dad's hand on my shoulder. He squeezes slightly, his way of letting me know it'll be all right.

"Mom, please," Javier begs. He squirms, but with the restraints he can't move more than a few centimeters.

Ben slips on plastic gloves. He opens a metal box. In large letters along its side I read: *En Cognito Downloadable Cognizance—Pediatric.* Shiny silver spheres sit inside. Ben lifts one of the "Cogs" out and sets it in what looks like a miniature ice cream scoop. He presses a button on its handle, and the Cog glows purple.

A tear falls down Mom's cheek, and her voice is higher than Javier's. "It's okay, little one. I promise you'll be fine. Be brave."

Javier's body trembles, and tears pour down his cheeks too. I squeeze his hand tighter and keep my thumb gripped on his birthmark.

"Almost done," Ben says calmly. Using the ice cream scoop, he slides the purple Cog along the base of Javier's neck, then holds it in place. "Only a few seconds now."

Javier clenches his eyes shut.

I lean in, and his eyelids flutter, opening to meet mine for just a moment. I move even closer. "See you when you wake up," I whisper in Javier's ear.

Javier sniffs, then squeaks back, "When we wake up—" and in an instant, he goes limp and stops breathing.

I let go of his lifeless hand and stand, collapsing into Dad's chest. Mom cocoons her arms around both of us. I use Dad's shirt to wipe my eyes, hoping no one but Dad notices.

The smooth female voice of the computer speaks. "*Stasis pod seven filling.*"

I can't look. I know the other children in their pods are resting peacefully, but none of them are my brother. Javier was talking just a few moments ago.

I keep my head buried in Dad's shirt as the clicks of Javier's pod being latched echo in the room.

"I'm sorry to rush you, but . . ." Ben says.

Dad eases me across the room toward one of the few remaining empty pods. "We understand."

I wipe my eyes on Dad's shirt again and look up.

Ben is moving slowly to stand in front of me. He tilts his head in confusion.

Mom clears her throat. Her eyes widen at me. What am I missing? I hurry to look down, trying not to be too obvious. Right in front of me, Ben's holding out the same bag he'd given Javier. I hadn't even seen it.

"Your clothes?" he says.

My hand shakes as I reach out to take it from him. "Thanks."

He glances at my parents. Did he notice? No one says a word.

"Petra?" Ben looks directly into my eyes. "Did you not see me?"

I bite my lip and drop my head. I glance up at Dad, and he gives me a weak smile, then looks away. This is so messed up. But I've ruined everything.

I set the bag down and can't help my desperate stare at Ben.

I feel my Mom push her arm forward in front of me, as if to protect me, but then Ben picks up the bag. He hands it back to me. "Let's get Petra dressed," he says, nodding at my parents.

Mom makes a hiccupped cry. "Thank you," she answers.

I can't help noticing Ben glance out the window toward the forest again. "We do need to hurry."

I walk behind the partition and open the bag. Sandwiched between the clothes is a silvery white cap like the kind swimmers wear. I imagine shoving my tumbleweed of hair in that thing, and know I'll look just like a brown Q-tip.

I try not to think of it. Why do I care about that right now?

I drop my clothes to the floor and pull on the shorts. They

skid to a halt at my thighs. With one final yank, I wonder if I'll wake up as a balloon animal, pinched off in the spots the suit covers. I hurry to slip the tank over my head before my mom can barge in to help me.

I pull the pendant Lita gave me out of my pant pocket and clutch it in my hand. The sun's silver rays poke into my palm. Metal tiles chill the bottom of my feet as I walk out.

My hand trembles as I hold my obsidian pendant out to Ben. "I can't lose it." My body feels like it's held together by strings that are splitting and fraying inside me.

Ben steps forward and takes the pendant from my hand. He gently sets my magic link to Lita inside a plastic pouch. "It'll be right here when you wake up," he says, smiling.

I can't catch a full breath. Mom wraps her arms around me, her breathing jagged in my ear.

She kisses my cheek. "I love you so much."

I squeeze her back, but there's a lump so large in my throat, I can't tell her I love her more. We move toward the pod where Dad and Ben wait.

"I promise you," Ben says to my parents, glancing toward the window again, "I'll do whatever I can to get them there safely."

I want to thank him, but it'll call more attention to how weird it is that he's going to spend his entire life babysitting me. Dad helps me step up into the pod, kissing my forehead. I lay my head all the way back, stretching to make sure no skin pinches or pulls. My entire body shivers just like Javier's, and I can't stop it.

Mom sets her hand on my forehead, and Dad stands next to me, holding my hand.

Ben pulls on new gloves and lifts one of the Cogs from the box. He sets it in the Cog installer and presses the button. It glows purple. "Botany. Geology. Standard core. Looks like we've got it all."

"And my elective?" I ask.

Ben's brow furrows. "Elective?"

I'm suddenly a lot colder. "Mom?"

Mom turns to Ben. "We arranged for Petra to have a mythology elective as she's nearly thirteen."

Ben sweeps his finger over his tablet and shakes his head. "I'm sorry, it's not here," he says. "The Lead Monitor finalized all the curriculum herself."

I think of the grumpy woman with the tight bun. Why would she leave them out? Pinpricks run up my spine. I need those stories. Without them, how can I be a great storyteller? The one word comes out wobbly. "Please—"

Ben gives me a weak smile. "I like stories too." He nods toward a desk in the corner. "More priceless than anything else on this ship."

I can't see distinctly, but it looks like he has a stack of librex there. Each of those are capable of storing thousands of holoscripts. "I'll talk to the Lead Monitor and see what I can—"

"Ben!" Dad interrupts, running toward the window.

Ben sets down the Cog installer. His eyes grow wide and he walks slowly after my dad. "We thought we had more time."

Dad sighs deeply and leans his head against the window.

"What's happening?" Mom asks, finally turning away from me.

I sit up in the pod but can't see what they see. I stand and walk toward the window. Dad tries to block my view, but not before I see a swarm of dark shapes running toward the ship from the forest. Many of them are carrying objects. I don't want to think of any of those dark objects being anything more than some garden tools the people found in the ranger station's shed.

A deep thud echoes near our window. Mom stands next to me and grips my hand again.

A soft robotic voice comes over the main speakers. "Closing main doors."

"What?" Mom's hand breaks out in a sweat. "Now?"

"We'll have to move even quicker," Ben motions with his head to a padded chair bolted to the wall. "Only one jump seat per room in this sector."

Dad directs me back to the pod. My parents both hurry to situate me into it, their eyes desperate.

Ben rushes, fumbling to activate the Cog again. Its fading purple light glows bright again.

Just like with Javier, the ropes cinch around my head, waist, and feet, holding me steady.

"Ready?" Ben says.

I blow out a deep breath but don't answer. I try to keep my lips from shaking. I bite the inside of my cheek. With the download, I would've had other stories. Not anymore. I will be just as normal as I always was. A tear trickles down one cheek.

Ben slides the Cog along my neck at the top of my spine, until it catches in the indent at the base of my skull.

I focus on my breathing in and out slowly and think of the most comforting thing I can. *The prayers of abuelas and mothers. Estrellas sin cuenta.*

"En Cognito's Cogs are biocompatible," Ben says. "She won't feel anything."

But I do. It gouges into my skin like a jagged rock. I need to stay still so this goes quickly. I swallow and wait for it to sink in and put me to sleep.

Ben pulls his hand away. Impacted-zit pressure burrows just under the surface of my skin. Suddenly, I can't move or breathe or speak or blink. Part of the Cog is working.

But something is wrong. I should be asleep. Eyes wide open, I can still see. I can hear.

I try to scream. Nothing comes out.

Ben swipes on the pod's screen. The system responds, "*Stasis pod twelve filling.*" Pinpricks like fire ant bites run over my skin as the cold gel seeps around my body and into my ears.

Gel pours over my tongue and down my throat. Seconds after it makes contact with each area, I no longer feel a thing there.

It hits the corner of my eyes, and a green glow covers my vision.

Ben's words are garbled, but I still hear them. This can't be happening. I'd rather be outside with the people attacking the ship than trapped like this. The only thing I can think of to help are Lita's prayers for me.

Estrellas sin cuenta . . .

"Why is she staring at me?" Mom's voice trembles.

Estrellas sin cuenta . . .

"That's a normal reaction. She's already asleep."

Estrellas sin cuenta . . .

Ben leans over, and with his gloved hands, pushes my eyelids shut.

6

I ONCE HAD A NIGHTMARE WHERE I WAS AWAKE BUT couldn't move. Mom said it was called sleep paralysis. Lita called it "subírsele el muerto," or, "dead person on you."

Lita was the right one.

If I could just make my hand move, knock on the pod, Ben would know. He'd know the Cog hadn't worked. I try to move, but nothing happens. Dead person on me.

"Dr. and Dr. Peña, I'm sorry to rush you," Ben says. "Let's get you both to your Monitor. "We don't have the jump seats to spare—we need to get you in stasis."

Choppy, muffled words from Mom tell me she's tucked into Dad's chest now.

"They'll be fine," Dad says.

Their footsteps echo away along with Mom's small sobs.

Stop! Don't leave me!

If I can't fall asleep . . . I'll be stuck like this. There has to be some sort of safeguard against this kind of thing.

Another thud booms. Why would they pay any attention to me when the entire ship is being attacked?

My mind tells me I'm already crying, but I know between En Cognito's Cog and the gel, my eyes can't make tears.

Hopeless, I curl up with Lita, drinking hot chocolate with cinnamon under a Santa Fe sky. Feeling her warm hand brushing along my head as she softly sings an arrullo.

Arrorró mi niña,
arrorró mi sol,
arrorró pedazo
de mi corazón.

Lita's lullaby blows softly into my ears like she's right there.

Ben's hurried steps return, another softer set of footsteps with him. Sounds of him working shift around the room. "You're the last, Suma."

I think of the girl with the unicorn horn hoodie.

"I know." The girl's words quiver. "My mom said we have to hurry."

"We do," Ben says. "I'm sorry she can't be here. It's an emergency." Just as he says it, another loud thud bellows.

"Just so you know, I'm not afraid," Suma says.

"I know you're not. But just so *you* know, it's okay to be afraid. If you were, that is."

"Well, FYI, I'm allergic to sulfa, so if there's sulfa in that gel I might explode. But don't be afraid. If you were, that is." Her voice is shaking, but she's trying her best.

Ben laughs. Under other circumstances, Suma sounds like someone I'd be friends with.

For a moment it's silent, then Ben says, "Ready? Count backward from ten."

"Ten." Suma breathes in and out so hard, I think she might throw up.

"N-nine."

"It's okay, Suma. You're almost asleep—"

Suma's hyperventilating halts abruptly.

"*Stasis pod eleven filling.*"

The slosh of gel filling her pod is directly next to mine. This is it! Ben will discover I'm awake! But instead of my pod opening gently, it vibrates with a massive jolt.

"*Prepare for takeoff,*" the system's computer says. "*T-minus ninety seconds.*"

Pounding steps boom from the corridor. "We did it, Ben. Everyone who made it on board is in stasis," a woman's voice says. I know it must be the Lead Monitor.

For a moment I'm relieved. We made it. But then I realize how many others were behind us on the trail.

"What about the third ship?" Ben asks.

"We'll be lucky if ninety seconds is enough for our ship to make it off the old planet. They've overrun the guard station. They've taken weapons."

"Screen on," Ben's shaky voice demands. "Show me ship three."

"There's no time for that," the Lead Monitor responds.

"My little brother is on—" Ben's voice pleads.

Mixed with more thuds, the sounds of stomps and running feet echo from the outside corridor.

"T-*minus sixty seconds.*"

"I have to go." The Lead Monitor's words shift into the hallway. The door shuts, and the commotion from the corridor is gone.

"Oh, God. Oh, God," Ben mutters. "Confirm youth pods sealed."

A long beep drowns out all the other noise. "*Confirmed. Pods sealed for takeoff.* T-*minus forty seconds.*" A hum like a washing machine escalates in volume until I think my ears might burst. "T-*minus thirty seconds.*" A hiss of air grows louder and louder.

Deep thumping now reverberates like someone hammering on the shell of a shuttle-port.

It has to be them. I imagine how desperate all those people left behind must feel.

"Confirm pod bases locked," Ben says.

Another beep. "*Confirmed. Bases locked for takeoff and flight mode.*"

I think of the wasted, empty pods. If they'd attacked the ship an hour earlier, our pods would've been empty too.

If only I could twitch one finger, Ben could still help me. He'd notice something wrong. He'd get me out and just put me to sleep once we were safely off Earth.

His muffled words sound right by my head. "Vitals down. Brain function intact."

My brain tells my mouth to scream, "*No! Help!*" Still, nothing happens.

"*Affirmative,*" the soft voice says. "*T-minus twenty seconds. Monitors, prepare for immediate takeoff.*"

Belts cinch and click from the corner in response. My chance is over.

Ben speaks in a whisper so low I can't make out the words. Is he praying? The ship shudders like chattering teeth, and I know we're lifting off ground into an antigravity hover.

It's followed by a shriek like a million forks on ceramic plates.

I imagine the attacking people flooding out of the forest like terrified mice, scratching at the sides of the ship to get on.

If I could, I'd let them all on. I picture the mom with her baby in that crowd.

The entire ship makes an electronic moan. It increases an octave at a time. "T-*minus ten seconds.*"

A throbbing pulsates deep inside my ears.

"*Nine, eight, seven, six, five, four . . .*"

The unmistakable jolt of the thrusters hits. "*Three, two . . .*" I can't be sure, but I think my numb body shifts so hard I hit the inside of the chamber.

A mountain-lion roar drowns out the computer's voice. Metal clanks like a rattling silverware drawer for a long time, before it stops and levels off into a steady purr. "*Gravity shell activated,*" the ship's voice says, meaning we've moved beyond Earth's exosphere.

I hear Ben unlatch himself. The chaos of the past few minutes is replaced by an eerie hum. Ben's mumbles and footsteps shift back and forth in the room.

Soon after, the Lead Monitor returns. "We're on course," she announces to Ben. "Now, it's just . . . time."

Ben clears his throat. "Any word on the third ship?"

"I'm sorry. I really am. I know your brother, Isaac, was . . ." She pauses. "Ben, we all had friends."

For a moment it's quiet. Then her voice changes. "Without the final ship . . ." she sighs. "There's talk about a change in the mission."

For a moment, I can't hear anything. Then, Ben's voice comes, sharply. "What?" he says. "What are you saying?"

"Without the politicians, the president . . . Ben, this is an opportunity to start over. A consensus." The Lead Monitor clears her throat. "From this moment on, we can create a new history."

7

I SPEND WHAT MUST BE AN ENTIRE DAY LISTENING TO Ben shuffle around the room. Mumble to himself. Cry. Fidget. Snore. And I am awake to hear it all. Will they open my pod hundreds of years later and find a babbling girl—green drool dripping from the side of my mouth? If I'm awake the whole time, does that mean my body keeps aging? Or will I just be so out of it I don't even know who my parents are?

I'm haunted by the Lead Monitor's words: *consensus, create a new history.* I know exactly where I've heard them and how it scared my parents. But what scares me more is what Dad said.

It's not about what they want, it's about what they're willing to do to get it. And now some of them have gotten onto the ship.

At what must be close to Ben's bedtime, I hear the distinct chime of a librex opening. "*Please select a holoscript.*"

"Might as well start at the very beginning," Ben says gently. "The first story ever recorded. *The Epic of Gilgamesh.*" His chair's legs scrape against the floor. "Some argue this ancient Sumerian tale's worth, but I think all stories have value. Readers and listeners should decide which stories speak to them or not."

I wonder why Ben is here right now. I mean, we're just lying in our pods. If his job for the day is over, why wouldn't he be hanging out with the other Monitors? But I think maybe more is going on. Maybe he's avoiding them for a reason.

I try to imagine how Ben feels. I still have my parents and Javier. What if Javier had been on the other ship? In that moment, I vow when we got to Sagan, I'll never let anyone separate me from him again.

Ben reads aloud the story of the great warrior king Gilgamesh, son of gods. Even though I can't see it, I know Ben has turned on the reenactment function and the holoscript is playing out the battle scenes. In my head I picture the ghost-like forms of Enkidu, a man like a bull, and Gilgamesh crashing right through our pods as they fling each other around the stasis room, until finally, Gilgamesh defeats him. As Gilgamesh and Enkidu then become friends, and embark on a journey, my mind is transported out of the ship's pod to the forests, oceans, and great deserts they travel to.

"Enkidu, my friend, I have had a third dream, and the dream I had was deeply disturbing. The heavens roared and the earth rumbled; it became deathly still, and darkness loomed. A bolt of lightning cracked and a fire broke out, and where it kept thickening, there rained death."

I swear I see the flash of the thunder flicker through my closed eyelids. Ben's words become dramatic and deep. I imagine him flailing his arms theatrically.

Ben goes on to read of the tragic end of Enkidu and Gilgamesh's pain of losing his best friend. He stammers the final words.

"Deep sadness penetrates my core."

I wish I could hug him. I understand. Even if my eyes can't make tears, my heart cries with his.

Ben sighs. "I think that's a good place to stop for the night." I hear the click of the holoscript turning off.

I wonder why Ben read it out loud if we can't hear the story in stasis. Maybe he needs to hear it as much as I did. Maybe he's afraid and needs something to help him feel brave. I wish he'd read *Dreamers*.

We're like the people in Javier's book. Scared. Hopeful. And maybe like the woman and her child at the heart of the story too. When we arrive to Sagan, we'll be shocked by its strangeness, but at the same time amazed by its beauty.

"And . . ." Ben says, "It's midnight Earth time. That makes it your birthday, Petra."

Is he right? If it's my birthday, that means two whole days have passed. Fire Snake has already come home to its mother, Earth. We haven't turned back, so I know what this means. It's over. Whatever is left of Earth is uninhabitable.

I'll never again snuggle into Lita, rub the soft underside of her arm, and listen to one of her cuentos while her chickens cluck in the background. I'll never stare out at the red, gold, and brown rocks that took two billion years to form. Lita, the Sangre de Cristo Mountains . . . all gone.

I wish more than ever that sleep would just take me away.

"I have a present for you, Petra. I couldn't get your curriculum approved, but since you're *technically* old enough for more downloads, and these are off the record . . ." Ben's footsteps drum away in the direction of his shelf full of librex. "I'll give you any basics I have. Greek, Roman, Chinese, Norse, Polynesian, Sumerian." He stops to take a breath. "Maya, Inca, Korean, West Africa, North Africa. And here's some more . . ."

My mind grins. He has more stories than I'd requested in the first place. Ben would've made a great teacher. If only my stupid Cog hadn't malfunctioned.

"What do we have here? This one's a classic. *Norse Mythology* by Gaiman. It's a better version than the historical stuff—you can thank me later. Well, actually, you won't be able to thank me. But I'm sure you'll figure out who the culprit was."

Poor Ben has no way of knowing all his efforts are for nothing. As long as I am wide-awake, I'll only hear the stories he reads out loud. But if he does one every night, at least I can keep those stories in my arsenal, along with Lita's.

"Complete works of Gaiman." Beep. "Douglas Adams." Beep. "Le Guin. Butler." Beep. Beep. "You know what . . . I really shouldn't filter. You can handle the more mature stuff, and one thing you've got is plenty of time. Vonnegut. Erdrich. Morrison." Beep. Beep. Beep. At least twenty more ring through the pod.

"Wish I could meet the future you, kid. You're bound to have some opinions." He laughs. "Good thing I won't be there for your parents to kill me." One lone beep echoes. "How did I almost forget R.L. Stine? Everyone needs a little creepy. That should do it for now," Ben says. "Happy Birthday, Petra! And . . . Enter."

A hum vibrates inside my head. It's the first physical sensation I've felt since the numbing gel.

An English accent speaks suddenly from somewhere deep within my mind, startling me. "*Before the beginning there was nothing*—"

It all soaks in instantly. Nothing like school, where I have to work to remember it all. This is just there, like the author, Neil Gaiman, is inside my head talking to my brain.

Ben! Thank you! If I have to be awake for eons, Ben just ensured I'll have his favorite stories to listen to. I might be nuts by the time we arrive to Sagan, but I'll be the best kind of crazy storyteller known to humanity.

"*No Earth, no heavens, no stars, no sky: only the mist world . . .*" Neil Gaiman continues in my head, but becomes more like a dream deep within my mind. The humming increases.

Heat. At the top of my spine.

Whatever Ben has done . . . I feel myself getting sleepier. Is the Cog finally working? If I could, I'd breathe a sigh of relief.

This is it.

When I wake up, we'll be on Sagan.

8

THE NOISES COME SLOWLY AT FIRST: SHUFFLES FROM every direction in the room. My mind is fuzzy, but I definitely hear something. If I'm awake . . . have we arrived?

Even though it feels like no time at all has passed, I can't wait to hug my parents. I can't wait to hold Javier and read him his book.

The ship still has the low hum of cruising through space.

Ben's voice trembles. "Please work . . ."

Ben? If he's still there . . . we haven't arrived at Sagan yet. The imaginary strings holding my heart in place start to snap. We're nowhere close to our new home.

Ben's fingers screech across a control panel. I think it's mine. "Please work," he repeats, this time raspier and more panicked.

Someone pounds on the outer door like a sledgehammer on a metal drum.

"No, no, no, no . . . Not yet!" Ben's voice skips like the first day I met him, when he found out his brother's ship had been attacked. "This has to work . . ."

More pounding.

I barely hear Ben's heartbroken words. "A world without story is lost."

The skid of the door opens.

"Ben! You were warned."

The clink of something metal dropping on my pod's shell rings in my ears.

"Stop fighting, old man!" the angry voice grunts. "Take his arms!"

Old man?

Thumps and cursing shift around the room until there's one big thud. Ben moans. The scuffling stops.

Someone sighs. "He'll have to be purged."

Purged?

"What was he doing at this pod?" A beep from my pod's control panel pierces my ears. "Did you see this? Petra Peña has remaining elective files in her system. Books from Earth; music, mythology . . ."

"Delete it all," a woman's voice says. "And make sure there's nothing else from before. The Collective's mission can't be compromised by one child."

"A new history," the other person says.

"A new history," she repeats.

Collective. A *new history.* It's them. But what are they doing? If this is real and they are wiping our memories . . . With all the risks, this is not one of those things my parents or the other passengers imagined could happen.

If I can have one final memory before they erase it, it has to be perfect and special.

Under a starry desert sky Lita wraps the blanket around our shoulders. She hands me a cup of cacao. "Close your eyes, chanquita."

I close my eyes. The smell of chocolate fills my nose.

"Only a sip," she says.

I know the cacao has caffeine or something Mom won't let me have.

"Set your intention. Proclaim to the universe what you will be," Lita says.

I take a sip. It's not as sweet as chocolate, and little pieces of grit cover my teeth. "What I want to be right now?" I ask.

"Now. Tomorrow." She rests her hand on my cheek. "Years from now."

When I am old, like Mom's age, I will always say what I really feel. I will wear long flowy dresses like Lita. I will let my hair grow as long and wild as I want.

"I am . . ." I bite my lip. "I will be . . ."

A tiny noise flutters deep within my mind, and I grow sleepy.

"*Reactivating pod twelve.*"

9

THE SUMMER I TURNED TWELVE, DAD AND I TOOK A shuttle from Santa Fe to Rockhound State Park, which was exactly what its name suggested, and also Dad's version of heaven.

Dad slips a helmet on my head.

"Seriously?" I raise my eyebrows. "Why do we have to wear these? It's not like the rocks are gonna fall from the sky."

"Because I promised your mother."

I whisper. "She's not here."

He hands me a small pair of leather gloves and whispers back. "I'm not stupid enough to cross a mama bear." He smiles and holds up the sunscreen.

I roll my eyes.

"She just wants us to stay safe." He proceeds to spray every last sliver of our exposed skin like Mom is standing right there.

Her constant efforts to keep me safe is like being vacuum sealed. But here with Dad, I feel like someone tore open a tiny corner of the bag.

We each pick up our rock hammers and a little pail. I follow as Dad walks toward a shaded ravine. He approaches a bank and tilts his head one way, then another. "This is the one."

He looks back at me and I shrug. "*Mmmh*, geology."

He winks at me. "I promise, one day, you won't just see this as science." He holds up his hammer. "You might even . . . dig it."

I bite my lips together and turn to hide my smile. We've barely walked a half kilometer from the park's entrance, but I sit down on the ground next to him, pull out my water bottle, and drink like we've hiked all day. Dad uses his rock hammer to explore a ten-by-ten-centimeter area. He stops to brush around a dark spot with his finger, chiseling around its perimeter until a rock comes loose.

He rubs dirt off its surface and grins. He examines it like it's a precious relic.

I set down my water bottle and brush my gloved hand over years of tailings. "What about this one?" I hold up a white one.

Even with the dirt coating, its surface has a glint of something more special and sparkling beneath.

"Quartz," he says. "But don't lose focus. We're here for jasper." He pulls out ten or so round beads from his shirt pocket and lays them in a row in the dirt. He holds up the deep-red rock he's just pulled from the bank. "When this one is polished, it'll be a great companion to the others."

I stare down at the hodgepodge of beads. "They don't look at all alike."

"That's because each piece of jasper has its own spirit. The rock will tell us who it is, not the other way around."

"But it won't match the others."

He pulls it out again and holds it up to the sunlight. A yellow vein runs through the crimson rock. The red is similar in hue to the stone he's just placed in his little pail. "They're not meant to be identical; they're meant to complement one another. Differences make things beautiful as a whole."

The rumble of tires on the unpaved road echoes in the ravine. We both look in the direction of the noise, and a truck speeds up the gravel road.

"I thought the sign said no driving up here," I say.

"It did." Dad squints. "Not too many come out here anymore. I imagine collectors make their own rules now." Two men wearing stiff new camo and matching pants step out of either side of the truck.

Dad nods in their direction, but they're too busy laughing at something we can't hear.

They open the backseat and pull out big five-gallon buckets.

Dad shakes his head and leans toward me. He speaks from the side of his mouth. "Great hunters of rocks."

I snicker.

The taller man wearing an old-fashioned baseball hat walks directly to the nearest bank. He doesn't scout or tilt his head back and forth, looking for where the best spot to dig might be. Instead, he runs a scanner over the hill's surface until it beeps. "Something here!"

He stands back as the shorter, squattier of the two holds up something resembling Dad's electric drill. He presses a button, and it squeals to life with a hum. He walks to the spot the scanner indicates and begins pummeling its surface with his drill. Within a few seconds, he reaches down into the tailings and squeals out, "Turquoise!"

Dad sighs. "There was a time when butchering a site was regulated."

"And now?"

"Pfft. Now? No one much cares about these rocks anymore."

"If no one cares, why did we have to hike out here? Why can't we just drive too, and use a scanner and mechanical digger and take what we want?"

He raises his eyebrows. "Because that's not who we are."

He pulls me into a side-armed hug and reaches out, taking a handful of dirt. He opens his palm. The dirt sifts through his open fingers; some falls to the ground, some blows away in the wind. A tiny gray rock is all that's left in his hand.

"You need to feel the dirt. Sense when it will give you a gift. And only take a few of what you need." He sounds so much like Lita and her ideas on food.

"But Dad, they found turquoise! It's worth a lot now."

"Who says what a rock is worth?" He hands me the tiny gray stone. "When my project is complete, what you and I have gathered will be more valuable to me than the Hope Diamond."

I sigh. "I wish we could stay longer to search."

"Don't worry, Petra. We'll come back." Dad knocks on the top of my helmet. "And when we find turquoise, it'll be with respect."

In less than an hour, the men are heaving their buckets of mixed rocks back into their truck. Dad shakes his head as they drive away. We continue looking for the perfect few rocks that will join Dad's other beads. By the time the sun dips near the horizon, he's found seven of our eight maximum the park rules allow.

Sweat drips down my forehead into my safety glasses, fogging them up. I've decided I'm done when I spot a tiny bit of yellow under the dirt. I use my rock hammer to chisel around its edges, then pry it up and brush away the surrounding dirt with my gloved hand. I pull out a piece of golden-yellow jasper with one narrow vein of deep red. I hold it up proudly to Dad and he smiles. I place it in the pail with the others. It stands out like a beacon, but also somehow blends in perfectly.

Without a word Dad sits down on the ledge we've been digging. He pats the ground next to him. I nestle in, and he puts his arm around me. Every so often he sighs as we stare toward the sunset. We're dirty and exhausted, but it might be the best day I can remember.

It begins to drizzle, and the smell of wet dirt fills the air.

"Hey, Dad?"

"Yep."

"Knock knock."

"Okay, I'll bite. Who's there?"

"Petra."

He lets out a deep sigh. "Petra who?"

I take an exaggerated deep breath in, inhaling the smell of rain in the desert. "Petri-chor."

Dad flops straight back onto the ground and groans.

10

THE SAME MESSAGE PLAYS OVER AND OVER FROM THE Cog inside my head. "I *am Zeta-1, Expert in botany and geology.* I *am here to serve the Collective.*"

I feel the En Cognito Cog slide out like they're pulling a burning ember from the back of my neck.

My mind slugs like I've napped too long in the middle of the day. How long has it been? Regardless, whatever that downloadable message was trying to tell me "I am"—isn't going to work.

My name is Petra Peña. We left Earth July 28, 2061. The "Collective" was going to erase all our En Cognito *programs. Ben was trying to save me and my memories.*

The shapes of people bustle around the room. There are too many of them. The room feels nothing like the calm of when it was just Ben.

What am I waking up to? Ben must be long gone. But I still remember what I think were his final moments. *Purged. A new history.*

"Finish draining pod twelve," a stiff voice says.

If they are draining the pods, we've definitely arrived.

A gurgling noise burbles by my feet.

Oh, God! Wait. I'm not ready.

Wasn't this what I'd wanted? To be here on Sagan with my family?

"Exciting. Is it not?"

"Place her on the table."

This isn't how it's supposed to happen. Dad and Mom should be here.

Is what happened like the mutinies that happened on ships long ago? Or is it something far scarier? I'm more afraid than the time I found a rattlesnake in Lita's chicken coop.

The rattlesnake's head appears behind one of the roosts. Adobo's feathery head drapes over her nesting box.

I sense them lifting me. I land with a wet thunk onto a spongy surface.

The ear-splitting buzz of the snake's rattle fills my ears. I can't move. I haven't even seen Lita approach with the hoe.

"Set her on her side. We are ready to restart organ function."

I want to scream out for them to stop.

"Engaging electrical impulses."

I picture Frankenstein. *No! Don't engage electrical impulses!*

Pain sears into my chest. My heart tha-thunks.

I cough and gasp.

"Vital functions intact."

Oxygen pours into my lungs.

It's all happening way too fast. My throat burns like lemon juice over strep. I need my mom. I try to open my eyes to find Javier, but I can't force them open.

The high-pitched whine of air through a vacuum fills my ears. Cactus plant pinpricks of heat run over my face in vertical strips.

Someone gasps. "What are those?"

"An Earth disease. Should we quarantine her?"

A woman's voice, smooth and twinkly like a wind chime, speaks. "I'd ask you not to mention that word in front of them."

"Apologies, Chancellor."

I think of the Collective from the news. *Erase the pain of the past.* How far did they go?

But the scientists and doctors on our ship, like Mom and

Dad, won't tolerate assimilation. They'll remember. They have to.

"Freckles." A finger rubs over the bridge of my nose. "Skin damage from their sun," the Chancellor says. "Without epiderm filters, this sort of physical anomaly happens."

Warm water flows over my cheeks. Then suction. Cool air hits my face.

The vacuum pulls onto my ears, and suddenly my muffled hearing is gone. Small beeps blare like sirens.

The robotic voice inside my head repeats the words, but this time fainter like a distant echo. "*I am Zeta-1, Expert in botany and geology. I am here to serve the Collective.*"

How many centuries has this loop been running through my mind?

I repeat the truth. *My name is Petra Peña. We left Earth July 28, 2061.*

If this loop was downloaded to my Cog, and it's still in my mind, but I still remember who I am . . . maybe whatever Ben was trying to do worked. Maybe the stories he downloaded are still in there somewhere too.

"Restarting electrical impulses to Zeta-2," someone says from the pod right next to mine. "Place Zeta-2 on her side."

The Chancellor's smooth voice is so close. "Can you tell me who you are?"

Someone coughs. "I am Zeta-2—" a voice I recognize as Suma's says. She coughs again.

"What is your role, Zeta-2?"

"I am Expert . . . I am . . ." She struggles to speak. "I'm . . . I'm cold." Suma stumbles.

"Is she defective?" a man asks.

Light filters through my closed eyelids.

I breathe in slowly. I know I shouldn't call attention to myself. But I force my eyes open. They burn like I accidentally rubbed them after deseeding a habanero. Bright light hits my eyes and tears pour down my cheeks. Things are foggy, but a group of five people surrounds Suma. Backs to me, they're each covered from head to toe with what look like HAZMAT suits. I look to where the window is, hoping to see either sky or stars, but the window's covered by a sheet of metal. The room that should contain three rows of pods lined up like an egg carton is nearly empty. I scan quickly for Javier. Hazy figures of at least eight people mill about the room, none of them small enough to be him.

They lift Suma out of the pod with gloved hands. Her body plops to a table between our pods. Excess gel drips to the floor.

Suma's eyes open lazily, and she flinches back, eyes wide in fear. "Momma?" Her voice shakes. "Ben . . . ?"

"Disappointing," the Chancellor's icy voice says. She drops Suma's Cog into a bowl with a metallic clink.

"Should we purge her, Chancellor?"

I don't know how to help Suma. There are too many people

to fight. I can suddenly feel my stomach again, and something inches up my throat. *Don't barf. Don't barf.*

The Chancellor holds up a new shiny black sphere. "There is no need for that. Place her back in the pod. With the upgraded download"—she leans over Suma's pod screen—"Suma Agarwal will be Zeta-2 for the rest of her life."

They lift Suma off the table and ease her back into the pod. She wriggles sluggishly in their arms like a dying fish.

The Chancellor leans over her, hinging rigidly at her waist like a stick bug. "Shame. Her reprogramming will take up precious time. We could have used her abilities for the first mission." She sets the upgraded Cog into its installer and presses the activation button. Then she slides the glowing purple Cog onto the back of Suma's neck and turns to the others. "This time we'll assure there's nothing left from before."

Our parents are going to demolish them . . . I hope.

I barely see the faint glow of the sphere as it melts into Suma's spine. She winces, whimpers, and goes still. Without a word, or bothering with restraints, they begin filling her pod with stasis gel. Suma sinks downward.

My heart is beating so hard in my chest, I know they'll hear it.

One of them starts to turn back around, and I slam my eyes shut.

I can't let them put me back in! What's the line? I *am Zeta-1 . . .*

Once again, water runs over my chest and stomach, then

legs. My body's lifted up, and I'm flipped over onto a new board, this one softer. They wrap me in a blanket.

"Scanning her brain."

A buzz vibrates my skull. Tiny beeping noises shift inside one side of my head to the other.

I'm terrified to open my eyes again. What scared Suma so badly? What could be so frightening? They're just people.

"Pod twelve—youth sector. Identify your role," the Chancellor says, so close I can smell her sweet hyacinth breath.

I couldn't answer if I wanted to. I can barely wheeze in air, let alone speak.

I have to do something to let them know I'm not "disappointing" like Suma. She lays her hand on my cheek. "Open your eyes, Zeta-1."

I crack open my eyes and force myself not to gasp.

Blood vessels and tendons weave like hoverways under the Chancellor's translucent skin. She brushes her pale, sickly hands over my forehead. *Don't react.*

I swallow hard. The person in front of me barely looks human. She looks more like the ghost shrimp I saw once at the Albuquerque aquarium. Just like the ghost shrimp in the tank, she's both beautiful . . . and horrifying, her veins glowing red and blue under pale skin. Her darker cheekbones arch too high on her face, leaving a shadowed valley to her jawline. And her lips, the color of lilacs, are too full.

Her eyes are so light I can see spiderweb capillaries behind her irises. She smiles.

Warm water drips off my forehead and into my mouth. I look toward the direction where Javier's pod should be. Like most of the rest, it's missing.

Dad's words hit me as if he's right there. "*What they want isn't so much the scary part, it's how they propose doing it.*"

Suma floats in glowing green gel near the door. How did it get to this point?

Whatever this Collective is, I just have to convince them long enough that I'm what they want. *Zeta-1, Expert in botany and geology. Here to serve the Collective.*

Everything will be fine once I find my parents and Javier. And whatever these people are, they can't make me forget.

My name is Petra Peña. We left Earth July 28, 2061. It's now 2432, and we've arrived at Sagan.

I'll do whatever I have to do to find my family.

11

MOM BRUSHES THE FINAL KNOT OUT OF MY HAIR.

"You literally named me after the Greek root of the word *rock*," I say.

Mom snickers. "Actually, your dad came up with it. But I thought it sounded pretty." I see her shake her head in the mirror, smiling. "He didn't tell me what it meant until after I agreed to it."

"*Rock*," I say. "My name means 'some old dirty rock.'"

"Your name is beautiful, Petra. Like you."

Strands of hair fall from the braid dangling down her chest. Her green eyes in the sun look bluer than usual, a layer of gold over the top. Freckles dot over the bridge of her nose. I'll never be as pretty as she is, but I can tell by how she's looking at me, she thinks I am.

"Besides, your name suits you. You're strong." I look up, and her eyes are welling up. "I don't know what, but you will be the foundation for something amazing one day."

I roll my eyes. "You don't let me do the things I want to do." I don't say out loud what I know is always in the back of everyone's mind too. My vision.

But how can I ever be the "foundation" for anything, if she won't let me try? Or if she's always steering me toward botany instead of what I really love? I know I could be a storyteller. Story generators are ruining everything. I can tell immediately if a book is written by a real person or a lifeless program. And all I want is for stories to feel real.

I fold my arms over my chest.

Mom finishes my braid and ties the holder around the end. "You don't have to like me all the time, Petra." She stands up and kisses me on the forehead. "My job is to keep you safe, so you can have the best life possible."

12

THE WOMAN'S VOICE IS SOFT IN MY EAR. "IDENTIFY your role."

I roll over and cough out a green loogie. I know I'm about to betray myself. "I'm . . . I'm Zeta-1." My voice comes out in a rasp. "Expert botanist and geologist. I am here to serve and obey the Collective."

Oh God! I screwed up the line. Not *obey*. Just *serve*.

A faded vein under the lady's see-through skin moves as she furrows her brow.

"Elevate her, Crick," the Chancellor says.

The man, Crick, lifts me to a seated position by my armpits. He places his cold hand on my chin, turning my face from side to side. "Fascinating," he says. Just like the lady, a vivid blue vein runs over his left eyebrow, like he'd brushed eye shadow way off course. And just like the woman, the lower half of his face sits in the shadow of his cheekbones. His lips are full, not from a makeup trick or fake-looking fillers like back home. Similar braids spiral over his scalp. I glance at the woman next to him, who shares all the same traits.

What happened to them in the last three hundred and eighty years? I think of biology class and Ms. Cantor teaching us about the peppered moths in England, their new color camouflaging them from birds among the soot. They'd evolved so quickly. Those moths were still beautiful.

This is nothing like that. I think of the lady's "epiderm filter" comment. Have they done all this to themselves? Just to avoid looking different from one another?

I swallow, cringing as my own saliva feels like I gulped hot coals. Crick lifts a shot-sized cup to my lips. Not knowing what to do, I take a sip, but tuck it in the side of my cheek. A tiny bit slips through, and the pain is instantly gone. I swallow the rest and shiver as a wave of warmth moves down my body. It's a little like Lita's cacao, only much stronger.

I have no idea how people with memory-wipe are supposed to walk or talk, so I sit quietly, holding my arms stiffly at my sides.

A little girl two pods away coughs too and gags up her own gelatinous lung slug.

"That's right. Expel it completely." A man gently pats her back. "Can you tell us your name?"

In a tiny voice, the girl answers, "I am Zeta-4, Expert in all things nanotechnology and surgical. I am here to serve the Collective."

She doesn't even cringe when the man pokes his translucent nose to hers, glaring into her eyes.

Zeta-4 looks as young as Javier. She sits stiffly while the man flexes her hands up and down at the wrist. "Her small fingers make her perfect."

Crick turns back to me and picks up a corposcope by its metal handle. He activates it, just like the pediatrician always did, and it flashes bright pink. He leans down in front of me, starting at my feet, then brushing it upward over my skin. Every so often he pushes it back at arm's length to look at its display.

As he passes it over my belly button going upward, I almost slap at his hand, then realize I need to keep my mouth shut and act the part.

Crick presses the end of the wand, speaking into the tip just like a holotack. "Heartbeat within normal limits." He proceeds upward.

Oh God! My eyes . . .

It's too low and out of my line of sight, but I sense him at my neck, then chin, then mouth . . .

When the Corposcope reaches the bridge of my nose, it buzzes and turns solid pink. It's over.

He leans in, staring. He's so close, and the room light so bright, even I can see the tiny blood vessels spiderwebbing over his pale irises.

"Chancellor? I think you will want to see this," he says.

I hold perfectly still, unable to inhale a full breath. I can barely move, and I think I understand what shock feels like.

She stares at the scope. "Hmm, defective." She presses its end.

The Corposcope speaks in rigid tone: "Ocular disease. Diagnosis: retinitis pigmentosa."

"Her eyes don't appear different than the others," Crick says.

The Chancellor sighs. "Many of their physical failings weren't outwardly visible."

I clench my teeth together. I understand my parents being a little protective, but I'm no failure.

Crick scans over my eyes again and shakes his head.

I can't believe I've come this far, and this many centuries away, just to have it end here. But we knew the rules, and still brought *my* disease to *their* new world. My parents swore and signed my false medical history. The other Monitors got rid of

Ben for a lot less. I breathe in and out slowly and tuck my shaking hands under my legs.

But I'm no aberration. If I'm going to be purged, I'm going to give them a piece of my mind on my way out. I unclench my jaw and open my mouth to speak—

The Chancellor turns to Crick. "It's of no matter. We are not interested in her eyes. We are interested in utilizing her brain."

I snap my head in her direction.

"Still, they are physically . . . unique," Crick says, sarcasm in his voice.

Look who's talking!

"But the Collective has taken great strides and risk to move beyond that, haven't we Crick?"

Crick's shoulders sink. "Yes, Chancellor."

"Just so we're all of one mind," she whispers softly in his ear.

He makes an almost imperceptible head nod.

"I believe we have done enough to absorb this one small physical variance, don't you?" She turns back, staring into my eyes. "They are so ancient; we must try to ignore their appearance. Thanks to us and their programming, their minds have some value, and that is all we are interested in."

"Of course," Crick says, setting down the Corposcope.

I stare at the Chancellor, unmoving. Maybe they aren't so bad?

Technically, these aren't the people who purged Ben. The ones before them did. And *this* Collective isn't judging me by my eyes like people back on Earth did. It's been nearly four hundred years, after all. Maybe they've changed.

Still, Suma is floating next to me in her pod, her brain being wiped anew. Like Dad said, what matters is how far they'll go. Right now, I don't care why they want us to forget. I just need to play the part until I can find my parents and brother.

Crick slips a weighted blanket over me. The blanket expands, and immediately more warm liquid begins pouring out of it, removing the last of the stickiness. Once my skin is free of the gel, hot air blows from the blanket's inner lining over my body, muffling the noises in the room.

Just like I was taught, I scan the room bit by bit. There should be eighteen pods here. Only four total are left, including mine; the little girl, Zeta-4's; the pod Suma's in; and one more.

Suma, aka Zeta-2, is back in stasis in the corner. So the last to be removed, Zeta-3, is being lifted to a seated position. As soon as he is upright, I see he's too thin and tall to be Javier.

"Open your eyes, Zeta-3."

I compare my freckled brown skin to the boy, Zeta-3's. His skin almost glows beneath his freckles. I refuse to accept that they want to name us all "Zeta." So, maybe just for me, in that moment I decide to come up with my own names for us all.

They pull off his cap to reveal a thicket of strawberry-blond hair. *Rubio.* And I have his name.

The Chancellor pushes a probe on Rubio's tongue and stares down his throat. "Remove them."

"Open your mouth, Zeta-3," Crick says.

Rubio does just as he's told. My breathing speeds up as an assistant wearing a mask and surgical gloves approaches him. A spinning noise and hum of a laser is followed by a burnt smell. It's a little too close to the reek of Dad burning chorizo and eggs on the weekend before we found out about the comet.

The spin of Crick's tool shuts off. Two singed pink nodules drop into a glass of fluid.

My throat clenches.

Crick holds them up like a curiosity, then sets them on the tray along with our blood samples. Thank God I've already had my tonsils out.

But Javier hasn't. Even if it means they reprogram me like Suma, I will not let these people poke and prod him like this.

The warm air flowing over my body stops. Crick comes to help me sit up again. His nails pull the baby hairs at my hairline as he peels back the rubber cap. My hair explodes out in a loofah of wild ringlets.

Crick's eyes widen as if my hair is going to attack him.

Luckily Rubio's lanky body decides at that moment to slump over during the medical exam. He collapses, still sticky, back in his pod.

"Assistance with Zeta-3, please!" the woman calls out.

"Normal reaction," Crick responds. "They've been in stasis nearly five units."

I do the quick math. If we've arrived, then each of their "units" is over seventy years.

"What should I do?" her panicked voice asks.

"Let them sleep," the Chancellor says coolly.

Seriously!

"With a bit more rest, they will be able to begin." The Chancellor is already setting a blue capsule inside Rubio's mouth. She lifts a green fluid-filled cup to his lips. The green fluid clashes against his hair like a Christmas wreath. "Drink."

Rubio swallows the pill with the green chaser. He lies back down and breathes heavily almost immediately.

They repeat with the little blonde girl.

Crick walks toward me. I open my mouth just like they did, hoping they'll think my trembling is a side effect of just coming out of stasis.

Crick slips the pill onto my tongue. I close my mouth, lodging the pill on the inside of my cheek. I take a small sip of the green liquid. It's not my imagination. I suddenly feel calmer and stop shaking. If they've figured out ways to control our emotions, I tell myself it's better to stay petrified and alert than accept any more of their drinks. I lie back down in my pod a little too quickly, hoping the snoring isn't too much. The pill swells on the inside of my mouth. I roll to one side quickly to mask the bulging chipmunk-cheek side of my face.

"Let us close the room to let them rest," the Chancellor says, walking out. Most of the people trail behind the Chancellor exiting the room. Crick and another woman linger behind.

"Exciting day, was it not?" the woman whispers. "Aren't they wonderful?"

The lump continues to grow slowly inside my mouth, creeping down my throat.

Crick clicks his tongue. I'm pretty sure it means the same thing as when Lita does it.

He sighs. "I hope they can perform." He walks toward the door. "There were not any decent Experts until the removal of the Epsilon an entire unit ago. Let us hope these have impeccable knowledge and compliance."

He turns off the light, and from the hall to the adjoining teen stasis room, a faint green light glows on the floor. More pods! Their conversation is confusing, but I can't waste time now trying to determine what their bizarre words mean. I need to see if Javier's been moved to that room. When I hear the door sealing, I lean over to the pod's suction tube, opening my mouth. The sludgy lump sucks down the hole with remnant stasis gel. I spit into the bowl just like the dentist's office and wipe my mouth.

My legs wobble as I tiptoe toward the green gel glow coming from the narrow hall. I know there's not much I can do right now until they remove him safely from stasis. I just need to see Javier's face.

I turn back just to make sure no one's awake or watching me, then continue down the hall toward the room. Unlike ours, it seems to be empty except for a mass in the back corner, with a faint green glow. Just like in our room, where a window should be on the outer wall, a metal insert obscures the view outside to the stars, and maybe my first view of Sagan. It's too dark, and my eyes are having trouble adapting. The low hum and faint beeps of controls keep a steady rhythm. I shuffle slowly toward the green glow in case I bump into something I can't see.

Without the constant swooshing of the stasis gel being replenished, you could hear a nanochip drop. When I reach the corner, instead of the pods filled with glowing green gel I thought I saw, I realize it's only some equipment and a monitor, emitting light from the ship's atmospheric reading station.

Not Javier.

No longer worried about knocking something over, I circle the empty room, wondering where they could've put him. I'll have to wait until they remove him or I find my parents.

I back up slowly toward my room, and right into something.

I yelp and turn around.

"May I help you, Zeta-1?" Crick inches toward me, the hall's blue light illuminating him like a glow-in-the-dark fish.

The tiny sip of the drink I took is suddenly not working. I tuck my shaking hands behind my back, unable to speak.

"You should be asleep," he says.

"Bathroom," I croak out between shallow breaths.

He smiles. "Come with me," he replies, leading me back through the hall toward my room. "I suppose we didn't think of that. Of course, you wouldn't know."

In the hall between our rooms, he presses a button, and a door slides open to a small open room, four toilets lined side by side like a row of desks in a classroom. "Nope," I say aloud before I can stop myself. Have they literally wiped awkward from our memories too?

"Pardon, Zeta-1?"

"Just clearing my throat," I answer, stepping inside. I hurry to slide the main door shut, leaving Crick outside.

Crick waits, whistling. Not a happy hum or pee-pee encouragement song. Just the three same flat notes over and over.

I close my eyes trying to imagine a trickling stream. After a minute of nothing happening, I press the expel button. I stand, looking for a sink. Instead, two glove-shaped sleeves made of the same material as the bath blanket are embedded into the counter. I slip one hand inside on the right, and just like the weighted blanket, warm water massages my hands, followed by warm air.

I open the door and Crick is waiting to lead me back to my room. "Would you like another sleep capsule or some tonic?"

"No!" I answer too quickly.

He waits by the door until I crawl back into my pod before leaving. Rubio's snores groan like an overcrowded hoverway.

I think of everything that lies between me and Mom, Dad, and Javier.

When I was little and staying at Lita's house, any time there was a thunderstorm or I had a nightmare, I would crawl into her warm bed and she'd tell me a story to calm me. Her cotton nightgown smelled of flowers and her breath of coffee and cinnamon. But the pod bed is cold and smells of disinfectant. I close my eyes and pretend the pillow is her chest.

Curled in her arms, her voice whispers softly in my ear. "En los tiempos viejos, there were two warring lands. One king had a daughter, Iztaccíhuatl, the white lady, who wore a long white dress and a red flower of the tulipan tree in her raven hair." Lita sighs like the daughter in the story, Iztaccíhuatl, was a dear old friend of hers. "Iztaccíhuatl," she elbows me softly, "or Izta as I like to call her, was promised to wed the arrogant son of the power-hungry high priest, but instead fell in love with a brave young tribal leader named Popocatépetl. And Popocatépetl fell in love with Izta."

Even before she told me "her version" of the cuento, I knew the legend. Popoca and Izta were on the wall of Dad's favorite Mexican restaurant on a black velvet painting. Well, that and I'd googled the story.

"When Itza's father sent Popoca off to war, the evil priest, plotting for his own son to wed Izta, lied and told Izta that Popoca had died in a fierce battle." Lita shakes her head. "With this devastating news, Izta drifted into a deep sleep of tristeza."

I roll my eyes. I already know Izta actually dies in the story. I sit up and give Lita a give-me-a-break look. "*Really?* She just fell asleep?"

Lita shushes me. "When Popoca returned he found Itza under her spell of sadness and deep sleep."

"But really, didn't she die in the real version?"

Lita gives me "the look." This is *her* story and she will tell it her own way.

"While Izta slept, Popoca carried her to the top of a snowy mountain. He created them each a mound and lit a torch.

Popoca formed a pillow of snow for Itza and surrounded her with the red flowers of a tulipan tree."

I also found on Google the next day that Popocatépetl is really a volcano, and the name is literally Nahuatl for "smoking mountain."

Lita narrows her eyes into a storytelling threat. "His fire and lava frighten those who dare come too close to his lover. So angry that being off to battle had cost him his eternal love, Popoca vowed to stay with Itza, lying next to her where he also sleeps, protecting his love until warring neighbors can settle their disputes without the costs of war."

Lita stares off into the starry sky out her skylight. "And to this day, they rest next to each other, waiting until the earth is peaceful so they can awaken and marry. Esto es verdad, y no miento. Como me lo contaron, lo cuento."

Even though I know the story isn't real, something about Popoca being so dedicated to Izta that he'd spend his life high atop a mountain, waiting with her, always gives me comfort.

Lita made it no secret she thought our world's leaders needed to swallow their pride and figure out their differences. But in the end, even with the comet coming, everyone had been out for themselves. They didn't have much time, but they didn't even try to pool resources to build a shelter, or maybe another ship. Everyone worried only about their own. And Izta and Popoca never got to marry.

I see Popoca and Izta on top of the mountain, Izta in her

white dress, the wind blowing her long black hair, a single tulipan flower tucked behind her ear.

Popoca holds her hand and smiles. But still they wait and wait and . . .

13

I YAWN AND RUB THE SLEEP FROM MY EYES. I SIT UP. Zeta-4 and Rubio are already dressed and standing at attention by the door.

I tumble out of my pod.

The little blonde girl is in line behind Rubio. There's a space between them. A neat French braid begins at Zeta-4's left ear and curves around the back, to where it twists into a pretzel bun on the opposite side, a lot like the Chancellor's. Even the kid's hair looks brainwashed. I hurry to gather my hair and braid quickly, trying to copy what Zeta-4 has done.

Both Zeta-4 and Rubio look a lot younger than me, and I wonder if that's why the Pediatric Cog didn't work on me. Maybe with its malfunction, I'm missing out on some sort of programmed routine. Apparently sleeping in isn't part of that schedule.

Tufts of hair I miss jut out like a staticky lion mane, and the pretzel bun falls out twice, leaving the braid dangling down my chest.

My hands tremble as I pull on my shoes. I can't believe I'm messing up my chance to find my parents.

I scoot in between them just as our bedroom door slides open. A waft of over-sanitized air blows over me. I glance over at Suma, who floats peacefully in her pod, having her memories of her home and mom stolen that very moment.

I stare straight ahead, expecting someone to walk in any second. As I'm trying to steady my breath, something soft brushes against my fingers. I flinch and glance down to see a ghost-shrimp boy younger than Javier staring up at me. His smile makes his face even more rounded, but just like the others, this mini-version shares the same violet eyes and pale delicate skin. He smiles even bigger. He's almost . . . cute. I know my vision isn't great, but the little boy must be even better at sneaking around undetected than I am. How did I miss him come in?

He leans in close to my hand, rubbing his finger over my arm.

"Voxy!" We both jump at the Chancellor's voice. "What are you doing?" she asks from the doorway.

The boy, Voxy, tilts his head. "These spots on her skin. What are they?"

She bends slightly, looming over him. "You are not supposed to be here."

Voxy quickly steps away from me. "I wanted to see the Zetas, Nyla."

Nyla raises her brow and clicks her tongue.

Voxy's eyes fall. "I mean, Chancellor," he says.

"Well, you've seen them now." She flicks her wrist, her long fingers scissor-blading out.

Voxy glances up and I meet his eyes. He smiles and I grin back before realizing what I'm doing.

The Chancellor turns back to face me, and I quickly stare ahead again.

She flashes what Mom calls a social-media smile. "Zetas, I am Chancellor." The sweet fig smell of her breath is so close it fills my nostrils. "I look forward to seeing what you all have to contribute to the Collective. We have much work to do and little time."

The Chancellor faces me at the front of the line, staring over our heads. "You will remain together as a unit until you receive your assignments." She turns and walks out our bedroom door into the hallway. "Come," she calls back like we're pets.

We pass the adjacent teen room, looking through the door where I saw the grumpy Lead Monitor hovering over the blond boy's pod that first day. We continue walking. Rooms which should contain other passengers in stasis, instead hold walls of hexagon bed tubes puzzled together like a honeycomb.

The Chancellor turns into the hall leading to the colossal open park. I see the big windows ahead and remember Javier yelling "Whoa!" and slamming his hands on the glass the first time he saw it. I think of the track and pools, the theater and cafeteria on the other side. How magical it all was. How lucky the "Collective" has been to live on the ship with all that cool stuff.

Instead, Mom's Hyperion redwood has been watching over the Collective just like Izta and Popoca watched over their people, waiting for peace to arrive.

My heart speeds as we approach the bend leading to the windows. Mom's redwood among a forest of green is just ahead. We round the corner.

I wince back from the brightness. I slow my pace, staring down, my throat dry. The central cavity of the massive room is so stark and white, I blink hard, thinking I must be in the wrong place. There is no park. No bushes or trees. The stage and theater are gone. The track and gym are instead walls of white.

The screens above that should show Earth's sky are empty. Only an expanse of bland, matte metal remains. The ceiling screens are not Earth's sky, only a blank field. The carpet of green grass, with its trails and Mom's tree, has been replaced by a floor of iridescent glass glowing from below. The cafeteria with cubbies filled with food and a wall of magnawaves is bare. Besides a few tables and white pillars, the main room is barren.

It feels twice as big with everything missing. A knot digs into the back of my throat.

In another life, I'd been sure that once the grown-ups were awake, we'd run and play and swim and watch movies until the settlement was ready for us on Sagan. My legs go numb, and I stop.

Rubio bumps into me from behind. "Zeta-1?" He taps me on the shoulder, and I take three hurried steps to catch up to the Chancellor again.

Below, I see a smattering of ghost-shrimp Collective mill around the empty room.

The word *Harmony* in bright green starts to flash across the otherwise blank ceiling. I'm sure I'm imagining it, but then *Unanimity* replaces it in purple.

Chancellor Nyla leads us into one of the glass elevators. She walks in ahead of us and turns to face us. As we descend, I stare right through her to the opposite side of the ship, where I know my parents are sleeping in their pods. All I want is to get to them, and Javier, wherever he is, and right now that feels impossible. I focus on my breathing, like we learned in yoga in PE, to keep myself from crying.

They've ruined everything people had worked so hard for. How could they destroy something so wonderful? Wasn't it supposed to be for them anyway?

We step off the elevator, and a man with an impressive double pretzel-loop on top of his head points at us, like we're some sort of exhibit at the museum of natural history. Along with the man, the main room is filling with others who look just like Chancellor Nyla, Crick, and Voxy—blonde braids twirling across their scalps. A watershed map of veins spread out under the surface of their skin. Same cheekbones. Same full lips.

I think of all the different colors of skin of the scientists, passengers, and Monitors boarding on the first day. I glance down at my own freckled brown arm. What have they done to themselves?

The first man bites daintily into a brownish-green loaf and sips pale liquid. Thanks to science class and Ms. Cantor's obsession with prepping, I know all about purified urine. I hope they haven't figured out a way to—

I'm so busy staring, I don't notice a boy barely older than me standing next to Chancellor Nyla. He holds a tray in front of me. The shape of his face reminds me of a kid at school—Cole Stead. Just like Cole, he barely makes eye contact, and probably only knows I exist because I'm taking up space in front of him in the lunch line. The same little brown squares and cups of yellow fluid are lined neatly across his tray. Rubio and Zeta-4 are already chewing what looks like a compressed prune square and drinking from their cups.

The boy nudges the tray forward. Everything within tells me it's not a good idea, but I actually feel like I haven't eaten in four hundred years.

Nyla glances over at me. "Is something wrong, Zeta-1?"

I think of Suma and how if I'm back in stasis, I won't be able to find my family. Rubio and Zeta-4 seem fine, so I grab a bioloaf square off the tray and quickly pop it in my mouth. If kale, hay, prunes, and vinegar had a baby, I'm pretty sure it would taste like bioloaf. Nyla is watching me, and I wonder if she has some secret skill of detecting lies.

"*Mmmh*," I mumble.

She nods. "We meet here for our daily rations."

I chew just enough so it's a paste. Bioloaf Boy who looks like Cole sighs and turns the tray, so the cups of liquid are facing me. I pick up a cup with mystery yellow fluid and stare down at it. I hope it's not like the green "tonic" from the night before. Bioloaf Boy quickly walks away.

Nyla turns to watch me again.

Before I can argue myself out of it, I lift the cup to my lips. With one gulp, I swallow. Thank God. It only tastes mildly of something like diluted apple juice, and I don't feel any sort of change in my emotions. Within a few seconds, the concoction of the two expands in my stomach, and I feel like I've eaten enough food to last me the entire day.

I burp bioloaf, and a waft of alfalfa and disinfectant fills the air around me. I blow it in Nyla's direction. The elevator in front of us opens, and Crick exits, remotely directing a cart.

Red, blue, green, and gold drinks fan out like a quetzal's rainbow of feathers across the six clear trays on Crick's cart. People clap and "*oooh*" like Crick is delivering each of them a luxury hovercraft instead of colored juice.

He directs the cart toward what was once the cafeteria, and we follow him until he's in the smaller open room connected to the domed great room.

One by one, Crick hands over to our group one of the trays filled with what he called tonic. "Your job is to keep the Collective tranquil," he says.

I glance at the crowd. They don't look like most people do going into a party. Other than the momentary outburst for the drink cart, no one looks particularly excited or annoyed. No one even pretends to be happy like Dad does before one of his work parties. They're all just . . . there. I'm wondering what kind of party this is supposed to be.

The Chancellor slithers between Crick and me. She takes a single glass filled with emerald-green fluid from my tray and lifts the drink to her mouth. She closes her eyes and drinks the entire glass in one smooth gulp, then purses her mouth, the liquid forming a thin, dark line on her lips.

She smiles and walks to the center of the room. Except for the clicking of her shoes, the room goes silent. She turns with a grin on her face just like a fox.

A distant echo of Lita's voice fills my mind. "You must always remember the story of the fox and crow. It is good to trust others. But there are some, like the fox, who will make promises to gain your trust. They are tricksters and will not have your best interest at heart. You must be able to sense those who have selfish intentions."

"How will I know?" I ask.

Lita kisses my cheek. "Listen to the story and learn from the crow's mistakes, for the crow did not see the fox's sneer, but only heard his deceptive words."

Lita squints just like a fox. "En el tiempo des nuestros antepasados, los animales hablaban. 'Pobre Crow,' Fox said. 'You seem to have demasiado queso to carry. Perhaps if you dropped some of your cheese, your load would not weigh so much.'"

"Wonderful news!" the Chancellor announces. "The biodrones have confirmed the atmosphere has sufficient oxygen."

An echo of thrilled caws erupts in the massive space.

"The water supply has shown only mild salinity," she continues.

Crick gasps. "This is it," he says softly to no one.

"Crow considered Fox's words. Of course, Crow was tired. And Fox's suggestion seemed so much easier than all the hard work he'd been doing."

"As the survival of the future Collective is what is most important," Nyla says. "The atmospheric evaluation will require a . . . test subject. A chaperone of our own to explore the planet with Zeta unit."

"And with that, Crow dropped his cheese, and Fox gobbled it up. Y se acabó lo que se daba."

"As you all know," the Chancellor continues, "Zeta unit has joined us." She motions toward Rubio, Zeta-4, and me.

I grip the platter as a roomful of eyes settles on me. My blood freezes, but I try to act natural—whatever "natural" means now.

"The drones were unable to collect the underwater plants.

So, the Collective will need to forage samples in person. Risk is high, so the Zeta unit will collect these among other specimens we need."

The glasses vibrate on the tray in my hands. I'm not sure if I'm terrified of the "risk" of being the first on the surface, or excited we'll be leaving the ship. But I especially love how she volunteers *us* for the dangerous part.

A man with wide eyes and unsteady breath approaches me. He grabs a glass filled with ruby-red fluid off my tray. The liquid trembles in his grip. He lifts it to his lips and chugs it down where the others can't see him. He wipes his mouth with the back of his hand. A streak of red brushes over his hand. He smiles, an instant happiness washing over him. He lifts a second glass to his mouth, this time green, washing away any trace of red.

He turns back, speaking casually in a low voice to Crick. "I hear I may have been the one chosen to accompany the Zetas tomorrow to the surface."

I think I've found the Crow.

Crick's smile falls. "Yes, Len." Crick places his hand on Len's shoulder. "Nyla has determined," he pauses, "for the Collective, you should accompany the Zetas."

"Of course." Len glances at Crick's hand on his shoulder and takes another drink. His voice shakes. "I am happy to do my part." He sets the glass down a bit too hard on the table and tonic spurts upward. "For the Collective."

Crick brushes a droplet of green off his face and glances around to see if anyone saw.

Nyla lifts her glass. "Everyone! Enjoy your evening. The near future will be difficult work, but it will advance our cause." She pauses, glancing in our direction. "And with it we will fix the errors brought on by our predecessors."

I grit my teeth. I know by "predecessors" she means my parents and the other passengers.

Chancellor Nyla motions to a man across the room. The man nods and waves his hand over a display. The entire room dims, and my vision dims along with it. A buzz vibrates through the air. Holographic stars encircle us. I set the tray down quickly on a table. Even though they know about my eyes, the last thing I need in the dark is to bump into someone I can't see, and spill a rainbow of tonic. I stand with my back to a pillar, hoping no one will notice.

The air begins to hum, then shriek. I recognize the morbid squeals as those NASA recorded of the radio waves of planets. Nyla closes her eyes and breathes deeply, like the sound waves are some New Age Meditation stuff Tía Berta listened to. The sound vibrates through my body. Mixed with the spin of holographic stars, glimpses of pale faces with red-tonic-lined lips wash by like anemic vampires.

A woman next to me smiles dully, a stack of empty glasses lining a tray next to her.

Nyla comes to stand next to Crick on the opposite side of the pillar. The planet noises are so loud I can't hear, so I slide closer, hoping my gray jumpsuit camouflages me enough that they won't pay any attention to me.

"Regarding Len . . . Chancellor, what if the atmosphere is not suitable for us?" Crick asks over the noise.

"The air is suitable. The water can be processed," she says with zero emotion.

He makes a tiny exhale and head shake. He's noticing the same thing I am.

"Yes, but is there anything *else* that could harm us?" he asks. "What about the things we can't measure? The things that may be . . . different for Len—us—than they were before."

She turns to give him a stern look. A star drifts over her face, the veins beneath her skin glowing blue as it passes. "Whatever decisions the Collective made long ago were made in our best interest. What we are now was what they were striving for. Unity demands sacrifice. Sacrifice comes with a price."

Crick nods as if he already knew all this and just needed the reminder. I'm sure they're talking about the alterations they've made to themselves. Lita always said there are costs when you mess with nature.

"We cannot know for sure until it is tested with one of our own," she says calmly. "But if the planet is incompatible with the Collective, we will leave."

Crick cranes his neck quickly at her. "Leave?"

"One of the other viable planets we've found is within two units," she says, looking away.

If it took us five units to travel three hundred and eighty years . . . ? I struggle to take a breath. Two units will be two lifetimes.

Crick looks away like he's calculating too. "But that would take—"

The people surrounding us drink tonic and poke at the stars zooming by them, clueless to the decision being made about their life.

"Sacrifice." Her voice stiffens. "That is what it would take. We have a duty to the Collective to find a permanent home, where we can survive without threats from anything or anyone that would harm us. We owe it to those who came before us, and those who will come after, even if it means we live out our lives on this ship searching for it."

My head swims. I lean my cheek against the cold pillar. A satellite passes slowly across the opposite side of the room. A few people follow behind it, staring curiously.

Crick turns his gaze back toward the holographic show. "Of course, Chancellor."

What does this mean for us? Zeta-4, Rubio, and I just serve them for the rest of our lives on the ship? Our parents stuck somewhere, hidden in stasis for who knows how long?

But, it's no worse than some environmental factor on Sagan that kills everyone. Nyla might be heartless, but she's right about making sure a planet is viable. And it sounds like she'll do whatever she has to do to protect her people.

I can't wait any longer. I need to get out of here and find my mom and dad.

14

DAD AND I UNLOAD THE BAG OF PEAT MOSS MOM ASKED for. We each take one end, and Dad pretends it weighs more than it does. "Not sure how I could do this without you," he says, making me feel valuable, though at nine I'm barely big enough to be helpful.

We walk with it through the back gate to find Mom and Javier asleep on a blanket on the grass in our backyard. The sun is quickly falling below the horizon.

Rápido saunters off toward his den near the trail leading into the desert.

Dad and I dump the bag of moss on the ground. Mom stretches and sits up. "Prince Charming and his squire, returning at sunset from their conquest, with a gift of sphagnum."

"I'm glad we survived our perilous mission to Home Depot."

"Well, I'd say looking around here, it was worth the life risk." Mom motions to her garden. "This is our medieval battlefield. I plan on dying with a rake or hoe in my grip."

Dad laughs. "Petra, we're counting on you to roll our dead bodies right into the raised beds for compost."

"Gross!" I yell.

Javier flinches awake and whines.

"I've got him." Dad picks up Javier and props him over his shoulder. Javier's pudgy feet dangle down Dad's chest. "I'll go give him a bath."

Mom picks up her phone and turns on the flashlight. "Wanna go on an adventure before bed, Petra?"

I nod quickly. Before Javier, it was just the three of us. And there were enough years between that I remember what it was like not have him come between my time with them.

"How about a fairy hunt?" She winks and gets up.

I can't help grinning. She knows how to lure me in. "Fairies aren't in the desert though. They're in forests."

"This *is* a forest. It's just a desert forest." Mom gasps. "Did you see that?" She whips her flashlight to the first tree on the trail and heads to it. It's covered in pink blooms.

"On the desert willow?" I ask, following her.

"Exactly. Well done." She smiles.

I try to imagine the flowers' petals are actually wings, but all I see are clusters of flowers. "I didn't see anything."

She ignores me and whips her flashlight in the other direction. "Ah yes, it must be. The elusive Sage Fairy."

I squint at the dark purple flowers on the bush. "I think I did see something."

"And the English think *their* lavender attracts fairies. It's got nothin' on our desert sage."

Daylight is fading and the sky is turning purple, with barely a ribbon of orange on the horizon. Mom points her flashlight up ahead on the trail. She puts her finger to her lips. "*Shhh.*"

I follow her lead, whispering, "Giant Pipe Cactus Fairy."

Giant arms of spiky green protrude into the sky. "There must be a fairy city as big as Albuquerque under that!" I say. And with that, my imagination's off and running. "I bet they have such huge parties. Each cactus arm has its own magical door of a different color." I point to the tallest cactus stem. "The largest glimmers gold. Fairies who enter must fly through an obstacle course of rose-thorn hoops that would tear their fragile wings. They have to dodge exploding chamomile that causes instant sleep and dripping honeycombs, one drop of which would gum their flight shut. But once through . . ." I lower my voice to a whisper. "Then comes the riddle." I narrow my eyes. "I am in each rainbow." I reach upward with my arms. "I am in the sky." I dip my knees. "In the oceans' depths." I wiggle my fingers. "And the feathers of a jay. What am I?"

Mom smiles, but instead of looking at me, she's scanning the area behind me for something else.

I bow. "That is correct, pixie. I am the color blue. You may enter." I continue, now oblivious to the surrounding desert. "Fairy gowns and suits shimmer like the wings of dragonflies. Fairies drink from cups the shape of lupine bells. Fountains of juice and nectar of all different colors fill their cups." I close my eyes. "Trees filled with fireflies twinkle with their glittering—"

Mom gasps again, interrupting me and pointing in the opposite direction. "What's that?"

I turn away from the magical fairy party inside the tallest cactus arm. Mom's flashlight is pointing at a very real shrub with little yellow flowers.

I sigh, "Creosote."

"Good job!" she says. "Isn't botany great?"

"*Mmmh*," I mumble, realizing what this really is. It was fun while it lasted, though.

She kisses my head and points her light back at the house. "And there lives the loveliest of all the fairies. Petra Fairy. And she needs a shower before bed." Mom catches my eye and winks. "Beat ya there."

She takes off running, and I sprint after her, terrified of the darkness.

15

NYLA AND CRICK'S CONVERSATION GOES QUIET. I LEAN around the pillar. Crick is closer than I thought. I pull back a bit, but not so far that I can't see the white orb that now fills the space beyond him. I recognize its pitted surface. I know if this hologram of theirs is astronomically correct, then behind the moon, I'll find . . .

A man with his braids twisted into a neat bun points and smiles. "Glorious!"

The 3D hologram spins like a massive blue-and-green marble. A few gasp at the planet only the youngest of us here have actually set foot on. It spins gracefully right in front of me. Even if it's no longer anything like *that* Earth, I still smile at the memory. On *that* virtual planet was my Lita.

My eyes fill with tears, and a yelp from deep inside me is drowned out by their wailing music. Rubio walks right by his own planet without giving it a second glance.

From the far side of the ceiling near the dome, a streak of light flashes. I turn and see everyone else has already noticed it, and are watching the show. The comet and its tail approaches slowly among the stars and the people standing around the room. Dinner sludges in my gut. I tell myself the hologram's not real. I can't just rush out and push Halley's Comet off its course. I can't make it un-happen.

The Chancellor waves her arm, and the glowing serpent speeds up its trajectory toward Earth. It hits the middle of the Pacific Ocean between Hawaii and Fiji. In an instant, a bowl of debris shoots upward. Arcs of light blast out in all different directions, like a firework exploding through the entire room. There are *ooohs* and *ahhhs* from the green-lipped Collective, like they casually witnessed a hard tackle at a football game and not the destruction of a planet.

In fast motion, a ring of fire spreads out from the Pacific Ocean east toward the United States, and west toward Japan.

The entire room fills with particulate. It soars through our bodies and then rains back onto Earth.

My throat tightens, imagining Lita somewhere in those dust particles. I've never fainted before. My lips tingle and the room tilts. I stumble to the closest table and collapse into a chair. If anyone sees my reaction, it's all over.

The music quiets, and Nyla walks to the center of the room as the lights come up a bit. Her features are softened by our planet's dust swimming around her.

She motions to where Earth spun peacefully a few moments earlier. "Today we celebrate our arrival to the new planet. What happened to the former world was not a tragedy. It was an opportunity to leave our past behind. Thanks to the Collective, not a single memory of a world filled with conflict, starvation, or war will find its way into our future."

My parents wanted a better future too. But Dad said exactly the opposite of how people needed to get there. "*It'll be our job to remember the parts we got wrong and make it better for our children and grandchildren. Embrace our differences, and still find a way to make peace.*"

"We are a single unit now, without past vices. We will no longer need to create a new history, for there is no past. Today's Collective and the new planet is our origin. The Collective will transform our new home to something far better." She holds up her glass. "To our new origin."

The space booms with all the Collective voices. "A new origin!"

I stare down at the ground. Even if my parents and the other passengers wake up, there are so many of this Collective.

I lay my head on the table. The screaming notes of the music turn back on. Intermixed with its notes, conversation and laughter begin again.

"Zeta-1?"

I lift my head quickly and wipe sweat off my lip. I look up to see Nyla. "I must be acclimating to the new diet, Chancellor. I apologize," I say, unable to look at her. "I will be back to help serve in a moment."

"That won't be necessary," she says. "Your duties for today are complete. You may return to your sector and rest." She pats my shoulder and I shudder. "If all goes well on your scouting mission to the surface, you will have even more important work when you return," she continues. "I think you will enjoy working in our laboratory complex."

I think back on the first day and the hold containing a shuttle and supplies. There were no labs back then. But I remember Ben explaining how he and the other Monitors were going to assemble them to be ready when we landed, for our parents to do their work.

"I am looking forward to it," I say. "To serving the Collective, that is."

She smiles and I force a smile back. I know as long as she's assured I'm using my knowledge to serve them, I'm safe.

"You can go now," she finishes.

She doesn't have to say another word. This is my chance. I walk toward the elevator and pass Zeta-4 happily holding out her tray as a woman exchanges an empty glass for a full one.

I enter the elevator and push floor 6.

I think back to Ben's words on the first day. "*I'm really sorry, Dr. Peña. They'll be just across the ship.*"

As the elevator rises, I draw a line in my head from our rooms to the opposite side of the ship. But between me and where my parents should be are the quarters of half the Collective.

I exit the elevator and scan in each direction. I let one long whistled breath out. If I'm caught—"I *just got disoriented.*" I pass my room and keep walking toward the back of the ship, following the mirrored route on the opposite side of the ship until I'm out of breath. The layout is identical to ours, and I soon find the room directly across. The door on this side slides open with the same *vvvvvttt.*

But instead of our parents' pods, the room's back wall is a stack of beehive beds, each covered in a warming blanket for a thin-skinned ghost shrimp. Collective clothing lies folded at the base of each bed.

Where are they?

I continue down the hallway and find identical rooms, but no stasis pods.

From further down the long hall, I hear voices. I stop for a moment, hearing them grow closer and closer and closer.

I turn and run in the opposite direction until I'm back at the center of the rear of the ship. I lean against the wall and scrunch my eyes tight, trying to decide what to do. I can go toward whoever is coming and convince them I just got lost. Or I can find a way to keep searching for my parents. I open my eyes. It takes a moment for them to adjust. I scan for the nearest door and see the familiar purple-blue light under a doorjamb in front of me. The voices are getting louder.

I step forward and open the door, stepping inside.

My footsteps echo on a metal platform. Light, the deep purple of the ocean and a reminder of the Pleiades Corporation, illuminates a stairwell spiraling downward into darkness. The door slides shut just as the voices outside approach. I hold my breath until they pass and fade away.

I take another step, and it echoes without seeming to end. I'm walking into my worst nightmare, a space of complete darkness without Mom, Dad, or Javier to hold my elbow. I grip the railing and take one step down. With each step, the stairs illuminate one by one, a purple-blue light sputtering to life. I count steps to take my mind off my imagination telling me someone is right behind. But there's no sign of a floor. "One forty-two," I whisper, "one forty-three." I continue with only my whispered words to comfort me. "Two seventeen, two eighteen . . ."

The echoes of my footsteps become more distinct until suddenly I'm standing on a tiny landing, facing another door. I press my ear against its jamb. Slowly, I pull open the door and enter.

I walk into what I recognize as the central hold we entered on the very first day. I start at one end and scan carefully. The shiny dark beetle of the shuttle ship squats at the far end near the entrance, exactly like it had four hundred years ago. I skim farther and see the plexiglass Habitrail lab complex Ben must've built, the one Nyla was talking about. I keep scanning to the center of the hold, where the warehouse rows of metal bins should be. But they're no longer there.

Instead, that section of the central hold is filled with row after row of stasis pods.

I smile and cover my mouth. At least a hundred pods. I wrap my arms around my waist and feel myself starting to sob.

I've found them. Now, I just have to figure out which ones are my family's.

Maybe I can steal a Cog extractor. Lift Mom's and Dad's heads and place it on the back of their necks. They'll start to wake up, so I'll need to suction their airway, but the stasis pods have the attachments right on it. The tough part will be lifting them out and cleaning them up when they're so groggy. But if I can get one of them out myself, they can help me with the other and then Javier. I watched them remove Rubio. How hard can it be?

Even if the Collective messed with my parents' memories, Mom will never forget our fairy hunt. Dad will remember "*Who's there? Petri-chor.*"

When I read Javier his *Dreamers* book . . .

Path lights pop to life as I hurry down the rows of pods. But then I realize that not a single pod is glowing.

With each step, my stomach twists into knot—*empty pod*—after knot—*empty pod*—after knot. All of them, dozens, each pod, empty and dark.

Orange utility buttons flicker on each nameplate. I lean

closer to read. *Flinn*. I zero in on the alphabetical order, moving to the next aisle. *Richter*. Then the next: *Quinn* . . . *Putnam*, *Peterson*.

I take a deep breath. *Pequin*. And finally, the next one . . . *Peña*. Like all the rest, it's empty. I hold my stomach and lean on the pod. The only sign of anything functioning is the flashing orange button. Something deep within tells me to leave. *Don't press it. If you don't, it won't be real*. But, I'm frozen.

I close my eyes, take several deep breaths, and reach out and press the button. The same smooth voice from the ship's intercom booms in the room as I stare into the empty pod. "*Peña, Amy. Memory erasure: fail. Reprogram: fail. Purged 7-24-2218*."

My knees buckle, and I fall to the ground. *Purged?* I grip the pod and gasp for air. I don't want to imagine what the word really means. But I know. Just like Ben.

I hunch over the edge of Mom's pod. My insides feel like they've been scooped out like a pumpkin. They will come looking for me soon. But I don't care now.

Everything Mom promised—our lives on Sagan together—vanishes. Mom will never brush my hair or kiss my forehead again. She'll never take me on a fairy hunt on Sagan that is sure to have even more plants and imaginary fairies than anywhere on Earth. Even if Mom and I weren't searching for the same things, we would've still been together.

I rub my hand inside the pod, hoping I'll be able to sense some part of her. But the pod where my mom slept is empty.

"Mom?" I whisper. I curl up on the ground next to it. Once, I think I hear a noise from the far corner of the hold, but no one comes.

I come to later. I'm not sure when. I crawl to the next empty pod. "Please, please, please," I whisper. I press the button.

"Peña, Robert. Memory erasure: fail. Reprogram: fail. Purged 10-28-2277."

I hug the bottom of Dad's pod. My chest feels like it's being crushed by a giant fist. My eyes burn, and I struggle to pull air into my lungs. This isn't fair. How could they have done this to so many people? My parents just wanted us to be together. I think I hear another noise, but I don't care.

The dates my parents were removed. They were an entire lifetime apart. I know Mom had been joking in our backyard, but that's how I would have imagined them in the end—lying side by side in our garden bed together. Instead, another image comes to my mind now. Each of them floating by themselves, out in a vast space. Not old, but how they looked the day we left Earth. Frozen and alone.

The bioloaf paste in my stomach heaves back up. Way more than what I'd eaten splatters onto the floor. I wipe my mouth and lie against Dad's pod.

I force myself to breathe and pull myself toward the next pod.

I don't want to look, but I have to know. Just like my parents' pods, the button blinks in a slow orange sputter over the nameplate. *Peña, Javier* is barely visible.

I step up to the pod. It's empty.

Javier too. They are all gone.

The screech of a metal door echoes out of the deepest section of the hold. "Who is there?" a gruff voice calls from the darkness.

I sprint out back the way I came, stumbling up the stairs with hot tears streaking my cheeks.

16

WHEN I RETURN TO MY ROOM THE PODS ARE GONE AND replaced with a beehive of backlit hexagon cells, just like all the Collective's quarters. Shadows fill two holes with the shapes of Rubio and Zeta-4. I crawl into the cell next to Zeta-4.

Tears pool on my plastic mattress. Why Javier? He was just a kid.

I would've been better off if the Collective's reprogram to my Cog had worked.

At least I'd be oblivious like the others. I wouldn't be lying here wanting to die with my family. If I tell the Chancellor I remember everything, she'll either purge me or try reprogramming me again. Either one is better than spending a life imagining what happened to Mom, Dad, and Javier.

Zeta-4 whimpers next to me in her sleep. Without her Cog, she and Rubio are no longer being fed downloads while they sleep.

She jumps, slamming into the wall of her bed and vibrating our entire honeycomb.

"But Mama, you promised only one shot! It'll hurt."

I sit up in my cell and hit my head.

All of Zeta-4's memories of Earth should be gone. Even in her dream, how can she remember her mom and going to the doctor?

I climb out and rub her arm to wake her up. She yelps and yanks her arm back.

I can't let her stay in well-check hell. I push on her arm, jostling her awake. She bolts upright and turns toward me. "Zeta-1, what . . . ?" She takes deep breaths. Her brow furrows, and she knocks her fist on her forehead like she's trying to jar something loose. "Odd . . ." Her chin trembles. "She wasn't real." She looks up at me, tears in her eyes. "Was she?"

I know down in the hold of the ship, there's an empty pod with her mom's name too. And somewhere deep in her mind, Zeta-4 is yearning for a mom she'll never know again. The memories of my own mom aren't in dreams though. At least Zeta-4 can pretend the pain isn't real. I can never go back and tell Mom

I'm sorry for scaring her on our way to the ship. "Go back to sleep," I whisper to Zeta-4. "We can talk about it tomorrow."

She lays her head back down. Her breath catches, and I know even though she thinks they're imaginary, she's still digesting her feelings. I think of what Lita would've done to comfort her. Will I just make it worse, like with Javier?

Mom's voice echoes in my mind. "*Really, Petra, this isn't the right time for a story.*"

I wish I hadn't refused to go on the ship the last day. And I wish those words weren't some of the last things Mom said to me. Zeta-4's body shudders. It's worth the risk. I rub her feathery hair.

My voice trembles.

Arrorró mi niño,
arrorró mi sol,
arrorró pedazo
de mi corazón.

I hurry to wipe my eyes.

Zeta-4 rolls back over to face me. "What was that, Zeta-1?"

I clear my throat. "It's called an arrullo, a song to help us sleep. I'm not very good at it."

"Aluro," she mispronounces. "I like it." She rubs the back of her hand over her eyes. "Zeta-1?"

"Yes?"

"Why do you think my dream made me cry? I shouldn't cry. Should I tell the Chancellor?"

"No!" I put my hand on top of hers.

The words from Mom and Dad's pods fill my mind. "*Memory erasure: fail. Reprogram: fail. Purged . . .*"

"Don't tell anyone about your dreams. They shouldn't be shared with the Collective."

"If you are sure," she says.

"I'm sure." I squeeze her hand. "Can I tell you something?"

Tomorrow, after I tell the Chancellor I remember who I am, I won't remember these stories anyway.

"What would you like to tell me?" she asks.

Rubio turns over in his cell, but his snoring continues.

"It is called . . . a cuento," I say. "It is to serve the Collective. But for now, we must keep it to ourselves."

"Cuento . . ." Zeta-4 says.

I begin just like Lita used to. "Érase que se era . . ."

Her brow crinkles. "What do those words mean?"

"They mean, like, the beginning. Once upon a time."

Her face goes blank. I realize she doesn't recognize the phrase in Spanish or English.

"All cuentos start with something to set the mood. And they end with a saying to finish it."

She nods as if she understands, but I don't think she does.

"Once, there was a princess named Blancaflor," I begin. It's not a standard fairy tale. Parts of it I'm not even sure how to tell in English. Lita said there was a time, when she was a little girl, she didn't dare speak Spanish in public, or share her stories where others could hear. A time when her language and the color of her skin could mean trouble. So, under a blanket of starry skies and piñon smoke, out of habit, she whispered her stories to me in Spanglish. Her own version, passed from her grandmother, and her grandmother's grandmother—each of them a slightly different version depending on what was happening in their world at the time.

I remember what Lita said about my stories. "*Never be ashamed of where you come from, or the stories your ancestors bring to you. Make them your own.*"

I will never be a real storyteller now like Lita. But for Zeta-4, I decide to tell one more. And for Lita, I'll make it my own.

I imagine her version combined with the Chancellor's sickly face and slithery words as bits of Earth flew into space. "*What happened to the former world was not a tragedy. It was an opportunity to leave our past behind.*"

I sit crisscrossed in front of Zeta-4's hexagonal bed opening. "Blancaflor's father was a strange king whose fear of the outside world turned him into an ogre. He had see-through skin and a voice like a serpent."

Zeta-4 flinches back a bit and snickers. Then I flinch back too, a bit shocked by her snorty response. I smile. Either they haven't blocked this part of her brain, or something in the story broke through to her.

"But Blancaflor was giving and kind and open minded to all she encountered, with rich reddish-brown skin like the Sangre de Cristo Mountains."

Zeta-4 closes her eyes and smiles. I know she's picturing it all in her mind, even though she has no idea what the Sangre de Cristo Mountains are.

I rub my hand over her soft hair. "And hair of blonde feathers like a snowy owl." *Feathers.* With that, I have Zeta-4's new name.

"Owl," Feathers whispers to herself, her forehead creased in a confused ponder for an animal we'll never see again.

"When a prince wandered into their . . . realm, Blancaflor saved him from her horrible father's control."

I tell Feathers of each impossible task the king gave the prince to perform for his freedom. And how, each time, Blancaflor was the one who gave the prince the tools he needed to complete his challenge. But in the end, the king would not grant the prince his freedom. And together, the prince and Blancaflor fled.

Maybe I'm going too far . . .

"As her father chased Blancaflor and the prince, each on one of the king's flying steeds, it was Blancaflor who took the comb from her hair, dropping it to create jagged mountains which erupted from Earth."

"Earth?"

I picture it spinning back at the Chancellor's party, green

and blue in their pale world. No color but their drinks. The heat in my chest rises. "Yes."

"Earth," she whispers.

I continue. "It was where Blancaflor and the prince lived. It was a planet."

"I feel like I've heard of it. But how does this cuento help us serve the Collective?"

I continue without answering. "Blancaflor then dropped a gold pin, which turned into hot desert sands like the Sahara. But the evil leader continued to gain speed. Blancaflor took off her sapphire shawl, making blue waves and white foam, like the Pacific."

As I speak of the ocean and its waves, Feathers' brow furrows. I realize I don't even know where she's from.

"Finally, Blancaflor delivered the prince safely back to his own home and family. The prince's father was grateful that Blancaflor returned his son to him . . ." *Make it my own.* "And the king was so impressed with *her* cleverness, he made Blancaflor his heir and next ruler of his kingdom. She chose the prince as her sidekick for his knowledge of the kingdom, where she ruled with intelligence and kindness. Blancaflor not only ruled the prince's kingdom, but went on to outwit her own ogre of a father, and any other tyrant or ruler who was unkind." I finish with, "Y colorín Colorado, este cuento se ha acabado."

Feathers sighs. "Will you sing me an aluro and tell me another cuento tomorrow?"

"Arrullo." I smile. "And only if you promise not to tell anyone."

She nods.

A different voice calls from the next sleep cell.

"I will not say anything either."

Heat runs over my face. I lean toward the next hexagon cell to see Rubio wide awake, head propped by his elbow. What have I done?

"It was wonderful," Rubio says. "I like Blancaflor."

Feathers falls into her pillow, eyes closed. "Me too, Zeta-3."

I rub her feathery head one more time and crawl back into my cell. "Me too," I say, much happier with my new version of Blancaflor.

This can't be the end. This can't be the way my story ends.

The room quiets, and their soft breathing and Suma's gel swooshing become the only noise. I close my eyes but can only picture my family's empty pods. And the casual voice: "*Purged.*"

What would my parents have told me to do? What if Javier could see me right now?

I know they'd want me to live. To fight. I can't stay on this ship any longer. I have to find a way to escape.

Lita would have told me to pray. But when I close my eyes and try to talk to God, I hear nothing. And I have nothing to say to Her right now anyway.

Instead, I imagine I sit under a blanket of stars with Lita; so many scattered in its darkness, if you squinted the entire sky would fill with glitter.

Or I'm curled around Javier, his soft GG Gang sweatshirt against my cheek, while I rub my finger over his constellation birthmark.

Then I'm with Dad, his arm around me, the smell of fresh rain on the desert floor and rocks enveloping us.

Mom brushes my hair from my eyes and points toward a desert sage; in my imagination, a purple-winged fairy flits toward us.

I know I can't live a life without my memories. If I forget them, it's like my family never existed. Tears drip down my face and neck until my hair is damp.

Feathers and Rubio deserve to have those memories of their families back too. What had they and their families hoped for? Had their parents promised them a new life on Sagan like mine had?

Rubio makes a loud snore just as Crick walks in carrying a stack of folded clothes. One by one, Crick sets dark gray jumpsuits at the end of our cells. Part of me is excited. They're for Sagan.

If I want to escape, I need to stay calm. "Hello, Crick," I say.

"Hello, Zeta-1," he says. "How are you feeling? You should be asleep."

"I'm better now."

"Wonderful. You have a big day when you wake up. It could be dangerous."

My heart pummels inside my chest. "I expect the Collective will be thrilled with what we are capable of." I hint at Chancellor Nyla's slithery voice. "I'm proud to be a test subject for the Collective."

He furrows his brow.

I roll over before he can respond.

17

I BONK MY HEAD ON THE INSIDE OF MY SLEEP CELL AS a soft voice speaks over the ship's comm system, jolting me awake. "Zetas, prepare to be escorted to shuttles."

In the reflection of the metal door, Feathers and Rubio are already standing at attention, jumpsuits straightened and zipped to their necks. Their hair is slicked back like a freshly raked garden. I jump up, quickly pull on my jumpsuit, and finger-comb out the tangles, weaving a loose braid. Strands of escaping hair tickle my cheek, and my jumpsuit lumps in spots.

I've barely tied my work boots when the door slides open. Crick faces us. His face glows with excitement. "Follow me, Zetas."

How did I oversleep? This is the day I need to be operating at one hundred percent.

I hurry to slip on my gloves and like the others, fall into line.

Crick marches us down the halls toward the elevator. Curious faces peek from rooms, and whispered conversations follow us around corners.

I stare out the elevator's glass to the main room where the park had once been, the floor emitting a pale white glow, like we're walking out onto ice which could crack apart and swallow us any moment. I glance toward the cafeteria where Nyla had the party the night before. The tables and pillars from the party are gone, leaving only an empty room once again.

In one tiny section of the main arena, at least twenty people form an assembly line behind a workstation of potted plants. My stomach knots. The only way it's possible for plants to be growing in space is with Mom's time-released nutrients, like she'd used in Hyperion's soil. I can't help staring as they snip off the larger leaves of what I now recognize as kale. They place those leaves, a scoop of protein powder, and then a glob of what looks like Mom's sourdough starter into a compression unit. Within moments, they remove a block like a puke-green Hershey bar and break off smaller squares.

Bioloaf Boy from the party approaches us holding a tray mounded with square sections. I'm not sure why they give him this task when we could just walk over and retrieve it ourselves. Feathers and Rubio reach out, each taking a cube. I do the same. I try to give a smile of thanks, but he's obviously still avoiding eye contact with me, so I pretend to be absorbed, observing the production line.

Crick comes to stand next to me, pointing in the direction of my gaze. "I can understand your fascination in our sustenance production, considering your background in botany," he says. "Brilliant, really. Vegetable, protein, and yeast. An indefinite supply of food."

"Yes. Removing only the leaves you need, leaving the rest to continue growing. And the yeast reproduces on its own asexually using budding." I clench my teeth. I'd seen the rations the first day on the ship. There should've been enough to last them another century. I want to tell him the seeds for those plants were meant to be cultivated on Sagan. I don't even bring up the protein powder which was meant for the passengers once we arrived.

The little boy Voxy approaches waving, Nyla at his side. His mouth widens in a huge grin, bioloaf coating his front teeth. I bite back a smile.

Nyla shoots him a quick glance, and he lowers his arm back down to his side.

Even though they are spread out, in the expanse of this main room alone, I realize, there are far more people than there should be on the entire ship. Rations meant for the Monitors were strictly planned out. But these people are no longer Monitors, and they aren't following the rules.

There's no way they could have sustained this many people and all the passengers in stasis on the ship. And then I realize, they never really intended to support anyone other than their Collective—which made those of us who were left far more disposable.

Many of the Collective scurry off after eating. Some remain, each cleaning a massive section of floor that looks like you could safely lick its surface. In a mirror image above, at least forty people dangle from the ceiling by harnesses, squeegeeing off the already pristine dome ceiling. The occasional *Harmony* or *Unity* flashes above, each purple letter larger than the person cleaning it beneath, like an ant holding a grape.

By the time I pull myself away from the show above my head, a workstation hinges down from a hidden pocket in the wall. One by one, like massive falling dominoes, more workstations lower from hidden pockets in the surrounding walls of the room. From the cargo elevator, the hum of levitating bins led out by people to each station echoes.

Ten people, five on each side, clean and fold sleeping blankets, sliding them into a bin. Another assembly line of jumpsuit repair falls into place. All working with a precision saying they've done this thousands and thousands of times.

The ship was set to be self-guided and able to go for centuries without maintenance. So beyond checking on our pods and Cogs, and getting things prepared for arrival on Sagan, the old Monitors like Ben were supposed to have the time and space to work on the things they loved.

Now it's all just busy work. Nothing creative or unique; nothing colorful or messy.

But still, even here, there are some stragglers. Like the teachers at my school who huddled on the playground during recess to chat over coffee. Here, they linger over bioloaf. I back away slowly from Crick, Feathers, and Rubio, who are silently eating their food, and Nyla, who appears to be trying to have a serious conversation with Voxy, so I can eavesdrop on the small group by the wall.

A man with wideset eyes like a hammerhead shark nibbles on his bioloaf. "*Mmmmh*," he hums.

I can't tell if it's a yes-hum to something someone just said, or a yum-hum to the bite he just took. But if bioloaf is all the guy's ever eaten, he can't possibly know how awful it is. He's never tasted mango-chile paleta or chocolate or Takis.

The woman next to him leans in. She's slightly shorter than Nyla and looks like she's making up for something with twirlier braids. "I hear they are sending Len." She clears her throat. "Len and I were in the same Collective creation batch as infants."

I glance at Voxy. I'd assumed he was Nyla's son.

"We even have the same duties. And planetary exploration was not one of them."

"What are you saying, Glish?" Hammerhead asks.

"I am saying nothing. Just a curiosity." But Glish suddenly shoves her entire cube of bioloaf in her mouth and walks away.

I jump as a hand takes hold of my elbow. I hadn't seen anyone approach.

"Shall we?" Crick says, smiling. He motions to Nyla, Voxy, Feathers, and Rubio. Nyla shoos Voxy off, and he slumps his shoulders, skulking away.

I choke down my bioloaf and follow them back on to the elevator.

We descend, sardines in a can, dark metal casing surrounding us for several floors.

The elevator bounces to a stop with a pleasant chime, and the doors open. We step out into the hold with our family's empty pods. My hands begin to shake, but I keep my face straight. *They are no longer here. They are no longer here.* And they've been gone hundreds of years. There's nothing holding me to this ship any longer. I know Feathers' and Rubio's parents are out here too. They trail behind Nyla and don't give the dark pods a second glance.

I think of Suma back in stasis. I can't help anyone.

Here in the hold, everyone in the Collective is just as busy with mundane chores as they are above. How clean does it need to be? It's as stark as the main level. No art. No music.

Crick clears his throat. "Any new developments from the drone reports, Chancellor?"

"Nothing of consequence." Nyla doesn't even glance his way. "There are strong winds in the habitable zone which come in eight-hour cycles. Nothing we are unable to time our scouting missions around."

I'm not sure what's up with Crick's constant questions, but it's obvious there's more going on than they're sharing.

I wonder if the first ship made it to Sagan. And if they did, were they able to survive? Could anything like what happened on our ship, have happened there too? The Collective doesn't seem to be in any hurry to find others from Earth.

We continue walking until we reach the entrance ramp of the ship. A lump forms in my throat as we approach the spot where Mom held my elbow the first day. But instead of the ramp like before, the entrance is covered by a metal tunnel-port into the shuttle which has been moved from its dark corner, just like Ben said it would be. Nyla leads us past watching eyes onto the shuttle.

I've taken plenty of transports on school field trips, but this is no public-school shuttle.

Fancy purple strip-lighting of the Pleiades Corp still runs along gunmetal floor and ceiling. Even the seats lining the sides are the original indigo blue of the luxury liner company. Instead of crammed rows of benches front to back like a school shuttle, though, there are only ten seats on each side, each as large as those in the cockpit. A lab station and cubbies with open sample bags run down the center of the shuttle. The vials and collection tools would've intimidated me before the hundreds of years of downloads. But the En Cognito program ensures I understand how each instrument in that bag works.

Feathers walks to a seat on the left side, plops down, and buckles herself in. Rubio does the same.

I take the seat directly across from Feathers. A moment later, Len, the man from the party who was drinking far too much tonic, walks in behind us fully suited up as well. I'm not sure if it's my imagination, but a fresh crease of the green tonic seems to line the corners of his lips. He sits away from us toward the back and closes his eyes.

Feathers blinks slowly, like this whole thing bores her. She sees me staring. "The Chancellor couldn't think of anything specific for me to do," she chirps in a high squeaky voice, "so I will be looking for raw material for nanotech. Do you know anything about carbon nanotubes?" I shake my head and purse my lips together, to hide my smile.

Nyla approaches me. She takes a deep breath and leans over. "Zeta-1."

I lose the smile quickly and nod. Hopefully soon I won't have to answer to that ridiculous title.

"Your job is especially important," Nyla says. "We need your expertise to help with defoliation."

Before we left Earth, I hadn't thought I'd actually have to use any of Mom and Dad's En Cognito program. This is when I would've been convincing my parents I wasn't meant to study the sciences. I was meant to be something else.

Of course, to settle on Sagan, they'd have needed to clear some of its plant life to build their settlement. But that would've been their job.

I think for a moment what I do know of herbicides, ranging from less toxic solutions like vinegar, salt, and dish soap to something like Agent Orange used in the Vietnam War. Obviously, I can't tell Chancellor Nyla I remember some of those things so specific to Earth's history. "Can you be more precise?" I ask.

She looks away. "We need to remove some of the native species. The Collective believes an airborne herbicide can kill foliage, without risking physical contact with dangerous flora."

I hadn't thought much of the Collective actually occupying the planet. I can't imagine them off the ship. I guess some part of me thought they'd land, but never leave the safety of their sterile world.

"Creating an airborne herbicide isn't a problem," I say, telling her the truth. "It's easy enough to do in the lab back on the ship," I say. "I will collect any plant specimens that might be resistant. For the Collective," I add.

She smiles at this.

"We are ready," Crick says.

"Well then." Nyla clasps her hands together.

She looks at each of us, but Len doesn't acknowledge her.

Nyla and Crick exit the shuttle, and the airlock door vacuum seals behind them. The shuttle grows eerily silent except for Len whispering something I can't quite make out.

Even though the cockpit's vacant, the hum of the shuttle's engine vibrates under my feet. The remote-pilot setting immerses the cockpit in a red glow.

I glance back at Len. His eyes are still closed. There's no way he could look paler, but his lips are unusually violet, and he looks like he might pass out.

The shuttle clanks as we shift off the dock and onto the launch rails. We jostle as it begins to make a ninety-degree turn to face the open launch portal.

My mouth drops open as a shimmering purple-and-blue abalone sky comes into view through the cockpit window. I know certain colors are harder for me to see, and I wonder how much more magical this looks to Feathers and Rubio.

I glance over, and Feathers has a smile on her face. Rubio's brow is furrowed.

"Fascinating," he whispers.

By their reactions, they're still not quite as blown away as I am. But obviously something within them, no matter how deep, can still be curious and impressed by something beautiful.

A low-speed blender hum kicks in and levels off to a high-pitched whine. Within a few seconds our shuttle is spit out like a sunflower seed. I'm sucked back into my seat as we catapult from the ship into the sky. Antigravity starts up, and the shuttle slows, then stops, hovering at the same level as the ship.

The shuttle trembles, a sign that back on the ship, Crick's hand piloting us remotely is doing the same. I can't confess to them I've piloted a hovercar a thousand times (mostly while sitting on Dad's lap and without Mom knowing), and could have gotten us to the surface with a smoother ride than Crick is doing right now.

The quiet of AG takes over and I can finally hear what Len is saying. He's whispering over and over, "For the Collective. For the Collective," while sweat beads up on his transparent skin.

"Helmets on," Crick's voice calls over the speaker. I suction the tracking corpomonitor to the back of my neck, the comm unit behind my ear, and then plug both into my suit. I reach behind my seat and slip on my helmet like everyone else. I hinge the helmet forward, and it seals with a *ffffft*. Fresh air flows from an air cartridge.

We pull away from the shadow of the ship and make a steep dive. My stomach plummets like I forgot it two hundred meters behind us. I close my eyes until we level into a flatter forty-five-degree descent. When I open my eyes again, Len is the only one with his still closed.

"*One thousand five hundred meters,*" the altimeter calls out.

From the cockpit, dark mountain peaks come into view. The more we descend, the greener they become.

From this height, I can see exactly what my father meant when he explained Sagan's tidal lock.

He picks up Javier and sets him on his lap. "Its orbital period is the same as its rotational period, locked in place by its red dwarf sun."

"So, it's always sunny?" I ask.

"Not as bright as if it had Earth's sun," he answers.

Below, this sky reminds me of twilight in Santa Fe. "*Four hundred meters.*"

"Sagan's dwarf sun is much smaller, but so close to the planet it creates a tidal lock," Dad says. "Not too hot for us, but warm enough to melt water from its colder side." He laughs like it's some joke only nerds understand. "Of course, we won't be taking trips to the dark side of Sagan, but the zone where we'll live will be just right for us."

"Like the story of the three bears," Javier chimes in.

Dad smiles and pinches Javier's nose. "Exactly why they call it a Goldilocks planet."

Far off to the east, the mountains turn white with snow in the shadows of Sagan's darker side. Just like Dad said.

"*Two hundred meters.*"

Directly below us in Sagan's permanent sunlight, though, lies a jungle tree canopy of Jurassic-sized leaves. Next to the jungle lies a lake, as turquoise as an image I'd seen of the ocean in the Philippines. If the entire tidal-locked habitable zone looks like this, I can't imagine a more beautiful new home for humans to live.

"*One hundred meters.*"

I scan the trees for any sign of dangerous predators. Elephant-ear-shaped leaves the size of our shuttle dangle from trees. That foliage could easily hide a T. rex. I suddenly see why a defoliating agent will come in handy, and imagining what could hide under the gargantuan canopy, I sort of wish they'd taken care of it before sending us down to the surface. Otherwise I wouldn't hesitate to rip off the tracking monitor and make a run for it.

The autopilot landing is even rougher than my first few times landing a hovercar on my own. We survive—the landing, anyway.

The door opens and the glow of the twilight sky fills the

shuttle. Rubio and Feathers are already unbuckled and grabbing their gear from the cubbies. Len takes his sweet time pretending his seatbelt is stuck.

The exit ramp lowers, and I gather my collection bag as well. Vials clink in my pouch as I try to steady my shaking legs.

I step toward the door to join Feathers and Rubio, who are staring out at the new planet. The lake as big as the desert behind Lita's house lies less than thirty meters in front of us. Instead of dust and tumbleweeds, mist slinks over the surface. Water laps gently on the shore, and a warm wind from the west blows through the elephant-ear trees all as tall as Hyperion. The trunks of the trees along the outside are all wind-bent toward the east.

In that direction—the planet's dark side—lie Sagan's icy mountains. On the opposite side of the lake, from a distant cliff face, gush three waterfalls of varying heights. There icy runoff from the eastern snowcaps meets the sun in the west, pouring into a river that feeds the glacier blue lake.

A humming like a cicada's tune whispers on the breeze.

A huge moon lies partially above the horizon, while another moon half its size hovers just behind. It peeks curiously over the bigger moon's shoulder, like a younger sibling. Above and behind them, a ringed planet glows yellow in the pale-purple sky.

And high above them all, looking down, is the red dwarf, just like Dad said. It's not as bright as Earth's sun, but the jungle and lake bask in its golden glow. Compared to my eyes, the others must be seeing something even brighter. But I can't imagine it being any more magical than it already is. I think of my lost obsidian pendant Lita gave me four centuries ago. This is the moment I would have held the pendant up to the sun. I would have whispered into the wind, "We're okay, Lita. We made it."

Would her voice have called back?

Oh, mija! I have waited so long to hear your sweet voice. I am with your ancestors. You see? Millions of stars apart and I am still here with you.

But I'll never know. My hands are empty. No pendant. No stories.

I'm so deep in my thoughts, I don't notice the others (except Len) are already at the bottom of the ramp. I follow and stop at the ramp's ledge.

The mountains here are not so different from Earth's. Everything my parents and the leaders had hoped for, happened. We made it. I am about to take a step onto a new world. But it's all wrong. My first step onto Sagan should be with Javier. A tear drops inside my visor.

18

CRICK'S MONOTONE VOICE SPEAKS THROUGH THE COMM unit connected to our corpomonitor, "Depart the shuttle, Zeta unit." I know I have to calm down.

Feathers takes the first careful step onto Sagan's ground of mossy carpet. She wastes no time retrieving a soil sample pouch.

I glance to either side. If I ran now, where would I go?

Dark patches pit the face of a rocky hill near the jungle. One much larger black spot is masked by leafy fern curtains. Adjacent to this potential hiding place lies dense forest. Only a few steps in and I could disappear. If I lost the monitor in my suit, they couldn't track me. And there's no body-cam on my suit for them to see where I am—I've checked. Even if they could, no one on the ship has ever even seen a single tree. I can't imagine they'd consider following me to search an entire forest of elephant-eared leaves. There's not enough tonic in the galaxy.

Rubio steps off the ramp and pulls an atmospheric reader out of his bag.

I take a deep breath and take my first step onto Sagan.

My foot doesn't sink into the ground like I expected. And my next step doesn't come back down at a normal rate. I take a tiny jump and hang in the air just a bit longer than I'm used to. I can only imagine the fun Javier would've had, seeing how high he could leap in Sagan's lower gravity. Instead, with the others already several meters away, my first moments on Sagan are alone. I have no one's hand to hold.

"This is not how this was supposed to be," I whisper.

"Repeat your last, Zeta-1?" Crick's voice comes through my comm unit.

"I—" I quickly pull out the toxometer to look busy. "There's remnant luciferin on this plant life," I say, telling the truth.

"Oh my," he squeals. But I'm ninety-nine percent sure he has no idea what luciferin is.

"Crick," Nyla admonishes.

I look around. I wish I had someone other than Crick sharing in the excitement. Yes, there are others around me. But the importance and happiness of the wonder of this planet has been brainwashed out of them.

"Take off your mask, Zeta-4," the Chancellor calls out, breaking the moment's silence.

"Yes, Chancellor," Feathers' high-pitched voice responds.

It takes me a moment to realize what's happening, but when I look over, Feathers is already reaching up to unfasten her visor.

Before I can scream out for her to stop, Feathers lifts it up without hesitating. I quickly step toward her, ready to throw off my own visor and attach it to her helmet. She takes a full breath. I'm too late. Cold crawls up my body like an army of ice spiders. But she breathes in and out, unfazed at what could've just happened.

I hope my heartrate and speeded breathing aren't registering in my corpomonitor. I glance at Len, who's watching curiously from the shadows of the entrance ramp.

They really don't want to risk going on-planet themselves. I'm a pawn—but one they need. For now.

Feathers sits on the ground and scoops soil into a sample pouch. She's apparently okay. So, I let my body relax.

"Len," the Chancellor's voice shows no emotion, "remove your mask."

I turn back toward the shuttle where Len stands on the end of the ramp. He moves nowhere as quickly as Feathers did. His hand trembles as he slowly unclasps and pries off his visor.

If Len trusts Nyla and she said the air is breathable, I don't understand his hesitation. But then I recall Nyla and Crick's conversation at the party.

"*The air is suitable. The water can be processed*," she said.

"*Yes, but is there anything* else *that could harm us?*" Crick asked.

Len takes in a shallow breath and waits. He opens his eyes and makes a nervous laugh. "The air appears fine, Chancellor."

"Zetas 1 and 3, remove your masks," Nyla demands from the safety of the ship.

If my only options are figuring out how I'm going to live on Sagan or returning to the ship . . . What do I have to lose?

I pull off my visor. Warm, humid air fills my nostrils—nothing like the hot, dry air of Santa Fe. The scent of grass and something fragrant like Mom's sweet peas fills the air. I think of the sterile, stale air of the ship. Now, I want more than anything to disappear into the jungle and never go back.

Spiky red flowers aim their petals toward the dwarf sun like a spiny crab reaching out with its claws. Feathers brushes mud off a metallic rock with her gloved hand and places it in a collection bag. Rubio holds the beeping atmospheric reader and carefully starts walking the perimeter of the lake. Unlike everyone else, Len just stands there, looking relieved to be alive.

I kneel at the edge of the lake to collect the underwater plant samples the drones couldn't reach. Underwater ferns weave in spirals toward the shore from the deeper water. A branch of the plant fans out toward the water's edge, close enough for me to touch. Beneath the water's surface, a glowing purple cluster emerges from the core of the ferns. It moves closer and closer. I hover my hand above the light and tap the water with my gloved finger. The iridescent cluster scatters below in an explosion, like a firework. Sagan's dimmer light makes it harder for me to see than the bright white lights on the ship. But I focus in on one of the singular purple creatures and trail it until it disappears behind the spiral of kelp.

I gasp and sit crisscrossed at the water's edge. I pull my hand back to my lap and wait. Within a minute, they've regrouped into the same purple constellation. One curious rebel rises toward me and the water's surface. It's so close, I now see tiny luminescent fins like a butterfly dimming to a pale lavender the closer it flutters to the surface. I place my hand above it, creating a shadow umbrella, and it glows the deep purple of an amethyst.

The water butterfly nibbles on the surface of an aquatic fern frond. If he's eating it, it's a good sign. I reach out and extract one of the fronds floating on the surface. The little organism darts back to the safety of its group. I hold the vine up with forceps and point the toxometer at it. The screen lights up, showing, *No toxin detected.* I reach out to get a larger sample and two water butterflies dart back to safety. "Sorry," I say, dropping the samples in a vial and placing them in my satchel.

"Zeta-1?"

"Just verifying something," I say, annoyed I can't even have this moment to myself.

I need to play the part, so in addition to the four bags of lake vines I collect, I fill two vials with lake water without another word and put them all in my collection bag.

I walk away from the lake and toward the forest and surrounding shrubs. Rubio is over two hundred meters to the east measuring the atmosphere, and Feathers is way too close to the jungle's edge, holding a rock up to the sun. They have no fear. The Chancellor's combination of Cog and tonic neural blocks have made sure of that. I hurry toward Feathers and pull her back from the jungle's edge, pretending to show her something.

That's when I see it. There, in the center of a flower. I'm sure it's a honeybee. It's far more orange than I remember. It buzzes off too fast for my eyes to trail. But I'm positive it was a . . .

That doesn't make sense. The higher oxygen levels must be affecting my perception.

"Did you see that?" I ask Feathers.

"See what, Zeta-1?"

I shake my head. "Nothing," I say.

Feathers walks toward the shuttle, and a drone approaches her. She clips her sample bags to its base, and the drone buzzes back toward the shuttle where Len still stands.

For a moment I consider the drones. Even standard ones have heat signature detection. Losing the tracker alone won't be enough. I realize if I'm going to have a chance for escape, even the jungle may not hide me.

I turn back to the jungle and flinch. A furry animal the size of a field mouse, but with eyes and ears as big as a chinchilla's, scurries over my left boot to nibble on leaves. The mini-chinchilla makes a tiny squeak and avoids a plant with bright-green, red-rimmed leaves, then dashes away, disappearing into the forest.

Unlike the other plants, I notice this plant doesn't have a single nibble mark or bug on its surface, even though its spread out everywhere. I pull the toxometer out of my bag and run it over the leaf's surface, careful not to get any on my gloves. The meter's screen lights up: LD50 *.001 nanograms per kilogram.* My heart speeds and I take a few deep breaths. Note to self: don't touch this stuff!

Even on Earth, the skin of a Colombian golden poison frog had a waaaaay lower LD50—the Lethal Dose needed to kill 50% of a test population. Theirs was 2 micrograms per kilogram. Even botulism, the deadliest toxin ever known, needed at least 1 nanogram per kilogram to kill a human. This little leaf blows them out of the water!

"Uh, Zetas? Crick?"

"Yes," Rubio and Feathers say in unison.

"There is a bright green plant with red-rimmed leaves. Please avoid."

"Affirmative, Zeta 1," Rubio answers. Crick murmurs a yes a few moments later.

I use forceps to fill three bags with the toxic foliage. I hold up a tiny leaf in the sunlight and whisper, "Sorry, little guy, but I'm going to have to send you off for testing."

Maybe if the Collective has their samples, they won't

waste time searching for me if I suddenly disappear. If I disable the tracker and find a place to hide my heat signature, they might assume I just fell victim to some unknown new planet danger. I glance at the dark gap ahead I saw in the rock next to the jungle. Definitely not landscape discoloration. Worth investigating. I move closer and hear Nyla clear her throat through the comm unit. If they're watching me, my bag is too full for them to ignore. I don't want to draw attention, so I load my samples onto a drone. It zips back toward the shuttle.

I take a moment to scan and see where everyone is. At first, I don't see Rubio. I keep scanning toward the east, and I see him. He's safe.

Len is still milling around, doing nothing to help. He paces back and forth, stopping to wipe his face and scratches his head. His nerves are obviously getting to him. He takes a few deep breaths and throws up green liquid.

Feathers runs her spectrometer over a rock and waits for it to show its contents. "Ah, graphite," she says. "Perfect."

I don't know how long I can survive out here, but I've decided: anything's better than staying on the ship with the Collective, knowing what they've done to me and my family.

Like the universe just heard me, from the depths of the jungle a swooshing noise and then screeching vibrate the air. High in the treetops, the elephant-ear leaves waver.

Len sprints up the shuttle's ramp like a Jesus lizard across a pond.

An entire flock of bat-like creatures with long flowing tails bursts out and swims through the sky in the opposite direction.

I want to tell Len to calm down. It's only a flock of harmless . . . somethings. But then again, how do I know? I ease away from the jungle's edge and try to act casual as I move toward the largest dark spot in the mountain's face.

I continue pretending to measure anything growing along the way with the toxometer.

Len's squeaky voice filters through our comms. "Bring me back up, Chancellor. I beg of you."

I continue until I'm close enough to see a curtain of vines hanging over the black area. When I'm within twenty yards, my heart speeds. It's obviously a cave opening. I just don't know how deep. I reach in my bag for a thermal imager, and sure enough, the area reads colder than its surroundings. The forest can't hide my heat signature, especially from an overhead drone. But no thermal scanner can read through rock.

At the base of the dark cave, the mini-chinchilla scrambles through the vine curtain. I use Len's distraction to pick up a rock and throw it into the opening. The rock *click-click-click-clicks* until it fades away.

Maybe no one is paying attention. I could throw the monitor into the lake. The cave will hide my heat signature. I'd be free.

I close my eyes and imagine myself back in Lita's arms. "*Can you imagine the fear* Blancaflor *must have felt?*" *She clicks her tongue.* "*Still she mounted the flying horse and trusted it to deliver her and the prince across a vast ocean. All the while the king on an even faster horse, flying at their heels. La que no se arriesga no cruza la mar." Then, she makes one long sigh.*

Lita said about Blancaflor: "*If you don't take a risk, you cannot cross the ocean.*"

I glance back toward the shuttle. Once behind those vines, they'll never see me. And Len wouldn't have the guts to even look.

I stand with my back to a tree out of their line of sight. It'd only be one step.

Chancellor Nyla's voice comes through the comm. "Zetas, we have enough for the day. Time to return."

I pull back a section of vines and peek inside. Just like the purple creatures in the water, the cave's walls glow. But here, the bioluminescence is turquoise like the glowworm caves in New Zealand. Maybe these caves continue for kilometers, just like those in New Zealand.

I cover the mic on the corpomonitor. "If I don't take a risk, I can't cross the ocean."

Someone touches my arm, making me jump. It's Feathers. I quickly drop the vines.

"Zeta-1?" she says. "Did you hear? Time to go back."

I turn to face her. She smiles up at me. Just like chick feathers, her baby hairs are plastered to her forehead from Sagan's humidity. And staring down, I realize it.

I can't leave her and Rubio behind on the ship to spend their lives with Nyla.

Suddenly, I know what Lita's words really mean. Blancaflor wasn't just brave because she crossed the ocean herself. She was brave because she took the risk in saving the prince. If I leave without Rubio and Feathers, that's not enough. Only if I take the risk and bring them with me, am I truly crossing the ocean.

But I can't stop there. Once I make sure we are all off the ship for good, I will remind them of who they are. Give them the memory of their families back. They can decide what they want to do after. But when I escape, they will be with me.

I take Feathers' arm and sigh. "Right. Time to go back."

I zip my bagful of vials and sample containers closed and walk toward the shuttle. When I reach it, I take a deep breath of Sagan's sweet air before I walk up the ramp and deposit my bag in the cubby, buckling in.

The shuttle vibrates as we lift to a hover. I stare out the window at the lake, the waterfalls, and the mountain peaks, until once again I'm looking at the abalone-shell sky out the cockpit window. It's even more beautiful than Santa Fe's, but my stomach knots in disgust knowing I have to return to the stark ship.

Len must be thinking the exact opposite, as we're going back to where he feels safe. But his eyes are closed and he's clenching his stomach.

A plan forms. I'll convince Rubio and Feathers I need their help researching inside the caves. Even better! I'll tell them I have a special cuento for them if they come with me. But I've got to figure out a way to keep them from telling anyone. Now that it's not just me, we'll need to hunt for supplies, and that will take longer. We need food, water, a place to hide and protect us from the cycles of windstorms . . . We can't just tear off onto Sagan and escape the moment we land.

Even if it has to be without our families, the three of us can still build a life of some sort on Sagan. Maybe, in time, even something close to what Mom promised.

As the ship begins to take off, a swarm of the bat-like flying creatures passes in the distance. Len's lip quivers, and he's taking quick breaths. Why isn't he calming down? They can't attack him here on the shuttle.

It might take years, but if I tell Feathers and Rubio everything about Earth, maybe someday they'll remember.

I close my eyes and imagine what our first night on Sagan in the cave will be like. I'll tell Rubio and Feathers stories. I'll tell them a little about Earth, slowly at first.

I glance toward Len, who's huddled in his seat at the back of the shuttle. He's shaking now.

His skin is covered in boils.

19

A WHISPER OF LITA'S VOICE FILLS MY MIND AS I STARE at a trembling Len. "*People do the most terrible things when they live in fear*," Lita says. "*But others are at their best*."

I've never seen a dying man, but I am sure Len won't make it back to the ship if I do nothing. One tiny sliver of the leaves I collected could kill all four of us. I wonder if Len touched something. Maybe it's still on him. Maybe it's an organism that could transfer to me.

I learned from Lita to cross myself before doing anything dangerous. Len wheezes. No time for blessings. I remove my helmet and unlatch myself and hurry to his side, unlatching his helmet too. I flick the lid off my bottle and pour my water over his blisters. As the last of it drizzles over his head, his eyes find mine, begging for more.

"Hurry!" I turn back to Feathers and snatch her water pouch out of her hands. My hands shake as I flip the top open and pour the entire bottle over him. "We need help!" I yell, knowing Nyla and the others can hear me. No one answers.

Len's eyes are closed, and his breathing is uneven. I grab Rubio's bottle. I flip open the top and hold it over Len, but not a single drop falls.

"I was thirsty," Rubio says in a quiet voice.

Water drips from Len's chin and he leans into the corner of his chair, trembling.

"I'm sorry," I say, feeling helpless. "We don't have any more."

I consider using the lake samples, but I can't be sure what caused this and if that would make matters worse.

I kneel next to Len and fight back tears, staring at him. He's nothing like us. But he's also just like us. A test subject for the Collective. He closes his eyes and his head lolls to one side. A cold shiver runs over my head. "Oh no."

I yank off my glove and hold my hand under his nose, feeling hot breath. He's still alive. I look out the window and finally the crouched praying-mantis ship comes into view.

Feathers nudges me. I stare down, and there's something I

haven't seen in her expression before. "What can we do to help him?" Her eyes sag.

Part of me is relieved. She feels bad for him. The Collective couldn't wipe empathy from Feathers' mind. I have hope I can find the real person inside her soon. But any relief I feel then vanishes instantaneously. What will Nyla do if she sees Feathers like this?

"You need to be strong, Zeta-4. Please don't be scared." I pat her helmet where her cheek is. "For the Collective?"

She clears her throat and nods. "For the Collective."

I glance toward the camera I'm sure is observing us.

Rubio has removed his gloves and is picking at the skin on the corner of his thumb.

"It's okay," I mouth to him.

Rubio looks back out the window even though we can no longer see the planet. For a moment, I don't feel so alone. Rubio, Feathers, and I are all still different from the Collective. Inside us, we all still have the best parts of what humans should be.

Len stirs and winces in pain, but the fear I see in his shuddering chin is the hardest thing to watch. I wish I knew what caused his sudden reaction and how to treat it. If it is from the alterations they've made to their epidermis, I have nothing to help him. Why does the shuttle ride back to the ship feel like it's taking so much longer?

I want to tell Len how unfair this is, but then he'll know I remember what it is to be compassionate and kind. Even if he's dying, he's still part of the Collective hive. He might tell the Chancellor.

The shuttle attaches into the ship with a thunk. The Chancellor calls over the comm, "Remain where you are." The shuttle rotates away from the launch port and is lifted back to its docking unit. Within moments, the airlock seals and medics in beefed-up envirosuits and masks come in with a gurney. They lower it remotely and lift Len on as it hovers a meter off the ground.

Len's lips barely move as he whispers to me, "Thank you."

I try to keep my face steady, but it's trembling like his chin and my eyes fill with tears. None of us move as he's taken away.

We remain in our seats. Crick's voice comes over the comm. "Zeta unit, leave your bags and exit the shuttle to the decontamination sector."

A moment later, we exit into the hallway leading to the hold. It's been replaced by a metal tube. Like hamsters we scamper through, nowhere to go but ahead. The tunnel ends with three separate entrances to rooms—all of them small and transparent like Mom's greenhouse.

I remove my suit and place it in the corner. I walk into the decontamination shower and scrub off, letting the warm water run over my face where they can't see my tears if they are watching. When I exit, I find a new jumpsuit hanging just outside the door. My skin is clear and my breathing fine, so if Sagan's natural radiation affected Len, it didn't hurt me.

Just as I zip up the jumpsuit, Chancellor Nyla approaches. She takes a deep breath. "I thank you for helping Len, Zeta-1."

"For the Collective," I say, hoping my eyes aren't puffy from crying.

She smiles. "While I appreciate it, I will ask you not to do such things in the future."

I know my face is pained like a dog straining against a muzzle. "Is Len going to be all right?"

She tilts her head and leans in toward me. The veins under her skin are the color of the glowing water butterflies. How can one creature be so beautiful and another . . . ?

"One is useful to the Collective, or one is not." She leans in, examining me. "You are useful and thus too valuable to put yourself at risk for one who no longer is."

If I say the wrong thing, this could go very badly. "I . . . I was sure it was an airborne toxin of some sort, perhaps one that could be washed away. I apologize, Chancellor. I thought it was the best way to serve the Collective."

She leans back, and I can breathe again.

"I will be introducing you to someone you'll be working with in the labs." Her eyes flick toward the far back corner of the hold into the lab complex. "Together you will create the defoliating agent."

I'd forgotten. I thought I'd be off the ship by now.

She glares at me with her violet eyes. And with that, she turns and walks away.

I wrap my arms around my stomach like I just got kicked in

the gut. *Only a few more days and we'll leave,* I tell myself. *A few more days.*

Rubio and Feathers emerge, hair still wet from the decontamination room. We walk past our parents' empty pods toward the elevator. Next to the elevator is the blinking blue light over the metal door Ben showed us on the first day. The locked enclosure over the latch should be easy enough to crack open with the right tool. Inside are the food rations and water filtration straws our ship's passengers were going to use to survive on Sagan.

None of us speak on the way up. I wonder if they are thinking about Len too. When the doors open to our floor, we all exit without a word.

We reach our quarters, and I collapse onto the edge of my cell. It's one thing to be strong when you have to be, but now I feel like I've crashed to the ground after running a marathon.

I pretend to happily take the sleeping pill Crick offers me. I lodge it in my cheek and then use the bathroom, spitting it out quickly. When I return to our room, Rubio and Feathers are already in their honeycombs.

I crawl into my cell. With the low rumble of Rubio's snores, I drift off.

*

LITA SITS ON A BLANKET, leaning against the trunk of a piñon tree in its shade.

"Ay, changuita. Come sit by me," she says, smiling. Her voice in my dream is as real as if she were really there. Wind blows her peppery hair.

As I nestle into Lita's chest, I don't want to go back to my sleeping cell. Ever.

Something pushes on my other hand. I stare down, and my tortoise nudges my hand with his nose. "Rápido!" I rub my hand over his shell.

Suddenly, Rápido jerks his head back inside his shell.

In the distance, a man with a rainbow headdress of feathers approaches. To his side, there's a small furry white rabbit.

"¿Quieres escuchar un cuento?" Lita begins. "You know the story of el Conejo and Quetzalcoatl." She motions to the man and rabbit who walk toward us, as real as Lita is real.

I think of the rainbow serpent god and the rabbit who saved his life.

"Yes," I say. "I know it. Quetzalcoatl visited Earth in human form. But he screwed up because he didn't know as a human he'd need food and water."

"And el Conejo saves him from his suffering," she whispers.

Quetzalcoatl staggers across the desert, reenacted in this weird dream just like a scene out of a librex. He collapses in front of me and Lita. Dust stirs in the air. The rabbit hops up to him and paws at his feathers and touches his pink nose to Quetzalcoatl's face. "You need sustenance," el Conejo says to him.

I nudge Lita. "This is the part where el conejo blanco offers up himself as food for Quetzalcoatl, right?"

Lita nods.

And just like the story I've heard before, Quetzalcoatl is impressed with the rabbit's willing sacrifice and generosity. Next, Quetzalcoatl won't eat the white rabbit. Instead, he is going to launch him toward the heavens where el Conejo's outline will remain on the surface of the moon, so all are reminded of the mightiness of such a tiny creature.

But this doesn't happen. Instead of following the story, the rabbit turns toward us. "You should follow me," he says. But he is not looking at Quetzalcoatl or Lita. He is looking at me. "I will save you."

"I do not need food and water," I say, rejecting his offer.

"I am offering you far more than that," the rabbit says. "Your sacrifice and risk shall be rewarded."

Although he doesn't say it, I know he's referring to Len. "But I don't think I saved him."

El Conejo turns and hops in the direction of the Sangre de Cristo Mountains in the distance. "Come," he calls back, motioning for me to follow.

That is not what el Conejo is supposed to do. I try to redirect my dream the way it's supposed to go, but nothing changes.

I look up at the moon.

"He's not there, Petra," Lita says. "He is there." She points to el Conejo hopping across the desert. The moon without his gray outline shines with the pale glow of the Collective's skin.

"You should see where he leads," Lita says calmly.

"But I'm scared."

"The one who does not take the risk—"

I don't mean to yell. "It's not an ocean, Lita!" I point at the endless desert. "I'll die if I follow. You even said once there are many tricksters—that Rabbit can be a trickster." I motion to Quetzalcoatl's lifeless form. "Look what happened to *him*. He followed el Conejo, and he is dead." My stomach churns as the Great One's body turns to dust, spiraling upward and away. "This is not how this is supposed to happen at all. Lita, why are you changing the stories?"

Lita laughs. "I am not changing them. You are." She nods her head toward el Conejo. "But if you take the risk and trust where the story is leading you, you might find the ocean you must cross."

The rabbit hops farther toward the mountain range, and my tortoise, Rápido, wanders behind the tree toward a hole dug into its roots. It is peaceful and calm. And my Rápido is right here. "Rápido, come back," I call after. But he crawls into a burrow beneath the roots, and disappears.

"Lita," I say turning back, but she is gone too. I stare out to find el Conejo. A tiny pinpoint across the edge of the desert disappears along with the mountains.

I am alone with only the desert. The tree is gone. Just a flat plain of dirt. Not even a whisper of Lita . . . or her story on the wind.

I'm scared and I hesitated. Now my chance is gone.

The ground trembles. Dirt spins in the air around me like it had around Quetzalcoatl.

"Lita! Come back!" I call out, sitting up in my cell. Even my awake mind knows maybe I've made a huge mistake and I won't get back the chance to follow el Conejo. Rubio snores gently in the cell above. Now that I'm up, it all seems so silly. "It was just a dream," I whisper, staring at the top of my cell.

Behind me, a clicking noise echoes. I roll over and sit up in time to see the door to our room slide shut.

20

I BARELY SLEEP THE REST OF THE NIGHT, WORRIED about who could've been in the room. Whoever it was that saw my outburst.

I take my time to make sure I have no hairs straggling from my braid. I place my collection bag over my shoulder and stand tall and straight at the front of the line.

We exit the elevator and I walk straight across the room to Bioloaf Boy. When I reach him, I don't even bother trying to get him to smile or make eye contact with me. I down half of the cube right away like it's a doughnut hole instead of horse food.

I see the smaller version of Nyla, Glish, is with the same morning bioloaf group not far away. I move closer and pretend to nibble on the rest of my cube just like she is.

"Who is next?" Glish says. "Was Len not just as useful as I am?"

I remember her saying she and Len were in the same Collective creation batch.

The man with the wideset eyes, Hammerhead, nudges her. "I'm sure you mean you are willing to sacrifice for the Collective, Glish. Whatever that may be." He glances from side to side and speaks in a low voice.

One of the group clears their throat and walks away nervously.

Hammerhead continues. "Without the Collective, there would only be war and famine. Our unity and agreement on all things ensures we will never return to the ways of conflict." He holds up his bioloaf. "We will never starve, because the Collective has eliminated diversity and demand for more choices."

How would he know? He's never been to a museum and seen art from Cézanne to Savage. Basquiat to Kahlo. He's never eaten in a universal commissary with choices from udon to bucatini, Irish stew to pepián. Just because someone says something over and over doesn't make it true.

And suddenly, after all this time, I truly understand what the word *dogma* means.

Hammerhead whips his eyes away from Glish. I follow his gaze. It doesn't go very far. Just behind Glish, Nyla and Crick are watching and listening.

I want to warn her, but Glish is already speaking again. "None of our work or service matters if we are not alive to reap the benefits—" Glish stops abruptly. She turns and notices who's behind her.

Nyla nods to Crick, and he walks away.

The rest of the morning bioloaf group goes completely still like a herd of deer. Glish doesn't move a centimeter—a prey sensing she's caught by her predator. Where could she hide on the ship anyway?

It's quiet for too long. When I finally see Crick return, he's not alone. Even from a distance, I can see he's dwarfed by the largest ghost shrimp I've seen so far, approaching next to him. I decide he's the Prawn. As he nears, I see his brow is furrowed in wavy wrinkles of a permanent scowl.

Crick remains with Nyla as the Prawn continues walking directly toward Glish. One of the men closes his eyes. The Prawn stands right next to Glish, taking her elbow.

Still, she doesn't move. "For the Collective," she says calmly. Without a struggle, she walks away with him, the Prawn holding her tiny elbow the entire time. They enter the elevator and within seconds disappear out of sight down the dark metal tube.

I look away. The words in the ceiling seem to blink faster. *Unity. Camaraderie.*

"For the Collective," Hammerhead says.

"For the Collective," the rest repeat.

No war. No famine. But at what price?

Getting away from them feels suddenly a lot more pressing.

I walk across the room toward the food assembly line. The boxes with today's excess are stacked neatly to one side, for later. And unlike the rations room, I don't have to safecrack a lock.

Glish's retrieval is the distraction I need. I open my bag and lean against the wall next to the stacks and stacks of bioloaf. I scan from side to side, making sure no one is near. I reach down and pick up a box. I'm about to slip it into my bag.

"Zeta unit!" Crick calls out. "Time to depart."

A buzz of voices fills the air. People look around excitedly, zeroing in on Feathers and Rubio. It will only be moments before they spot me too. I look down to my side to slip the box in my bag.

Voxy stares back up at me.

This time, I am the frozen deer.

He holds a finger to his lips. "I get extra hungry too sometimes." He shoves two extra boxes of bioloaf into my bag. "I will not tell." He smiles and runs away.

My heart laser-pongs in my chest.

"Zeta-1!" Feathers waves her hand in my direction from across the room.

I hurry to zip the bag's flap shut. I wave back and stay close to the wall, walking toward the elevator, hoping the two extra boxes in the bag aren't a dead giveaway. I enter the elevator first, pushing my bag behind me.

Just as before, Nyla, Crick, Feathers, Rubio, and I descend to the hold and follow the same path toward the shuttle.

We round the corner, and the Prawn walks toward us from the airlock. But now, Glish isn't with him.

No one makes eye contact as he passes, like nothing at all has happened. It's been less than five minutes. Is that all it took to make a problem disappear?

This time, Feathers, Rubio, and I alone enter the shuttle. I keep my posture rigid and don't look back toward Nyla and Crick. I hurry to stash my bag and buckle in. It's no longer just about me. Today has to be a scouting mission for when we all can really run.

The ride down is quiet and somber, and I catch Rubio staring at where Len sat the day before.

Just like the day before, we attach our corpomonitors and comm units and exit down the ramp, but unlike before we no longer wear helmets. The same warm air hits my lungs. The same golden light falls over the jungle and lake. The moons and ringed planet have not moved. It's as magical as it was yesterday.

I step off the ramp. "Hmmm, interesting," I say loudly so it registers for whoever's listening through the comm. Then I fake curiosity and head in the direction of the jungle and the cave that lies beyond. I hope they are only paying attention to my vitals and not my movements while on the surface. Within a few minutes' walk I see the vines, still waving in the wind which has just finished its eight-hour cycle. I make sure I'm sheltered from view behind the cover of the massive tree, push the vines aside, and step inside.

The walls shimmer with bioluminescence. But my eyes are taking too much time to adapt. I stand in the cave's entrance, with only the sound of my breathing. *Please don't let Sagan have bears.* I rub my gloved hand over the cave's wall, and just above my head I find a ledge. I run the meter over its surface. It's dry and there are no readings of toxins. I quickly stash the three boxes of bioloaf and calculate it will only last us a few months. But there are years and years' worth of filtration straws and additional rations if I can find a way into that room back on the ship. I hurry back out and wait behind the tree to let my eyes readjust to the light. I step out and scan. Feathers has followed me partway and is crouched by the lake, brushing debris off a stone. Rubio is even closer to the shuttle, loading a collection bag onto a drone.

I move away from the cave so I don't attract attention. The last thing I need is them searching this area when we finally escape. Near the jungle's edge, I find the red-rimmed plant that could kill me with one nibble, and fill another pouch just to make it look like I'm working. I take four samples of the mossy ground cover and snip off several pieces of a fallen elephant-ear leaf. I place them each in their own sample bags, sending the drone back to the shuttle. I gather more water samples and lake plants. If I really will be working in a lab, why not test the hopefully edible plants and water before we escape?

Just like the day before, once decontaminated, we're sent back toward our room, passing the rations room holding exactly what I need.

I'm about to crawl into my cell when a body with long black hair sits up inside my hexagon.

"Suma!" I yell out.

"Excuse me?" she says with a gravelly voice.

My breath hiccups, knowing I don't have to live my life on Sagan wondering if she was stuck in stasis another four hundred years. I want to hug her. I hold back my tears. "I mean, I was going to say . . . Sum . . . Some-someone is in my bed."

"I'm sorry. I'll move," she says. I'm having a hard time keeping the huge grin off my face.

"No, no. Stay where you are."

"I'm Zeta-4," Feathers says, introducing herself. "Expert in—"

Suma interrupts, rubbing her hand over her closed eyelids. "I apologize. I'm just so tired." I remember how I felt coming out of stasis. Suma's done it twice now.

"We are just so glad you're back," I say.

They all turn their heads toward me.

"I mean . . . we could use your help in sample collection . . . for the Collective," I say, realizing my mistake.

Luckily, they all seem to accept the explanation and turn away.

Feathers crawls into her cell next to Suma. And Suma lays her head back down. "I really am sleepy," she says unironically.

Rubio smiles, inching toward the door, then quickly closes it. "Theeeen we should get ready for bed. Zeta-1 will tell us a cuento, won't you? Please?" he begs me. He motions toward Suma in question. "So Zeta . . . ?" He waves his hand at Suma again. "Zeta . . . ?"

"Zeta-2," Suma responds.

"Zeta-2," he says. "So, Zeta-2 can sleep."

I hold in a snicker.

Suma lies back in my bed. "What's a cuento?" she asks before I can say no.

My stomach twists in a nervous knot. Now, I need them to hear the stories. Hopefully, these stories from Earth will remind them of who they are and who their families were. But if they do remember, I pray they don't decide to share with someone outside this room. They all watch me, waiting. It's worth the risk.

"Oh, you'll see," Rubio chirps out, pulling his mylar blanket up to his neck.

I sit on the floor and face our honeycomb. I stare at Suma. I hadn't realized how worried I was about leaving her behind so the rest of us could escape. Now, we're all together, and we all have a chance. Except we'll need even more food. And I can't sneak down to the rations room in the hold while they're awake.

I take a deep breath. "Había una vez."

Feathers sticks her head out and cranes her neck around peeking into Suma's cell. "That's how you start a cuento. To set the mood."

Suma nods at her.

Feathers pulls her head back into her cell. "Continue," she motions to me.

I clear my throat. "There was a poor old couple called los Viejos," I begin. "They had very little, no food, a tiny home." I think of how we are sort of like los Viejos, except the three of them don't know it yet. "They were different than most of their neighbors in appearance, in the foods they ate, the things they loved. But they were willing to accept and share with others."

Then I think of the promise Mom made me about Sagan, "*We'll start over, like on a farm.*" And what is stopping us. "However, their neighbors were cruel and selfish and wanted everything to themselves and those like them. One neighbor in particular, a purple-lipped woman, had slowly taken away all hope they had for a large farm by stealing their land for herself and those like her."

Rubio shakes his head in disgust.

In Lita's version, an awful man stole from the old couple's dreams, but from now on, this story lives on through me and my new version.

I stand and pretend to knock on a door. "One day, when a beggar from a far-away land came to the old couple's door, they fed him the last of their corn. Then their dry scraps of tortilla." I hold my fingers to my mouth, pretending to eat.

Feathers and Rubio are sitting up and Suma has her chin cupped in her hands.

I lift a pretend drinking glass to my mouth. "Then all the water they had left." I wipe my mouth sloppily and let out a greedy sigh. "When the beggar had eaten it all, he was still hungry, so they gave him their own dinner." I hold up my pointer finger. "'To reward your kindness, I will offer you a gift,' the beggar told the old couple. Los Viejos' eyes sparkled like the stars."

Feathers, Sumas, and Rubio's eyes light up as well.

"The old couple could not remember the last time they'd been given any sort of gift. The beggar told them, 'Near the end of the mountain range to the north you will find a four-armed cactus with a bright-pink flower. Behind the cactus within the ravine is a hidden cave. Near the end of the cave you will find a jar filled with treasure. This will be the reward for your kindness.'"

Feathers tilts her head. "Is this on the planet Earth like your last cuento?"

Rubio knocks on his cell adjoining Feathers. "Hmmm, probably in the Andromeda galaxy, also known as Messier 31. It has two trillion planets! Even so, you shouldn't interrupt a cuento, Zeta-4," he says. "Go on, Zeta-1."

I can't help smiling at hints of their personalities the Collective couldn't erase. So far, I think we'll all get along.

"When the beggar left," I continue, "the couple decided they would travel to the ravine and the hidden cave as soon as they could find enough food to walk the long trip. What they didn't know was that the mean and selfish neighbor was listening to the beggar's tale"—I point to our room's door—"right outside their window!"

Suma gasps. "That is unfair!"

I nod calmly. "Yes. The mean neighbor rode through the night toward the mountain range on a donkey she'd stolen from los Viejos. She found the cactus and the bright-pink flower, the ravine, and the cave. She walked, then crawled to the cave's depths until she came upon a ceramic jar. When she lifted its lid, a scurry of horrific insects crawled over her arms, stinging her. She cried out as the tarantulas and scorpions and wasps stung her body. She crammed the lid back on the ceramic jar and rode home, welts and hives covering her body, the closed bug jar in her sack."

Feathers' mouth is ajar—Suma's holding her blanket over one eye, even though I'm sure they can't know what half the story means.

Rubio tilts his head. "Tarantula, a type of arachnid. What species is this one?" he asks.

Suma and Feathers both turn toward his cell at the same time. "SSSSSHHHHH!"

"When the neighbor arrived back home," I continue, "she snuck to the house of los Viejos at night and dumped the jar of atrocious bugs into their kitchen window."

Rubio gulps. I want to laugh. A tarantula doesn't faze him, but "atrocious bugs"?

"'That is what you get, you old fools,'" I say in a grizzly voice. "'That will teach you to trust and feed a strange, foreign beggar,' she said, riding back to her home."

I take a moment to let the horror of the crawling bugs on los Viejos' kitchen floor sink in. It works. Suma's knuckles are white. Rubio is even paler than usual, and Feathers' forehead ripples as much as the Prawn's.

"The next morning," I continue, "the old woman went to the kitchen to boil water to cook nopales, hoping the meager cactus would be enough for the long journey to the cave. But when she stepped onto the kitchen floor . . . she let out a yelp."

Rubio and Feathers inhale.

"When the old woman reached down to see what the sharp thorny object was in her foot, she pulled a diamond from her heel. Scattered about the floor, like hundreds of glimmering insects, were diamonds and rubies and sapphires, the bugs transformed magically from the kindness within the walls of their home."

Feathers clasps her hands together and giggles. I see the excitement in her eyes for something she doesn't entirely "understand." She still "feels" the thrill of the treasure.

"Los Viejos gathered the gems, only selling enough to buy land"—I imagine what I've seen of Sagan—"surrounded by jungle with a lake as blue as an aquamarine gem. And kept the remaining stones so they would always have enough to grow fruit trees and crops. And so it was, y asi fue word spread if any people—from any land, rich, poor, or just tired—were hungry, they only needed visit the home of los Viejos."

I sigh like Lita always did at the end. "Este cuento entró por un caminito plateado, y salió por uno dorado."

Feathers peeks over the edge again into Suma's cell. "That is how a cuento ends. A saying to close out what you've heard."

She lies back down, and one by one, thankfully, they sink into their beds. I turn off the light. Soon, Rubio's familiar snores fill the room.

*

I SNEAK TO WHAT WAS ONCE the teen stasis room and find a metal calibration tool from the drawer below the ship's atmospheric monitor, still glowing purple. Where most could just look at it in the dim light, I have to run my finger along its edge. Thinner than a flathead screwdriver, it's perfect for prying open a domed cover to a lock.

Even though the elevator would save me time, I sneak to the back stairs to avoid curious eyes through the elevator's open glass. Just as I had before, I count the two hundred and eighteen steps and open the door. My footsteps echo across the hold until I reach the flashing blue light above the metal door. It blinks as brightly as it did three hundred and eighty years ago on the first day, when Ben pointed out the supply room. I pull out the calibration tool and jimmy it under the lower edge of the cover. But instead of the resistance I'd expected, the plastic dome pops off immediately. It falls to the floor too fast for me to catch. Bouncing twice, its clinks echo in the hold. I flatten my back to the wall and wait. When no one comes, I turn back to the door.

I must feel like la Vieja did, picking the diamond out of her heel and finding the jewels. My hand trembles as I reach out to pull on the latch. Unlike all the others on the ship sliding open easily, this door creaks open slowly from disuse. My footsteps echo as I step inside. The dim overhead light flickers to life.

My stomach plummets. The back wall, which should contain a hundred lifetimes of food, is empty.

I tiptoe across the space until I reach the shelves. Bare. Not a single meal remains. The parasites have already scavenged even the last emergency rations meant for the passengers when we arrived on Sagan. I think of my few boxes of stolen bioloaf and wonder how we're going to feed ourselves.

On the lowest shelf, at least, purification straws are stacked neatly. I unzip my sample collection bag and scoop straws into the bag until I have enough to filter water for our entire lives.

If my suspicions are true and the lake plants I saw are edible, maybe we can survive. Except, of course . . . we'd be eating lake plants. I take a deep breath and turn to leave.

A door just outside in the hold slams shut.

Now, I am Glish. Frozen like a deer as the slim figure walks slowly toward me.

The same deep voice I'd heard in the hold the night I found the empty pods calls out. "You are not supposed to be in here. The Collective has restricted this area."

A man with wrinkled brown skin and a long white beard blocks the path to the elevator. It takes a moment for me to scan him from head to foot and process what I'm seeing. He's wearing Collective-issue boots and jumpsuit, but is also wearing gloves and has lab goggles on the top of his head like a hat. I take a step back, startled by someone who looks like a skinny, brown Santa. Finally, an adult from home!

Just like when I was six and with Santa at the mall, I want to run and hug him. But I know better. I wonder who he was on Earth. To be so old and still make the final cut. He must have invented something revolutionary back home.

I thought all the adults were purged when their reprogramming failed. But they were able to reprogram him, so maybe like with Feathers and Rubio, something about his mind was easier to manipulate?

"Hello," my voice catches. "I am Zeta-1."

"May I help you, Zeta-1?" the man asks.

"I was told I will be working here." I shift my bag filled with straws behind my back. "I'm not supposed to start yet, but I got anxious." For a moment, I let myself hope he's faking the reprogram too, but the Collective must trust him enough to leave him alone down here.

"Understandable," he chuckles. "They told me you were coming, but not until after the next scouting mission." He turns to walk out. "You are off course though. Let me show you our lab."

I flinch back. "*Our* lab?" This must be the person Nyla was talking about.

He leads me to the farthest-back corner of the hold where the lab complex is. When we arrived on Sagan, these labs should've been bustling with scientists like my parents. But it's just the two of us now, me and the old guy.

He walks into the last lab on the left. Rows and rows of petri dishes line the walls behind him. Agars of different colors radiate like a rainbow.

"Here we are," he says, opening the door for me. His smile is kind, and his long hair pulled into a ponytail makes him look more like a poet than a scientist.

"Thank you," I reply quietly. I think for a moment if he was taken out before or after us, and if there might be anyone else with him. "Ummh." I step toward a lab station and set my bag down. "Are you the only scientist?" I ask carefully. "I mean, are there any others, like you . . . me . . . us?"

"Just me now," he answers, and I wonder if there were any other adults like him who were successfully reprogrammed.

"Can I ask what you are an expert in?" I point to the rainbow agar. "I mean, what are you working on?"

"Life on a ship for so long can be difficult. My primary role is to help administer the tonics, thus stabilizing any mood the Collective may encounter." I think of Nyla's "party" and all the people drinking one tonic and another and another. He scratches his temple. "But to answer your question. There were five in my Epsilon unit."

"Epsilon?"

"I am Epsilon-5," he says. "I used to know any chemical equation or macromolecular synthesis without hesitation. But with age, I am becoming less useful."

I think of what Chancellor Nyla said about Len and being "useful or not." I'm sure "Epsilon-5" would be purged any day if they knew what he just told me. But if his mind's already slipping, that must be why he was so easy to reprogram.

"This way," he says, leading me into the next lab. The door is vacuum sealed, and hazard suits hang on the walls. Then I see why. My collection bags filled with red-rimmed leaves, the ground cover, and even the huge leaf samples hang on a rod in a glass refrigerator. My vialed water samples are sitting in a tube rack.

"Come." He takes my elbow and leads me like we are taking a stroll through a park. He can't know about my vision. He shuffles slowly, and I wonder if he is using our arm-lock as an excuse for me to help support him. We end at a blank wall. We stand awkwardly for a moment and he smiles. He presses a button, and the entire wall shifts back and into a pocket, revealing a wall of glass. Outside light from the moons and dwarf sun in the purple sky fills the room. I step to the window and look below at rivers and lakes and green. From here, I see we've barely explored the habitable zone during our sample collection missions. My lake with the butterfly fish is one tiny lake among hundreds.

"It's beautiful," I say.

"Yes," he replies. Then he sighs. "Of course, I will only be seeing it from here."

"Why do you say that?" I ask.

He shrugs. "The Chancellor believes this is where I am

needed." We stand for a moment in silence. "I *would* have liked to see in person what creatures the planet has."

I feel bad knowing we'll have to leave him, unless Nyla has a change of heart. I feel even worse that Nyla will keep him from exploring Sagan himself.

"There are wonderful creatures," I say. "For instance"—I hold my thumb and pointer finger ten centimeters apart—"the lake holds millions of tiny, winged fish."

He grins, and one of his back teeth is missing. "Tell me."

I realize it's all real, but it feels like I'm telling him a cuento. "The water butterflies swim in swarms and conceal their magnificent purple glow by hiding among a home of dense vines."

He leans in, his smile dropping. "What do you think they are hiding from?"

My heart speeds at the valid question. "I hadn't thought of that," I answer. And now I'm wondering what other creatures lurk in the lake's water.

"When you return to the surface, will you learn what they're afraid of?" he asks, with the eyes of a curious child.

I nod. But the truth is, if I can gather enough supplies, even if I discover what the water butterflies hide from, I may not return to tell him. A pit settles in my stomach along with the lie. I like Epsilon-5.

The lab door slides open, and Chancellor Nyla strides in. "Ah, Zeta-1, what are you doing here?"

I shove my bag with the straws behind my back. "I—I wanted to see the lab and check on the samples, so I'd be prepared."

She comes to stand next to us. She reaches over and pushes the button, the window sliding shut to a solid wall again. "Then you've already met. Since I have you both here, I can orient you to your project."

"Yes." Epsilon-5 walks to the workstation and reaches up toward a bag of poisonous leaves.

"Don't!" I quickly lower my voice. "It's highly toxic. I gathered it so we'd know how to eradicate it, for the Collective."

"Excellent," Nyla smiles. "It appears you both understand what we need." She turns to me. "How long will it take you to create the defoliator?"

I think of the massive elephant-ear leaves and poisonous plants, and the tests I need to run. "Not long," I answer.

"Yes," Epsilon-5 says. "We make a good team." He smiles at me, and I feel like he just punched me in the stomach with his friendship. How can I help him? As Lita would've said, he's not long for the world anyway. And the world he and I were part of is gone.

Nyla stands in front of me. "As soon as it's ready, we will send the Zetas back to the surface to test it." She points to my hanging sample bags. "Zeta-1, was it really *useful* to collect so much of this one plant?"

Before I can stop myself, the words are out of my mouth. "One leaf could kill every person in the Collective. I thought you might find it a priority to eradicate it," I say.

She makes a fake shuddering motion. "Frightening," she says.

I can have her defoliant ready in a few days. Then Suma, Feathers, Rubio, and I will never be Zetas again. I won't let Nyla or the Collective ever have an excuse to find the four of us useless.

21

MY HANDS TREMBLE AS I STRUGGLE TO TUCK THE DECADES' worth of filtration straws under the mattress in my beehive cell.

Nyla lingered so long watching me and Epsilon-5 begin our defoliator project, I didn't have time to test the samples.

I glance at Suma, Feathers, and Rubio snoozing. The four of us still have hope. But I wince thinking of all the food meant for us, gobbled up by the Collective. The image of raw billowy water vines fills my head. I crawl into my cell and close my eyes. Dancing empanadas and cheeseburgers sneak out of the vines to taunt me, then rush back into its spiral, hiding out of my reach.

I tune out the prancing food and run through my plan. I only need to keep playing the part long enough to create Nyla's defoliant, so she'll send us back on the surface like she said she would. I have to hope that they got the information they needed with Len, and when we go out again, we'll be alone.

Once we're off the shuttle, I'll convince Feathers, Suma, and Rubio to follow me to the caves. Like the Pied Piper, I'll lead them farther and farther away from the transport and the Collective with my stories. I feel bad about misleading them. But they deserve to know everything about what's happened to our families. I'll make sure they know the truth. They can decide with their own minds then how they want to live.

I need to sleep, but when I try counting sheep, it just makes me miss Lita's farm. I need something boring to count.

Lake-vine pozole (without chicken). Lake-vine cereal (without milk). Lake-vine pizza (without cheese). Lake-vine candy (without sugar)...

*

A WHITE BLUR OF FUR DARTS from the corner of my vision.

The rabbit faces me. Lita's words remind me, "*The trickster may be the one who leads you if it serves his purpose.*" El Conejo hops across the desert toward the mountains. Everything is moving too fast again. I need more time to think.

Suddenly Lita is next to me, and Rápido's right next to her. "Ah, mijita. Welcome back. Why are you not following him?"

I fold my arms over my chest.

Lita shrugs and raises her eyebrows. "Of course, you should stay here where you are comfortable and safe."

"Why wouldn't I stay with you?" I motion to the mountain ahead where the rabbit leads. "It's horrible out there. The desert could be dangerous."

"That is not danger. That is life . . ." she says, "a journey. You will only know if you follow."

I stay right where I am under the tree. Lita is already fading. The rabbit grows smaller in the distance.

I can't risk losing it again. "Fine," I say. I pat Rápido on his tiny head and push myself up. I turn to hug Lita, but she's gone, and when I look down Rápido is fading into a mist.

I jog after the rabbit like I haven't in years. Here, in my dream, I'm not afraid of tripping over something I can't see. Far ahead in the distance, el Conejo scampers toward the mountain glowing red in the afternoon sun. He scuttles into a hole at its base.

All the trickster has done is lead me to the middle of nowhere. No curtain of vines hiding a glowing cave for escape. No magical lake with shimmering butterfly fish.

I turn back and face the empty desert. Maybe if I return,

Lita will reappear. I walk back slowly toward where the tree had been. Then, from behind me, the echo of guitars and fiddles twang. I turn back around. Just like Lita's home, the faint melody of ranchero music is coming from deep within the red mountain. I run toward the melody. "Wait!"

The strumming of the guitar grows louder as I approach. So loud I feel the vibration in my body, then a thump on my back.

"Wait! Wait! I'm coming!" I yell after el Conejo. Something thumps on my back again.

But even as I say it, the music softens and the mountain fades, as I am pulled back through the desert, into darkness, and into my bed.

Thump, thump, thump on my back.

"Please, wait!" I wake up, still saying the words out loud. I sit up in my cell to find two small violet eyes staring back at me. I gasp and jump back.

"Voxy, what are you doing?"

He flinches back too. "I'm sorry." He points to a dark corner behind Ben's desk. Rubio lets out a snore. "I come here to listen to your cuentos. But I always fall asleep like everyone else." His shoulders slump. "You were yelling. I didn't have a choice. I had to wake you up so no one would come in and find me."

All this explains who I heard leaving our room the night before.

I swallow and my throat is dry. "Does—does anyone else know you're here?"

"I have to sneak. Nyla would never allow me to come listen."

Prickles run up my neck and over my head. "Voxy, you can't tell anyone."

He makes a grimace. "Oh, I won't. If I tell Nyla about what you say in your sleep, then I have to tell her why I was here." His eyes go wide, and he places his right palm up. "Then I *have* to tell her about the cuentos. The Collective would never let me out of their sight. I would never hear one again." He bows his head.

Even though we'll be gone soon, this is still dangerous. And I talk too much in my sleep. "You shouldn't come back here."

"But where else can I hear a cuento?"

He sounds just like Javier, begging for me to read him his book. Voxy is becoming less like the Collective, and it's me and my cuentos' fault. I should be happy, but it's the worst feeling. I think of what could happen if he's caught coming here. Even if it's just the next night, it could ruin everything.

"I'm sorry. But I can't let you sneak in here anymore."

Voxy's head drops. "It is not fair. The Collective has no cuentos, only rules. I mean, Nyla read one to me once. Not a cuento, like yours." His eyes widen. "This one was a relic and was in what's called a book, made of paper—"

"Wait," I interrupt. My heart beats faster than the time I thought a barrel cactus was a gnome, on one of Mom and my fairy hunts. "You saw a book?" I haven't seen a single shred of anything remotely related to Earth. Anything I could hold in my hands to remind me of home.

"I saw it once in our room," he leans in, whispering. "With other relics."

I think of how Voxy must have been created like Glish had said. But unlike the others, he is the only one his age. I realize I don't know anything about him.

"I'm not supposed to talk about the relics anymore," he says.

I try to hide my excitement, but I don't think I do a good job. "Voxy, how many relics are there? Can you show them to me?"

When he looks up, he arches his eyebrows. "Zeta-1, if I show you where they were, do you promise to keep telling me your cuentos?"

I nod. "*Mmmmh.*" The nod and mumble are still a lie.

He holds up a finger to his lips. "*Sssh.*" He beckons me with his hand and jumps up, scurrying toward the door just like the white rabbit. This time, I follow without hesitation.

22

VOXY SCURRIES DOWN THE HALLWAY TOWARD THE EL-evator. He actually moves like the rabbit.

"Wait," I call after, same as before. "Where are you going?"

The elevator pings as he presses the button.

Panicked, I whisper as loud as I can, "Someone will see us."

"Blancaflor wasn't afraid of her father seeing her leave with the prince." Voxy puts his hands on his hips. "Los Viejos would not have worried about a few Collective if it meant finding the treasure."

"How long have you been sneaking into our room, Voxy?"

He doesn't answer.

I roll my eyes and hurry to his side. At least if someone sees me with him, they won't think I'm wandering alone. "I think you just want the cuentos," I say.

He shrugs unapologetically. I take a breath and follow him into the elevator. If he really did see a book from home, it's more valuable to me than all of the diamonds and emeralds and rubies scattered on los Viejos' kitchen floor.

He presses floor one, and my heartbeat speeds even more. Five entire floors separate us from the treasure. The door closes and my eyes lock on the floor indicator. Voxy smiles at me as we descend.

Five . . . four . . . three . . . The elevator chimes.

The door opens to the wrinkled-brow ghost shrimp who dragged Glish away. The Prawn raises his eyebrows, and his already crinkled forehead puckers to ramen noodles.

"Hello," Voxy says, like our outing is perfectly normal.

"Hello?" the man says, staring at us.

"Are you coming in or not?" Voxy asks boldly. What kind of power do bedtime stories have over him that he'd risk our safety like this?

The Prawn steps inside with us and presses floor two.

The three of us face the elevator door, and it closes.

I laser-lock my eyes on the glowing 3.

He turns to Voxy. "Does the Chancellor know you are . . ." He glances at me.

Voxy huffs annoyedly at the man and turns a cold shoulder. "Do you really think I would disobey the order of the Collective? Are you doubting the Chancellor knows everything that happens on this ship?"

Two . . .

"Of course not," the Prawn says. Then he whispers, "Pardon the inquiry."

I barely move or blink or breathe until the elevator door chimes at the second floor and the Prawn steps out.

The door closes, and we continue down. "This is a horrible idea," I mutter.

Voxy smiles and the door chimes for the first floor. He walks confidently out of the elevator and diagonally through the main floor of the ship. We are nowhere near any of the Collective's living quarters, so I'm wondering exactly where he could have seen the book. We continue toward the front part of the ship, as far from my room and the safety of my cell as I could be.

A few people are still at stations, folding blankets, cleaning floors and ceilings, preparing bioloaf and mystery diluted juice drink.

I'm not sure if it's Voxy's confident posture, but no one gives us a second glance.

We turn down a hall, but only a single door lies at its end. Above the door, the outline of the faded letters spelling *Seed Vault* have been removed.

An antique keypad like the one Mom had on her greenhouse is next to the doorlatch.

Voxy presses 2061, the year we left Earth, and the door slides open.

The room glows dark blue like the ship had before. In the center of the room lies a bed.

"That's where the Chancellor sleeps," he says matter-of-factly.

I gulp, then cover it up with a cough.

Then Voxy points to a room off to the side no bigger than a coat closet. "My room."

I walk to Voxy's door and peek inside. One tiny honeycomb cell is wedged inside, leaving no room to even stand. Empty plant seedling trays and irrigation tubes lie stacked on floating shelves.

I remember Mom's friend, Dr. Nguyen, but think Voxy's tiny closet is way too small to be the universal seed vault where Mom contributed New Mexican corn, squash, and beans.

I scan the main room with Nyla's bed. Besides her bed, there are only the usual rounded walls; no sign of any vault. And definitely no book. Even if Voxy saw a book and other "relics" from Earth, they aren't here anymore. He's young and his memory could have been from any part of the ship. I don't have time to be hunting for something I might never find. "Voxy, I should be getting back."

"No!" he yells. "I know it was in here. But it was so long ago. I told Nyla I'd seen it and asked to keep it, and she told me I must have dreamt it. It was real, though."

He paces back and forth in the doorway of his closet. "I read it right here." He points toward the front of his cell. "It was magical," he whispers, looking up to meet my eyes. "Like your cuentos. The people and places in each one are all so different from one another. They decide who they will be or what they will do or where they will go without being told by the Collective. And the people in your cuentos don't live in a world without"—he pauses—"cuentos."

I think of how Voxy and I are not so different. My parents and the original Monitors (except for Ben) were imposing En Cognito programs on me for which I had no interest.

Voxy sits on the edge of his sleep cell, and his shoulders slump. "The people in your cuentos and the people in the book I read, they do things I'd never be brave enough to do."

Even if it's risky, I can't let him think this. I put my hand on his shoulder. "You were brave enough to bring me here."

His chin is still on his chest, but his eyes peek upward at me.

"You're trying to find something good for yourself, even if the Collective tells you it's dangerous," I say. "You are trusting your gut. That is good." If he breathes one word of what I'm saying before we leave the ship, it's over.

"Well, I do not know exactly what that means," he says. "But if it means I want more cuentos, then what you say is true, Zeta-1." He drops his head. "Anyway, she must have hidden it all, but it was here. I promise."

I sigh and sit next to him, patting his knee.

"The lady in the storybook had her own baby back when there were parents," Voxy continues. "They left their home for a new land."

I'm so startled, I miss a breath. Javier's book. I can't help grabbing his hands.

"Voxy! You have to remember where it was."

His eyes widen and he shakes his head. "It was here. I am sure of it." His eyes gape even more when I hurry to my hands and knees and put my cheek to the floor, looking under his bed.

And that's when I see it at the back of his cell. A thin strip of Pleiades purple strip lighting in the shape of a door, just like the one at the back of the ship leading to the hold. I rise up to my knees and point to the back wall. "Voxy, what's behind that?"

"Nothing," he answers, giving it a glance. He crawls through his cell and knocks on the wall. It echoes.

I crawl in after him, and the two of us are crammed in his honeycomb side by side. I run my finger along the inner edge of the strip lighting, then wedge my fingernails in the crack. I pry until one of my nails splits off at the quick. But nothing budges. I feel around the dark wall and find a switch for turning on an unattached irrigation tube.

I yank down on the switch and it cracks off and shatters on the floor. Voxy and I exchange wide-eyed glances. If Nyla decides to check under his bed, we're busted.

We look back to where the switch had just been. A glowing button blinks from deep within the hole. It's too small for my finger, but . . .

Voxy forces his pinky inside until I hear a click. The door's edge creaks and with a suctioned pop, shifts backward. Cold air and the waft of a comforting smell blast me in my face. It takes me a few moments to place it, but then there it is . . . the Piñon Elementary School library.

As the wall slides into a pocket, a sliver of golden light from inside the room falls over Voxy's sleep cell. The door cracks open just wide enough for an adult to squeeze through sideways. Voxy dives headfirst through the opening before I blink.

I follow Voxy and slide out from the end of his cell and onto a frigid floor. The cold air and metal floor tell me what I need to know. We've found the seed vault.

Voxy stands in front of a single workstation in the center of a room the size of my entire house. The golden light I expected to be a lamp is not. Instead, a basketball-sized holographic sun throws off a yellow glow. Earth, Venus, Mars, icy Neptune, Uranus, and the rest, even Saturn with its rings, all spin slowly in the far corner of the room. It's not exactly to scale, but it's definitely Earth's solar system.

Below the twirling hologram lies an entire wall of seed vault drawers containing Earth's plant life.

I look at Voxy's smiling face standing in front of the work-station. A ceramic Christmas tree, mounted with a photo of a freckle-faced girl with a missing front tooth, sits on the middle of the table like a centerpiece. A pair of baby shoes dangle by tied laces from a drawer handle. In the glow of the fake sun, framed family pictures and yellowing birth and marriage certificates are attached to the other walls, like a shrine to Earth.

Voxy makes a fist pump I'm sure he's never seen before. "See! I knew it was all real!"

I think of Nyla and all her talk of "forgetting our past" and "the consequences of those who came before us." She scolded Crick for even referring to Earth.

"Do you know where she got it all?" I ask, trying to sound innocent, but my voice cracks.

"I am not sure." Voxy scratches his head. "But we are not to mention relics any longer."

My stomach roils. I can't tell him these things represent what we loved the most: our home, our friends, our families. I can't explain that Nyla and those who came before her stole these things from people like me and my dead family.

Even with the mementos and pictures scattered throughout the room, this can't even be half of what the passengers brought with us. I open a drawer on the workbench. My stomach lurches. Labeled *Downloadable Cognizance: Defective*, rows of Cogs sit lined in tiny holders like rings in a jewelry store. Each of these Cogs is laser marked with initials and dates spanning hundreds of years.

I look around and notice sealed, unused boxes against a wall. I go closer and see they're labeled *En Cognito Downloadable Cognizance—Pediatric* and *En Cognito Downloadable Cognizance—Adult*. They blink as they sit charging next to an ice-cream scoop installer like Ben used. If knowledge is so dangerous, why does Nyla have others ready to be used socked away here? Who does she plan to download these Cogs to?

"Where do you think the book is?" I ask.

Voxy shakes his head. I walk from picture to picture, certificate to certificate, looking for anything belonging to my family.

Voxy's voice calls. "Zeta-1?"

I turn, and Voxy's standing at an open seed drawer with a huge grin on his face. I walk toward him and the drawer he holds open. I look down. Interspersed with plundered foil bags that once contained frozen seeds, personal belonging bags hang from metal brackets like a file cabinet. The bags are the same ones Ben handed Javier and me to place the few precious things we were taking with us. Lighted tabs jut from the top.

A loud pop echoes in the room, and we jump. Icy air spouts from four slotted squares above our heads, a reminder that this room was intended to preserve seeds.

Voxy lets out a breath. "You've seen it now." His eyes dart back toward his sleep cell. "We should come back another time. I'm not feeling so brave anymore."

He's right. Nyla could come any second. My legs are shaking, and not from the cold either. But if I'm leaving the ship, this might be my last chance to find my belongings.

"Just a moment more," I say.

I lean over the drawer to see backlit tabs—*Yancy, Meg.* The magnetic seal opens with a click as I pull on its edge. Inside, Meg Yancy's diamond ring glimmers back. I close her bag quickly.

Voxy taps my shoulder. "We should go now," he says.

I can't leave when I'm so close. But even in the chilly room, sweat beads on my forehead. "You stand guard by the door," I say.

Voxy bites his lip. But he nods his head and goes to stand back by the room's entrance.

I try two drawers higher. *Riese, Marcus.* I move to the next row. My hands tremble as my fingers run along the top of the bags, stopping at the lighted O: *O'Neal, Jason.* Then . . . P: *Patel, Aashika*, P: *Peña* . . .

My stomach is a swarm of wasps in suspense.

I reach out to grasp Javier's pouch. I ease open the top of his bag. His jeans and GG Gang sweatshirt are still crumpled inside. The smiling Wally the Wooly mammoth, Hypacrosauras, and dodo bird on the front of his sweatshirt are faded.

I reach in and knock my knuckle on something hard. I slide out Javier's book and hold it up. On the cover, the woman with longing eyes and red hair scarf stares back at me. *Dreamers* runs in loopy script across the top.

"That's it! That's the book!" Voxy bursts out from his watch station at the door. "I told you!"

The lump in my throat grows bigger. I hold Javier's book to my nose and sniff. Even after three hundred and eighty years, the book smells like home. I turn to ask Voxy to hold it for me so I can search more, but I realize I can't let go of it.

I tuck the book under my arm and go to the next tab.

Peña, Petra

I slip my hand deep inside the pouch. Metal pokes under my fingernail. I wrap my hand around it and pull out my pendant, now tarnished black. I grip it tightly to my chest. They've all been gone so long. My chest tightens, and my eyes burn with tears.

I slip it in my chest pocket and place my hand over it, closing my eyes.

There's another startling pop as the cooling units shut off. I open my eyes, and Voxy is standing next to me.

"We have to leave now, Zeta-1," he declares.

I sniff. "Right." I start to close the drawer.

Voxy holds his hand out for Javier's book. "We have to put it back."

"No," I snap before I can stop myself.

Voxy jumps back. "Now we know where the room is. We can come back and read it later."

I know this won't be an option.

But I also know I can't risk ruining my escape if Voxy gets cold feet and tells Nyla I took one of the relics.

Voxy opens the pouch for me, and I let it drop back in. Something about letting the book go feels like losing Javier all over again.

Voxy smiles and turns back to the door. I turn to follow

him, then stop. I can't leave it behind. And what about my parents' belongings? What did they bring with them? I never even asked.

"What is it, Zeta-1?" he asks.

"It's just—"

"Voxy!" Nyla's voice calls.

We freeze like Lita's fainting goats.

Voxy rushes to the door, diving through the opening into his cell. The door slides shut seconds later, leaving me in the room with only the glow of Earth's spinning solar system in a cold mist.

My hot breath comes out in a fog. I grip my pendant. *Please don't let them catch me when I'm so close.*

"Yes, Nyla?" his muffled voice replies.

There's a moment that's too quiet.

"I mean, Chancellor," Voxy says. "Can I ask you something?"

"Of course, Voxy."

I hear him crawl to the front of his cell.

"You told me the relics were my imagination," he says. "I know that is not true. Why don't you want me and the others to know about them?"

Why is he doing this? It's like Javier, when Mom walked in on us eating Oreos before dinner. He smiled with little black flecks all over his teeth. "*We aren't eating the cookies you hid behind your succulents, Mom.*" Mom stared at her succulents on the kitchen counter. I'm sure Nyla is staring at the door behind Voxy's bed.

Nyla sighs. "Voxy, you must understand that all I . . . and the Collective do is to keep us all safe, including you."

I hear him giggle.

"You are correct though," she says. "But you need to forget about the relics. Nothing good has ever come from those things. Human possessions that were once part of the old Earth contributed to greed and selfishness. That led to unhappiness. Unhappiness led to conflict. Do you understand?"

"Yes, Nyla. I understand."

This time, she doesn't correct him on her name. I wonder if he believes that Javier's *Dreamers* book could ever be something that led to greed or war.

"Nothing can come between you and protecting the Collective. One day, it is possible you and I may have to take on more knowledge than you could dream of. Even in a Collective, the burden of hidden power falls on a few." I think of all the unused Cogs in the drawer. "But for all to possess that knowledge is dangerous. For now, for the Collective to be successful, we must control that knowledge, and only impart it to a few. And those few must be conditioned to serve implicitly, and absolutely, like the Zetas."

It is quiet for a moment. "But what happens when there are no longer any Zetas?" he asks.

"Do not worry. We have been working for years on a new Collective creation batch. It is all for a purpose. You will soon have others closer to your age. Those we can also utilize to advance our science and who are programmed to serve unconditionally."

Something scrapes on the floor, and I think their conversation is over.

"You and I, let us erase all that unnecessary knowledge and the possessions that distracts us, so that only see one another. And if when we look at one another, we see ourselves, there can only be peace."

Hearing the way she presents it, I'm not sure many would disagree with her.

"Come with me," she says. "There is a meeting and I'd like you to be there. It is how you will learn and understand."

"Now? Can I start learning another time?" Another uncomfortable silence follows, then, "Yes, Chancellor."

I hear footsteps, and all goes still. I know she is wrong. She has spun her words to fit her beliefs. Did Nyla have someone who taught her, as she's teaching Voxy?

If I don't escape before they come back, I'll be trapped in this frigid room all night.

With only the glow of the miniature sun, I tiptoe toward the opening—so seamless, the only way I know where it is are the walls on either side covered with Earth mementos, the slim door itself bare. I look for a switch or tiny hole like the other side, but find nothing but pictures and certificates. "No, no, no," I whisper.

Most people would stand back and zero in on a tiny hole. But even if I had more light, the wall is so covered with pictures, certificates, and art I'd freeze to death scanning it bit by bit.

I take a guess and run my fingers along the exact spot the lock was located on the other side. Over it a baseball card of the first female pitcher in the majors hangs in a plastic mount. I lift it off its hanger—and see the same round hole. Too narrow for my fingers. I go back to the workbench for a holotack, but it's empty. I glance down at the baseball card and pull it out of the plastic sleeve labeled with its owner's name on a sticker. I roll it up. "Sorry," I whisper, knowing the card must've been valuable to someone named *Foster, Niles.*

I slip it into the hole and the door slides open. I hurry to crawl through. Thankfully, Voxy's cell is empty, and I push the card in the hole on the other side, closing the door again. As it's shutting, I stop one more time. If I go back for all my family's belongings and get stuck, having parts of them won't matter if I'm reprogrammed and don't remember them at all. I exit Voxy's cell, peeking into Nyla's empty bedroom.

Nyla's bedroom door to the hallway is closed. I push on the latch, but it won't depress at all. The same keypad lock sits on this side of the door too. I wipe sweat off my head. *Please work.* I press *2061* and the latch doesn't budge. If Nyla comes back, it's over. If they chose *2061* for the year we left . . .

My finger shakes as I enter *2442* for what should be the current year. I push on the latch and it clicks, the door swinging open. I dart out and approach the open belly of the ship within ten seconds. I straighten my back and walk confidently right down the center of the main floor.

I'm halfway to the elevator when I hear Nyla's voice. Her

"meeting" is taking place near what used to be the cafeteria, and I have no choice but to walk right by the group to the elevator leading back to my room. Nyla stands at a podium, her back to me. Voxy sits in front and I see his eyes trailing my walk, but he doesn't break out of character either.

"We are exploring several options," she says. "However, a tidal-locked planet has limitations for colonization."

I continue walking, eyes straight ahead. "The optimal habitable zone is very specific. We are nearly ready with a defoliant."

Great. No pressure.

I reach the elevator and press the button.

"But nonetheless, there are many other obstacles to staying in this region," she continues. "And although we are doing our best, if they cannot be remedied soon, we will seek out another planet."

My heart sledgehammers in my chest. But once we're on the surface, I don't care where the Collective goes. As long as they go.

I step in, press 6, and face the door.

"One of those obstacles are hostiles," Nyla continues. The elevator door begins to slide shut. "With whom we have no intention of making contact."

What! They sent us down there with hostile beings? I reach out to smash the Open Door button—

"Our first scouting missions in the zone have avoided these First—" The door closes, cutting off her speech.

The elevator is already rising. But I heard it. *First.*

But first what? I hadn't dared hope the first ship had made it. Even if it had, with the Collective in charge? I hadn't thought finding others somewhere on a new planet was even an option. Dad said the first ship would create a settlement in the habitable zone, and we'd have to locate them from space using panchromatic imagery. Otherwise it'd be like looking for a needle in a haystack.

I want to jump up and down. But they'd see me through the glass. A laugh slips out, and I stop myself. Then I realize no one can hear me. I laugh harder than I have in hundreds of years. Sagan isn't quite as big as Earth, but I'd given up hope the terraformers were still alive, let alone possibly near us.

If the First Arrivers are in the habitable zone, it might take years—and gagging down a lot of lake vines. But if they are there, I will find them for Feathers, Rubio, Suma, and me.

The elevator chimes for my floor, and I run to our room and hurry inside, catching my breath. My roommates are all still asleep, Rubio's snoring the only sound.

I rush to the bathroom and turn on the fan, a smile still plastered on my face. I pull out my pendant and rub it on my clothes to clean off the tarnish, but it leaves black streaks. I hold it up to the light.

I think of Lita's words. "A *doorway to bring lost ones together.*" Between finding my pendant and the news that there could be other humans on Sagan . . . if a heart can thump out of a chest with happiness, mine's about to explode.

23

THE NEXT MORNING, I WAKE UP BEFORE EVERYONE else and sneak to the privacy of the bathroom. I brush my hair to one side and section it into three.

This is it. Now, with my pendant, I will be able to talk to Lita. I have everything. The sooner I create Nyla's defoliant to rid the planet of the dangerous plants, the sooner she'll send us back to check its effectiveness, and the sooner we can escape. The First Arrivers may be alive too.

I braid my hair tightly, not a single scraggly strand left behind.

I walk into our bedroom. Suma stretches and yawns. "Hello, Zeta-1."

"Hi, Sum—Zeta-2." I grit my teeth when I say the Collective's stupid name, remembering what Nyla said about Suma just before she stuck her back in stasis. *With the upgraded download she will be Zeta-2 for the rest of her life.* Not much longer, Suma.

Suma slips on her jumpsuit. "What have you been assigned today?"

"Oh, just de-leafing the planet," I answer. "And you?"

She sits up tall. "I will be creating fuel for the ship."

I think of what Nyla said about obstacles and leaving for another planet. Is this why they need fuel? How soon is this going to happen?

"Why?" I ask, wondering if maybe they've given her some sort of hint.

Suma shrugs. "I do as the Collective asks."

I have to work faster.

Rubio interjects in a voice as monotone as Crick's. "I will just be ensuring the Collective has the proper oxygen composition to breathe."

Feathers stands up and straightens her jumpsuit. "Well, I will ensure the Collective has nanomeds to keep their bodies functioning, so they can breathe in your clean air, which is of course irrelevant without a healthy pulmonary system."

I snicker and pull on my shoes.

Feathers sits next to me. "I really liked the cuento you told about los Viejos and the shiny gems and stones, Zeta-1. Especially the ending when they lived by the river and planted fruit trees and crops and the children from all the neighboring towns arrived to run and play through the orchards." She sighs. "I'd like to see an orchard someday."

I turn my head quickly. It's a great addition to the story, but I know I didn't mention children running or playing in orchards.

Rubio continues, "I liked how los Viejos helped the poor and homeless after the great pandemic."

Tingles run up and over my spine. I definitely didn't mention the great pandemic from back in the twenties. If they're remembering things from home, it's great. But my gut tells me now it's better for them to remember *after* we're on Sagan.

I put my finger to my lips and make eye contact with each of them. "*Ssssh.*"

They all stare back. This might be my last chance. I know it's a risk, but . . . "When we go on the next scouting mission, you all have to follow my directions. If you do, I promise to tell you as many cuentos as you want."

"Why?" Suma asks.

"We shouldn't question why," I say confidently. "The Collective is one." I know the statement is vague, but it sounds a lot like something a member of the Collective would say.

Feathers and Rubio nod, but Suma stares right at me like my words are simmering in her mind.

Rubio speaks to himself in a quiet voice. "Hmmm, more cuentos . . ."

"I agree!" Feathers blurts out smiling. "I will follow your directions." She stands up, arms at her sides. "It's to help the Collective."

Suma's brow furrows. "Wouldn't the Collective inform us all if there were a change in command?"

This is tricky. But if I can create the defoliant, we could be back on Sagan within a day. It's worth it.

My heartbeat quickens and I turn toward Suma boldly. "The Chancellor asked me in private." I think of the cave. "I'm to take you all to a prospective settlement site to test its safety. We are not to mention it in front of anyone yet, to manage their hopes. But if we succeed it will be a great success for the Collective."

Suma narrows her eyes at me.

"If you want more cuentos, you have to agree," I say.

Rubio purses his lips. "I agree."

Feathers squats down and peers up hopefully at Suma. "Zeta-2? Please."

This might be the one chance for us to escape. I can't let Suma influence the others.

I raise my chin, remembering how Voxy spoke to the man in the elevator. "Unless, of course, you doubt what the Chancellor says is best for the Collective's survival."

Suma doesn't answer, instead focusing on braiding her hair. When she's finished, she sighs deeply. "I think—"

The door slides open, and Crick walks in, hands interlocked at his waist. "Zeta Experts," he says through blue-lined lips. We follow him out and to the main level for our daily meal.

Just like every other day, I take my square section off Bioloaf Boy's tray. And just like every other day, he doesn't acknowledge me.

The assembly line is creating the Collective's food like always. I debate sidling up to the finished bioloaf stack and stealing more. But I can't afford the risk at this point. One group elsewhere repairs pristine jumpsuits, while another cleans the already clean, glowing floor. Like tiny specks of floating dust, people hang from their harnesses far above, cleaning the ceiling.

The bioloaf chat group still stands off to the side. Again, I move closer. Now, without Glish, Hammerhead and the others in their group are back to a dull chatter.

It takes Feather, Rubio, Suma, and me less than a minute to eat our daily ration.

I think of the time my family spent at the kitchen table eating meals. Mom would sip her coffee slowly and metronome her head back and forth, doing her crossword. Javier would ramble about a new Gen-Gyro-Gang member, or argue with Dad for ten minutes that he knew you could reach your brain if you picked your nose hard enough. All this compared to the forty-five seconds we spend downing bioloaf.

We finish and follow Crick out as he leads us to the elevator and into the hold. "Big day . . . big day," he says.

This day is way bigger than Crick could know. If I can just finish the defoliant in the lab without suspicion, or without Suma spilling to Nyla what I've just told them, we'll be on Sagan permanently within twenty-four hours.

The doors open, and the hold is buzzing with ghost shrimp. Like a choreographed dance, vacant pods are being floated from the center of the hold, while metal supply crates take their place in the belly of the hold in preparation for offloading.

One by one, the pods are lined up like a white-bricked garden border along the perimeter. Barrels of glowing green stasis gel dot between every four pods, a reminder they can still be used if necessary. I wonder how close Nyla is to creating our replacements. My meal churns in my stomach like sour milk.

Crick leads us past the blinking blue light of the empty ration room.

We continue past all the bustle and back toward the quiet research labs.

"Zeta-2." Crick motions toward a lab. "Do you need assistance?"

Suma scoffs and raises her eyebrows. "No."

I swear she side-eyes Rubio as she walks in, closing the door behind her.

Crick nods in approval. "Well then. Next," he says, continuing deeper into the lab sector.

When we drop off Rubio, he claps and mumbles, "Now, I can get to work."

Feathers walks ahead without Crick and me. She makes a

sharp left into a lab where her nanomaterial collection bags are already stacked on her lab table. Each rock and stone is sitting in its own petri dish next to a spectrometer. She waves over her head and shuts the door.

"H*mmpf*," Crick says, hopping back as the door slams in his face.

Crick and I continue toward the back corner of the lab area. "I hear you ruined my surprise," he says.

My heart skips. I clear my throat. "Surprise?"

"The Chancellor tells me you've met Epsilon-5 already."

"Oh y-yes," I stutter. "I couldn't wait. Sorry."

"Well, you are fortunate to have a partner. He is quite talented."

I'm even more curious now who the old scientist was back on Earth, for Crick to know of some special talent.

Crick opens the door. But Epsilon-5 is not there. The lab smells of burnt chemicals. The low hum of a centrifuge decelerates until it stops.

An incubator is set way too high at thirty-seven degrees Celsius, which makes no sense for a defoliant to kill Sagan's plant life for terra-forming. This is exactly the kind of delay I can't afford. I hurry over, and the sensor beeps as I reset it to thirty degrees. I know it's not Epsilon-5's fault. He doesn't know I'm in a hurry. And I feel worse being annoyed with him when I have to leave him behind.

"Well, looks like you are comfortable here. Is there anything else I can assist you with?" Crick asks.

I wave my hand like he's a gnat, shooing him off like the others did.

He sighs and sits on a bench just inside the door.

"Did you need something?" I ask.

"No, no," he answers. "The Collective would just like updates."

"Of course." With him watching my every move, it won't change what I need to do. I'm ninety-nine percent sure he has no idea what all of us are doing in the lab anyway.

I use the opportunity to verify what Nyla said, by testing one of my lake-water samples. I place one sample in an empty centrifuge so I can analyze the particulate. But for the rest, I unseal a test-strip kit. Within an hour I know it contains an unknown parasite similar to cryptosporidium, but no heavy metals. I filter the water through a straw and it easily removes the parasite. I test the particulate and the sediment is nothing more than sand, making it completely drinkable with the filtration straws.

It also means I know exactly how to treat the lake vines. I open the top drawer of the lab station, and sure enough, there's a flint lighter. I can't believe with all this technology, in a ship that traveled across the galaxy, the same flint lighter from my seventh grade chemistry lab is what they have on the ship. I grab two and several replacement flints and cram them quickly in my pocket.

I begin cooking up some lake vine soup, boiling in a 500 ml beaker. When I know it's boiled long enough to kill any cryptosporidium, I block Crick's view and pick a smaller piece out with forceps. I close my eyes and say a quick prayer, lifting it to my lips, and chew. It's a little slippery, and it's no sopa de nopal, but I'd take it over bioloaf. I pat the flint lighters in my pocket, feeling like I've already accomplished two things we'll need. Food and fire. I mentally fist pump and suit up to start on the defoliant.

I decide to spend the afternoon determining how to kill the stuff that can kill us first. But when I open the refrigerator where my sample bags of red-rimmed leaves were hanging, they're gone. I turn back to Crick. "My foliage is missing."

He raises his brows. "*Your* foliage?"

I recognize my mistake immediately. "The rest of *the Collective's* samples are here, but not the one I need first."

He nods. "I'm sure Epsilon-5 will have an answer for you."

I smile. "Of course." But my stomach flutters like it's full of water butterflies. "I'll begin with the other samples first."

I consider what defoliant will work on both the harmless ground cover and the elephant leaves. Sure enough, there's plenty dichlorophenoxyacetic acid as well as trichlorophenoxyacetic acid stocked in the lab. Enough to obliterate every last plant and animal on Sagan. But the chemicals in these Earth defoliants killed most fish and mammals too, as well as humans. Just like the chemicals that made up Agent Orange. Apparently, the Collective isn't so against all relics and things "Earth-like."

Instead of using something that might harm us, I mix a concoction of a surfactant, NaCl, and a chemical derivative of acetic acid—aka Dawn dish soap, salt, and vinegar. It might not have the speedy results Nyla wants, but if it could keep Mrs. Tronsted's hosta plants from creeping into Mom's berries, it should kill the huge-leafed plants and ground cover without contaminating Sagan's water and soil.

I place samples of leaves and ground cover in petri dishes and spray my environmentally approved potion over each.

It's late afternoon and I'm already halfway done when Epsilon-5 returns. He smiles, "Welcome back." He shuffles toward the workbench, one foot slightly turned in like Papá's after his stroke. He's already suited up, but his lab goggles are on top of his head.

"Thank you," I smile back and set the already-dying plant samples in front of him.

"Trichlorophenoxy—?"

"I didn't need to use it," I reply, smiling.

I show him the ingredients I used. "It will allow for quicker habitation for the Collective."

He nods. "Good work, Zeta-1."

Crick stands. "So the task is completed?"

Epsilon-5 answers for me. "Of course not. We need to conduct a control and then calculate a few variables."

I hand Epsilon-5 an Erlenmeyer flask, and he hurries to the opposite side of the bench like we're reading each other's minds.

He looks over the partition to Crick. "This could take quite some time."

He's right. It could take some time. But I wonder if he's

annoyed by Crick too, and I think Epsilon-5 and I would have been better friends than I first thought.

Crick sighs. "I will check on the others' progress and be back." He exits the lab.

As if we've worked twenty years together on an assembly line, Epsilon-5 and I snip samples, preparing dishes without needing to tell each other what we are doing or what to do next. The only pause is when I notice him grabbing his hand occasionally, to steady a tremor.

After a few minutes, he peeks under the partition. "You know, we were interrupted by the Chancellor yesterday."

I think of how beautiful the view onto the planet was, but know Crick would grow suspicious if we had the window open when we should be focusing on our work.

"I was wondering . . ." Epsilon-5 says.

"Yes?"

"Did you see any other creatures besides the water butterflies?" He smiles, and my heart sinks. If anyone deserves to see Sagan's creatures, it's him.

I smile back and he returns to his work.

"Well, I did meet a furry, round-eared fellow," I say, knowing he won't understand the term *mini-chinchilla*. I hold up a pipette bulb. "About this big."

I look up to see his gap-toothed grin.

I hold up a rubber stopper. "Ears this big."

He laughs. "Do you think the creature was dangerous?"

"I didn't see any animal life on the planet that's dangerous," I answer.

His tone is suddenly a bit more somber. "Nothing at all?"

"Not so far," I answer honestly.

"Hmmm." He continues clipping samples for our control.

"It scurries about," I continue, "eating every last leaf to fill its little round belly, except . . ." I point to where the red-leafed samples had been. "Except of course . . . Do you know where the sample bags in that refrigerator are? We need to test those next."

"Oh, I forgot to mention. The Collective decided to have me use it all right away to create something else."

I flinch back, not sure why he used every last sample of the deadliest plant in galaxy history to test an herbicide. He must have misspoken and said *create* instead of *test*. "And did you finish already?"

He lets out a breath, eyes wide. "Oh yes. It didn't take long at all." He shakes his head. "Dangerous to work with, but easy enough to extract."

"Extract?" I blurt out, hoping he's confused. "Don't you mean eradicate? To test an herbicide?" I think of the incubator setting when I came in. Set to grow something. My face numbs.

"No. The Chancellor was specific," he says. "Create an airborne toxin with a short half-life. One immediately effective but then leaves the air safe for human inhabitance. They must have found a life source that posed an obstacle to the safety of the Collective. A creature so threatening they'd put everything else on hold to create such a deadly toxin."

Suddenly I feel like I'm in zero gravity, untethered from my surroundings. While I was celebrating in the elevator that the First Arrivers were near, I hadn't considered the Collective was conspiring to exterminate the "hostiles."

"What have we done?" I whisper. I set down my flask before my shaking hand drops it. But I already know what we've done. They must have a good idea of exactly where the First Arrivers are. And when we return to the surface, if we escape and find them, what's to stop the Collective from using the poison on all of us?

My only choice is to find the toxin Epsilon-5 has made and try to destroy it. And I have to do it before we leave tomorrow.

"I've spent an entire unit helping them with their moods." Epsilon-5 motions to the tonic. "I was more than happy to ensure their new planet is safe."

I think of what I know about the Collective. They are afraid. They've been clear they will eliminate anything posing harm to them. But they don't even know yet if their epiderm-filters—

"Wait." Suddenly Epsilon-5's words hit me. "You've helped them an entire unit?" Pinpricks run up my back and over my scalp. If Epsilon-5's reprogramming is as good as it sounds, I know how hard it is for him to lie. He's been out of stasis . . . "Over seventy years?" I whisper.

If Epsilon-5 has been here that long, he was younger than me when they took him out of stasis.

"As I already explained," he says, "when we began our work, there were only a few Deltas still living. Before the Deltas, the

Gammas performed those duties for the Collective."

I take slow breaths in and close my eyes. All the kids put in stasis the same day as me . . . All of them, living out their lives with no memory of home or Earth or their families. If they weren't already purged. My face trembles uncontrollably.

Epsilon-5 sets his sample in the incubator and returns. He takes off his goggles and removes his gloves, setting them on the table.

The laboratory lights hit a brown mark on his hand. Something about the speckled blotch is familiar. I lean in closer. On his left thumb, a birthmark smattering of freckles in the shape of a constellation dots across his wrinkled left thumb.

I wobble and grab the edge of the table.

Epsilon-5 hurries to hold out his hand. "Let me help you."

I grab him and slump onto the chair. I pull his hand close and rub my finger over the mark like I have a thousand times before.

My voice trembles as I say his name that hasn't been spoken aloud for centuries. "Javier?"

24

EPSILON-5, MY BROTHER, TILTS HIS HEAD. "I DON'T UNderstand."

I can't help the hiccupped cry. I wipe my eyes and look away. "Oh God." I turn back to him. Even with what they've done to his mind, I see it. Under the wrinkles and white hair is my brother.

"Zeta-1?" His voice sounds slightly less stiff. "What is it?"

His eyes look like they did when I stubbed my toe on his bed, all those years ago.

Now the skin sags over Javier's brown irises, milky with age. He looks toward the hold. "I'll get help."

"No," I say. "Just . . . just give me a moment."

"Would you like some tonic?" He shuffles toward the shelves of red, green, blue, and gold bottles.

I can't breathe. He's even older than Papá was when he died.

I watch him in disbelief as his shaky hand pours red tonic from the bottle into a cup. I want to tell him to slow down as he rushes back across the room.

He pulls up a stool and sits next to me. "I should call for medical assistance?"

I push the drink away. "Epsilon-5, do you remember how you got here?" My voice is still shaky.

He speaks slowly, like Lita recalling a childhood memory. "The Collective decided when to bring us out of stasis so we would be of most value, just like you and the other Zetas. But . . ." He sighs. "The other Epsilons grew old." He sets one hand over the other and squeezes, bowing his head. "All gone now," he says.

Suma, Feathers, Rubio, and me . . . we are the last.

I need him to still be the Javier who said he'd be my eyes. Who would've done anything for me and me for him.

I now know what Lita meant when she said someone's blood was boiling. Even if Javier doesn't remember, I'm not leaving him here so he can die serving these people.

I wipe my face with my sleeve and calm my voice. "Epsilon-5?"

He holds out the glass of tonic to me like he doesn't know how else to help me. I take the cup and set it back down. I want to hug him or shake him or scream at him—to remind him of who he is. Now that we have the defoliant, the Collective will have us return to the surface once the winds are calm.

"You know we're going to the surface tomorrow?" I continue. Even if Javier can't grow up with me, we will make the most of the time we have left together.

"Yes," he says. "A scouting mission. I cannot wait to hear what you—"

"I will need your help," I say.

His eyes widen. "My help?"

"Yes. There's nothing to be afraid of."

"I'm not afraid. I will do what I must to serve the Collective." He shakes his head. "But I won't be going to the planet. The Chancellor made clear my service is needed here."

I clear my throat to keep my voice from shaking. "I agree we should do what we must to serve the Collective. And I will explain to the Chancellor why I need you to accompany me to test the defoliant."

But what good is it if he's on Sagan with us, just to have the Collective release the toxin, killing us all? "I was also wondering . . ."

He leans in. "Yes?"

I can't hesitate. I have so little time to destroy it. "Can you tell me where you stored the toxin?"

He tilts his head in question.

"Just curious," I say.

He nods. "I placed it—"

The door swings open. Nyla and Crick enter.

They stride over, and both Javier and I straighten our posture.

"The defoliant is nearly completed?" Nyla asks.

"Yes," I say before Javier can speak. If he says the wrong thing now, it's over.

She smiles at us. "You two have accomplished both tasks as quickly as I expected you would."

"There's just one thing," I add. I motion toward where my missing red-rimmed leaves had been. "I believe I can improve upon the toxin Epsilon-5 created for you."

Nyla stares at Javier.

"Zeta-1, are you saying what Epsilon-5 created is deficient?" Crick asks.

Javier stares past them toward the hold, I'm sure trying to determine what he could've missed.

I step toward them. I don't like the way Nyla's glaring at Javier.

"No, no," I answer quickly. "But I *can* decrease the half-life while simultaneously making the potency tenfold." I have to buy some time while I figure out how I can destroy it.

Nyla walks past us slowly toward the blank wall hiding the window. She presses the button, and the wall slides inside its pocket. A golden glow fills the lab. "But Epsilon-5's toxin is already prepared and ready for use," she says, staring down at Sagan's surface.

"Yes," I call after, "but while the toxin is effective, no human will be able to occupy the planet for quite some time."

Arms crossed over her chest, Nyla is perfectly still. No one speaks. What is she devising now?

I take a hesitant step in her direction like I'm approaching a tiger. "By reducing its half-life, you will be able to occupy the planet far sooner," I go on, hoping she won't be able to resist. "And with the increased potency, not only will no animal life within kilometers survive, it will be over almost instantly."

Her shoulders raise and lower with a deep breath.

Crick stands next to her. "Shouldn't we wait to see if Len—the results on our epiderm-filters. It won't be long now. Perhaps we will not need to use the toxin at all, if we must leave."

Nyla stays looking out at Sagan. "Even if we leave, who is to say the Collective will not need this planet for ourselves in the future?" She turns and holds Crick's eyes. "Better to eliminate all threats now for what may come, even if it is units and units away."

Everything Dad said was true. To achieve their goals—to have no starvation, or war—they are willing to do the worst kind of evil.

I speak in the most convincing monotone-Collective accent I can muster. "I *will* need access to the toxin supply to make the changes." My vision fishbowls like we've taken too fast a turn in the hovercar. "For the Collective," I add.

The room is still except for the quiet hum of the centrifuge.

Finally, Nyla nods at Crick, and he walks out.

I point toward the defoliant she'd asked me to make—my concoction of Dawn dish soap, salt, and vinegar. "We've finished this for you though," I say, including Javier so she won't think he's useless. "It will clear most of the ground cover within a few days."

Crick walks back in the room and hands me a slotted metal tray, filled with tiny vials of bright-green liquid the same color of the toxic leaves. He sets it on the lab bench.

Javier mumbles to himself. "Perhaps I set the incubator improperly."

I can't tell him yet his poison was the deadliest ever created, but once I get us out of this, I will tell him how truly brilliant he is. Even though he could've potentially ended humanity as we know it. How could he know the "dangerous creatures" they want to exterminate are passengers like us and our parents?

"Epsilon-5?" Nyla lays her hand on his cheek. I choke down my urge to smack her hand away.

His voice is soft. "Yes, Chancellor?"

"Do you still feel *useful*?" Her voice is quieter than his, but her words make my blood freeze.

Javier's brow crinkles up. "Well . . ." he hesitates.

I think of Ben, and how the first Monitors so long ago purged him when he was "not useful." I jump between the two of them and face Nyla.

"Actually, it was my error. I changed the temperature setting."

Nyla tilts her head.

"Crick saw me," I say.

Nyla turns to Crick, and his eyes widen. "Why, yes. Zeta-1 was rather insistent something was set improperly."

Nyla takes a deep breath, tilts her head, and nods, seeming to accept the explanation. "It's understandable. Your newly upgraded brain is learning to flex its muscles."

"Yes, Chancellor, that's exactly it." I clear my throat. "And because my mind is sharpening day by day, I was going to ask if Epsilon-5 could accompany me to the surface tomorrow. We make a good team. My knowledge, combined with his experience."

I look over just as Javier's grips his hand to steady a tremble, then slides the toxin casually to the opposite side of the bench with the defoliant. The vials clink as his hand pushes the rack.

My voice is as shaky as Javier's hands, but I can't make it stop. "His assistance is what would best serve the Collective."

She squints at me. "Is there something else you would like to—"

A clank, followed by a crash, echoes from the other side of the workbench. My breath catches as we all stare at a rack of toppled test tubes.

For a second I think this is how it ends for the entire ship. I let out a breath when I see a few bubbles from the spilled dish soap.

"Pardon me," Javier says, stooping to pick glass off the floor from my weed killer.

He's not making this any easier. I have to hurry and get him off this ship.

Crick clears his throat. "Chancellor, the Collective is waiting to discuss our strategy." He nods discretely at the bright-green poison.

Whatever that "discussion" is, if it involves their plans, I need to be there. How did it get so bad so quickly?

Nyla's nostrils widen with her breath. "I trust you will have our improved toxin ready within the day." She turns back and hits the button on the wall, sucking out the golden light of Sagan's sun and moons as it slides shut.

Nyla strides out of the lab, Crick in her wake.

I hurry to Javier's side and brush broken glass on the tabletop into the bin.

Except for the tinkling of shards, the room is quiet. I want to tell him I'm sorry for making him think, even for a second, he wasn't as valuable as everyone else.

"Do you really know of a way to increase the potency?" he asks.

I still can't tell him the truth.

"Epsilon-5?" I say.

"Yes?"

"From now on, I will present the information to the Chancellor."

He stares at me, mouth slightly ajar.

I cringe, but I have to protect him any way I can. "It's . . . it's what is best for the Collective," I say, using the only method he might accept. I bite the inside of my cheek. This is for his own good, and I'm running out of time. I need to destroy the toxin without watching eyes. "And," I hesitate, "I think I will work faster alone to replace the ruined defoliant."

He glances at the pile of broken glass. "You are right." Javier's knees crack as he stands. He smiles at me. "I am growing old. I trust you will let me know if there is any way I can still be helpful to the Collective." He ambles slowly out of the room.

I watch him leave, swallowing the lump in my throat.

Everything in me says to run after him, hug him, and tell him how sorry I am. But I don't have time. Once I finish what I need to do, I can spend the rest of his life making it up to him.

I hurry to the workbench and rest my gloved hand against the vial, whose contents could kill me ten thousand times over.

As I pull my goggles down, I scan each shelf for something which could render the toxin useless. The answer is dilution. But there's not enough water on the ship to dilute this concentration of poison. I'd need an endless supply of water and oxygen.

"The gel preserves tissue indefinitely, removing senescent cells and waste. It not only provides nutrients and oxygen the body will need for such a long stay in stasis, but lidocaine in the gel numbs nerve endings,

making the colder temperature comfortable upon awakening." If the best antidote for poisons is dilution, what better dilution than a chemical designed to add water and oxygen constantly for hundreds of years?

Once I do this, I've started a timer I can't unstart. No matter what, we'll have to be off the ship tomorrow before they discover how I've sabotaged their plan.

Walking confidently into the hold, I pass bustling workers who don't give me a second glance. I walk to the closest barrel next to an empty pod, its orange flashing button highlighting *Fu, Jie Ru* over and over. I syphon a quart of green goo out of a barrel in the hold and return to the lab.

I walk swiftly back to the lab knowing Nyla's meeting is already starting. I hurry in and close the door, setting the stasis gel next to the toxin. I pull on a full coverage suit and slip on new gloves.

My fingers tremble. Quickly, before anyone comes in to question me, I pipette stasis gel in each vial. I run to the lab next door and find a toxometer. I come back and point it at the first vial. It flashes, then reads: *LD50 .001 nanograms per kilogram.* It blinks next, showing it is recalibrating. *LD50 .0015 nanograms per kilogram.* It's working—the amount needed to kill fifty percent of the population is increasing, meaning it's becoming less effective. I wait a few more excrutiating minutes. *LD50 .003 nanograms per kilogram.* The stasis gel is diluting it, but . . .

"Not fast enough," I whisper. I rack my brain. Potassium superoxide? A bottle of it is stacked next to the other chemical supplies right in front of me. It makes sense that they'd have the super oxygenator even early astronauts used on a space ship. But the unknowns of an explosive powder mixed with the toxic solution are too risky.

I scour the lab and see the standard oxygen nozzle inside the contained glovebox system. It won't be fast, but it's the best I can do now. A steady flow of oxygen hisses out as I twist the knob. I carefully place the vials inside and seal it off.

Masked head against the plexiglass window, I slip my hands inside the gloves and remove the lids from the toxin. I turn the light off in the unit and press *opaque*, hiding what's inside. I stop at the door and stare back, hoping when I return to check on the toxin, the LD 50 will be *0.000 nanograms per kilogram.*

25

JUST LIKE THE NIGHT OF THE PARTY, THE GHOST shrimp are gathered in their thin-skinned glory in the common area, Chancellor Nyla on a pedestal at the far end. She looks so small from this distance, but it doesn't make her any less frightening.

Halfway to Nyla, a three-tiered rainbow waterfall of tonic sits on a table the size of my bedroom back home. Tonic of every color trickles down one glass at a time, filling lower glasses. The lowest glass barely has time to refill as people pick them up to drink. Each time, Bioloaf Boy is ready, setting an empty glass down to take its place.

Even though the people are spread out, it's the most occupied I've seen this level of the ship.

Projected behind Nyla is a backdrop of Sagan's gold-and-purple sky. A hologram of the three-tiered waterfalls I'd seen on the planet pours from the mountain. And then I understand their bizarre version of party décor with the tonic display.

High above on the projected ceiling, the words *Sacrifice*, *Commitment*, *Accord* flash intermittently.

Nyla waves her arms, and in an instant, just like when we stood among Earth and the moon and Halley's Comet on the night of the party, Sagan's surface suddenly surrounds us. Instead of the colossal white room, forests of swaying trees and rippling turquoise lake water fill the space, like we are right there. Every so often there is a glitch from faulty drone film.

A man reaches down to pet a mini-chinchilla. Another woman from the morning bioloaf group leans at the lake's edge, observing the purple glow of a swarm of water butterflies where the pale floor normally would be. Even if it's virtual, they don't deserve this.

Nyla waves a thin arm in front of her, and one of her hands passes through a projected elephant-ear leaf. "Welcome, Collective. It is with great pleasure I can announce our plans."

I made it in time. I hurry forward, easing my way through the web of people, stooping to hide along the way. I see Hammerhead near the front and continue forward until I stand behind him.

I still can't know if what I've done in the lab will destroy the toxin. And I'm even more unsure if I can convince Nyla to let Javier come to Sagan with me.

"With our arrival, comes trepidation." Her voice doesn't sound so worried though. The long journey has compromised the Collective's physical state. Changes made to our genetic makeup by our predecessors were done to protect us.

"I have just learned that one of our Collective was lost to research on the planet," she says, matter-of-factly talking about Len.

Hammerhead drops his head for a moment, then takes a sip of his neural-block cocktail. His face when he looks up is completely blank.

My heart flutters like I've drank too much of Lita's cacao. I already know what this means. If Len has died, the planet isn't safe for them. They won't stay. But like Nyla said, they'll still prepare the planet for the future. I have less time than I thought.

"We've determined the cause was an unanticipated reaction from the closer proximity of the dwarf sun to our epiderm-filters. This setback is not one of disappointment. It is only a temporary change of plans, until we can reconfigure our epiderm-filters and return." A transparent target in the shape of a laser scope pops up on the hologram behind Nyla. She motions to where the bullseye zeroes in, over an area below the lowest waterfall. "Our search drones have located the exact location of a habitable settlement."

My heart ricochets in my chest. A mix of mumbles and sporadic clapping fills the room. The person in front of me points directly at the targeted spot below the smallest waterfall. The gap leaves a direct path to Nyla's line of sight. I crouch a bit lower.

"I understand your confusion," she continues, "as our goal was avoidance of the hostiles. It still is." She holds up a small cube, smiling like it's some wonder bonding agent on an infomercial. "However." Light hits the cube. "Before we leave, we will ensure peace, by eliminating any chance of a future war."

Like the Tower of Terror at Disneyland, it feels like the ground falls out from beneath me. Inside the cube, a vial of toxic, green poison glimmers. I force myself to remain calm, hoping the container's airtight. How did she sneak it out? That one vial could kill every person in the ship—not to mention every last terra-former, and me, Javier, and the other kids—if I don't destroy it. But there's no way to get back into the sealed glovebox right now without exposing myself.

"If the Collective returns to this planet one day, it will be with a corrected genetic makeup to our epiderm-filters. This could take several units, but we can ensure this settlement will belong to the Collective and the Collective alone. It is truly a kindness to humanity to halt those who would destroy *this* planet, as they've done to their own. A new origin!"

"A new origin!" booms in return.

She who does not take the risk . . . I step out among the crowd like a raven in a flock of white doves. I lift my hand in an awkward wave.

Nyla's pale eyes dart toward where I stand.

"Pardon me." She steps down from the pedestal and strides over, holding the enclosed vial casually.

Air whistles through my teeth as I slowly let out a deep breath.

Nyla approaches me, her eyes watching me curiously. "Zeta-1. Why are you here? Is everything all right?"

I smile and point calmly to the vial like it's a lost ingredient for cookies. "I noticed we were missing some of our critical supply." I clear my throat and reach out, carefully sliding the container from her spindly fingers.

She watches me curiously as I slip it safely in my pocket.

"Incubation times are crucial for potency," I say.

She reaches up and places her icy fingers on my cheek, just like she had done to Javier. "You are clever . . . for your type."

My type? My teeth clench, but this isn't the time.

"Perhaps not clever enough." I hope my fake sigh isn't overdoing it.

Her scant eyebrows scrunch together. "What do you mean?"

I copy her eyebrow scrunch, mimicking concern. "I worry our final mission to test what we've created might suffer without Epsilon-5 accompanying me," I say, feigning disappointment. "His experience would be helpful." I pull out the vial and hold it up for emphasis. "There is so much to do, and so little time. I will need to centrifuge, then transfer, then back in incubation, then—"

She leans in, smiling. "Of course."

"Of *course* . . . Epsilon-5 can accompany me?" I ask hopefully.

"No," she says. "Of *course* you can return to your work." She tucks a loose strand of hair behind my ear. "There is no need for another scouting mission."

I swallow. They're leaving immediately.

I take a step away from her, pocketing the vial again. "I will get to work," I say. I turn, walking swiftly toward the elevator and not looking back. I pass the waterfall of tonic. Bioloaf Boy has one hand perched over his brow, staring up at something flying among the holographic elephant-ear trees. A stream of tonic overflows from a glass and onto the floor in a pool of red.

If I want to live . . . if I want Javier to live, and for the kids to have a real life, I have to sneak us all off the ship. Now.

But first, I need to get Javier's mind back so he'll agree to go.

*

I HURRY TO MY ROOM to retrieve my collection bag. I stash my hidden straws inside and roll up my mattress, spreading a blanket over the top. It worked when I used to sneak onto the roof to stare at the stars. But here I don't have a Josefina American Girl Doll's head to pry off and tuck under the blanket as a decoy.

True to form, Rubio is sawing logs, and Suma and Feathers are sleeping peacefully below him in their cramped cells. It hits me this will be their last sleep on the ship. After tonight, they will breathe in the fresh, sweet pea–scented oxygen of Sagan while they sleep.

Feathers rolls over in her cell. I stare down at her round, pink cheeks. Javier was her age when he was taken out of stasis. I can't imagine her growing into an old woman here on the ship. The Collective stole Javier's youth, stuffing him down there in that stupid lab. The thought of someone spending all those years alone makes me feel seasick. I can't let that happen to them.

Getting Javier back feels impossible, but I'm willing to die trying. Whatever I'm going to do has to happen in the next few hours.

I pick up my sample collection bag, hoping it will also help me look official. I carefully slip the last vial of toxin inside, next to the rolled-up baseball card I found on the wall in the seed vault.

When I enter the elevator, I look down and see Nyla's meeting has ended. But no one has left. They mill about the holographic magic of Sagan, sucking down tonic from the rainbow waterfall after the news they're going to spend the rest of their lives on this ship. As if it reads my mind, the word *Sacrifice* flashes across the Collective's subliminal ceiling.

I exit the elevator and hoist my bag over my shoulder. I walk along the periphery of the party through Sagan's jungle, toward the seed vault.

Voxy's at Nyla's side again. He sees me but doesn't break character. He's not just along for the ride tonight, though, like a.

little kid tagging along. He's standing in a way like he's part of the official proceedings. I hope Nyla's words in their room that night did not get to him. With what he knows, he could ruin everything. But I also feel sick thinking of what he will become. I nod at Voxy and continue walking until I reach the end of the room, then the hall, then their door.

I press *2061* and hurry inside. I crawl through Voxy's honeycomb cell and hold my breath as I slip the rolled baseball card into the tiny hole. The door slides open. Just like before, a blast of cold Piñon Elementary–library air hits my face. Gold light from the hologram of Earth's solar system glows eerily in the frozen fog from the corner of the room.

I nearly trip over my own feet rushing toward the seed vault drawers. Javier's lighted tab file is still gapped open. The book is exactly where I dropped it the day before. I pull it out and slip it into my collection bag.

The tab directly in front of mine and Javier's reads *Peña, Robert.*

My vision fogs over with tears. I'd been so worried when we left about what I got to bring with me, I didn't even know or care what my parents brought. I reach to Dad's bag in and pull out his rosary. Each jasper bead of red, yellow, or a combination of the two he'd chiseled down, polished, and drilled himself. Just like he said—all so different, but complementing one another into the most beautiful rosary ever created. And the bead I'd found, golden yellow with a red vein that I thought wasn't good enough, just above the cross. I can't swallow.

Like Dad used to do in church, I place a bead between my pointer finger and thumb and rub my fingers over its surface. I move on to the next and realize Dad's patience is in every last one of these beads. His love and kindness flows over its smooth surface into my fingers.

I slip it over my head, and it weighs heavy on my chest. I wonder how the whole Jesus thing works if we're on a different planet on the opposite side of the galaxy in another solar system. If Jesus was the son of God and God was the god of the universe, does it work here too?

I pull out a picture of Lita and Papá. Lita's wearing the white flowy dress my bisabuela made. The one I hoped I could wear one day. A flower crown of red, orange, and yellow roses and peonies sits atop her wavy, black hair. Papá wears a tan suit, and they cling together arm in arm, their mouths wide with laughter.

I find my own bag and pull out my jeans and T-shirt, cramming them into my collection bag.

Peña, Amy. I slip Mom's wedding ring onto my finger, and it fits. I smile at Mom's librex titled *Will Shortz's Two Lifetimes of* New York Times *Sunday Crossword Puzzles.* I picture her at the kitchen table, coffee in one hand, holotack in the other, punching in letters. "Clever!" she'd yell out, and shake her head as the librex chimed out the tune indicating she'd solved the crossword. By the time the Sunday puzzle arrived, she was grumbling at the puzzle and poking harder with the holotack.

Feathers, Rubio, and Suma should have mementos of their

parents too. But I don't have the time to look. Then I remember Nyla's words, "*Suma Agarwal will be Zeta-2 for the rest of her life.*"

I go to the first seed drawer and find *Agarwal, Suma* and open the bag. I pull out a folder labeled *Top Secret* in kid handwriting. I open it and find pages filled with unicorn stickers and drawings. Unicorns dancing, unicorns singing, unicorns farting rainbows . . .

I pull out Suma's clothes. Sure enough, her lavender sweatshirt with the silver foam horn spiraling from its hood is there. I ball up her magical sweatshirt and jeans and shove them to the bottom of my bag.

The next lighted tab is *Agarwal, Preeti.* I peel open the top, and the faint whiff of lilac escapes from the airtight bag. I lift out a baby book and open it. I press the first page, and the book chimes. The 3D hologram instantly projects in front of me. Suma is cuddled between two ladies, one I recognize from the first day when they passed us on the trail. Page after page, I press to see the holograms showing Suma with her moms, playing at a park, eating pizza with a number 5 birthday candle in the center, running alongside as she learns to use a hoverboard. In the final hologram, Suma is a little older and it's just Suma and the mom I saw. Suma, eyes pointed upward in an eternal roll, the other side of her face in an annoyed scrunch as her mom kisses her cheek. I swallow over a golf ball lump lodged in my throat. I know once she's free of the Collective, Suma will give anything to have that kiss. I wonder what happened. Did her parents divorce? Did her mom with the dimples die? I think of how even though it's not what I hoped, I still have Javier. Suma is alone.

I wish I knew Feathers's and Rubio's last names to bring something of their family back for them too. I won't let them feel alone though. Javier and I will be their new family.

As I tuck Suma's baby book into my collection bag, I walk back toward the vault's entrance. Just like before, I crawl through Voxy's sleep cell, poking the rolled baseball card into the hole so the door slides shut behind me.

I struggle to pull myself and the full collection bag back through his cell. I set the bag down and pull myself to standing.

I lift my eyes to find Voxy in front of me. I hadn't even seen him. I put the bag on my shoulder, like my sneaking into the vault is perfectly normal.

"What are you doing?" he asks.

"I wanted to look again. And you were busy with the meeting."

"We had an agreement. You have not told me a single cuento yet."

I don't have time for this. Especially if Nyla might have gotten to him. I suddenly understand why Lita's stories were sometimes . . . more persuasive when Javier or I refused to go to bed.

Voxy harrumphs and crosses his arms over his chest, a lot like Javier did with Lita. "You promised."

"Fine." I sigh. What would Lita or Tía Berta do right now? "Do you know the cuento of la Llorona?"

"What's that?" Voxy asks.

I turn and click my nails at him. "She's the weeping woman. And she comes to steal children who do not behave and go to sleep."

"Why would a woman with unstable emotions steal a child from their cell?" He grips his chin. "And where would she take them?"

I realize the story doesn't work when the person hearing the story has only lived on an enclosed ship. "Let me start over.

"Érase una vez a woman made the mistake of falling in love with a man who was as rich as he was arrogant. She adored him so much she had children with him. But this man did not return her love, so she drowned her children and then herself."

Voxy flinches back, eyes wide. "What is drowning?"

I ignore it and continue. "She roams the earth with pointed teeth and glowing eyes, looking for her children. If she finds a child awake, she will mistake them for her own and take them!" I lean in. "She might even devour them." I realize how different and creepy a lot of Mexican folklore is. Love, humor, pain, magic, lost souls—all woven to create stories most cultures might sugarcoat.

I don't even know if that was the right version. But it was Lita's version and the quickest and scariest I know. It works.

Voxy's eyes gape like la Llorona is standing right in front of him. "That was horrifying."

"Close your eyes and go to sleep, Voxy."

"I do not think I can. What kind of cuento was that?"

"The kind to make you sleep," I answer.

His mouth turns down, and his eyes sag as he looks away. "Now, I will never sleep again."

"I have to go finish some work. I promised the Chancellor."

Voxy stares up at me with his lower lip tucked inside his mouth, like Javier used to do.

"Okay, one more." I pick him up and place him in his cell. I pull his blanket up to his neck and tuck it under his sides. "Había una vez a tiny ant yearned to do something more than carry corn all day."

Voxy lets out a breath, settling into his pillow. "I don't know what an ant is, but this cuento sounds less terrify—"

Footsteps approach from the hallway outside.

Voxy whispers, "It's la Llorona." His nostrils flare.

I grab my bag and rush to the door's entrance, flattening my back against the wall. Voxy peeks out of the top of his cell in his room, and I hold my finger to my lips. The door slides open and Nyla walks inside.

"Hello!" Voxy yells, drawing attention in his direction. She walks toward him without seeing me.

I hold my breath and slip around the doorjamb into the outer corridor. I wait for the door to slide shut with them inside and run as fast as I can, taking the first turn to the elevators.

Safely inside the elevator, I push the button for the hold. I pull Javier's book out of my collection bag and clutch it in my hands. Will this even work? If Epsilon-5 doesn't remember he's Javier, what will he do? I lift his book to my nose and breathe in the faint smell of Javier's bedroom. It has to work. I place it back inside.

I continue down until I'm at the level of the hold.

The elevator door opens, and I step out. All the containers have been moved near the entrance ramp for a transfer to the surface that will not happen now. But this has left the center of the cavernous hold dark, except for the faint glow of stasis gel barrels between empty pods around the perimeter. I hurry to the closest barrel and pry open the top. My hands shake as I remove the last vial from my bag. As my fingertips hit the stasis gel, they tingle and burn before going numb. I can't afford a mistake. I hurry to grab gloves. Placing the vial back in the gel, I pop the top open, and leave it inside where they'll never find it. I slip off the gloves and toss them in too.

Sealing the barrel shut, I take a relieved breath. The only other sign of life is a faint light from Javier's quarters in the back near the lab.

My footsteps echo as I walk toward his room. How alone he must feel, confined to this gigantic space without anyone to talk to, or sing with, or eat with. I think of how this would have terrified seven-year-old Javier. Did he ever laugh or cry again after they woke him up?

With each step, my heart races faster than el Conejo's little feet across the desert. I reach his door and raise my hand to knock.

My arm freezes in place. What if he's angry? What if he blames me? What if . . .

His door opens, light hitting one side of his face. "Zeta-1? What are you doing here?" His voice echoes around us.

I drop my hand to my side.

He points a shaky hand to the collection bag. "Ah, I see you've come to work. I won't disturb you," he says, placing his trembling hand behind his back.

Smiling with his hand tucked behind him, he looks just like he did when he stole my Easter candy from my basket and thought I didn't know exactly where it was. Back then, I wanted to tackle him and grab it. Now, I know that somewhere inside Epsilon-5 is my little brother, hiding my chocolate egg behind his back. Somewhere inside he's still Javier, and he wants to live.

I take shallow breaths and stare up at him, unable to speak. I want to reach out and take his hand, make him remember, tell him I won't let anyone hurt him and he no longer needs to hide.

But what would a flood of memories do to Javier after all these years? My memories feel like yesterday. He's lived a long life without them. Would he even want to go with me? He might like my descriptions of what I've seen on Sagan, but he's known nothing but this ship for ninety percent of his life. In so many ways, I'm still older than the old man before me.

No matter what, he's still my responsibility. And I love him.

If I can't convince him to leave the ship with me, it's over for us. I won't leave without him.

I set the collection bag on the ground.

"Epsilon-5, do you remember anything before stasis?" I ask.

Javier tilts his head. "I have told you. There was nothing before—"

"That's not true," I say, before I lose my nerve. My throat is dry, and I try to swallow. If anyone notices me missing from my room or watched my elevator go down instead of up . . . This is my last chance.

If I can give him his own memories, he will have his own story back. The stories we tell ourselves make us who we are.

"Do you remember the time I gave you dog food and told you it was granola?" I ask.

Javier tilts his head. "Wha—?"

"Or the time we stole one of Papá's cigars and tried to light it. You held the lighter but ended up singeing my hair." I smile.

He closes his eyes for a moment, then stares off toward the hold.

"Or when Mom found Rápido injured on a walk in the desert behind our house, and you and I dug him a den so we could keep him, but then we hit the sprinkler system with the shovel and flooded the backyard."

He closes his eyes and shakes his head. "Zeta-1, I do not understand."

I sigh and lean over, pulling out his book, catching a whiff of home. "Epsilon-5? May I read you something?"

His forehead creases.

"Just for a moment?" I take a few steps back and plop down crisscross applesauce just like we always have, except Javier definitely won't be curling up on my lap now. "Please? It will help the Collective," I say.

His brow crinkles again for a moment. He stares curiously at the book and sits down next to me. "For the Collective."

I lay it gently on his lap.

My heart pounds as he stares down at the cover.

His smile falls, and he reaches out to touch the monarch butterfly on the cover. "I . . ." He runs his fingers over its orange and black wings. Javier's skin is the same color of the woman and baby on the cover. He stares back at me, his brow furrowed. "I . . . I'm . . . I'm not sure—"

Tears fill my eyes. I've read it to him a thousand times, but this will be the last if he doesn't remember me.

Javier tilts his head and leans in closer. He whispers, opening to the first page, "*Dreamers.*"

My voice shakes. "One day we bundled gifts in our backpack and crossed a bridge outstretched like the universe. And we made it to the other side, thirsty, in awe."

Page after page I read, searching his eyes for recognition. Just a spark. I read louder when they enter the new land, the things they did not understand, the fear, the mistakes. Searching, like we are, for a place to belong and feel safe, until they found a new and magical home. I turn to the page with the child sitting on his mom's lap. Just like Javier and I used to. I turn again to the page where the orange-and-black monarch sits atop the page like he could take flight any moment. Javier touches it like he always has. Every. Single. Time.

Suddenly the old man before me is my little brother again. I choke out the final words. "Books became our language. Books became our home. Books became our lives."

When I finish, I hold it out to him, the words catching in my throat. "Would you like to hold it, Javier?"

His chin trembles. He nods, and a tear falls down his cheek.

I don't move or speak. Mom always said you can never know exactly what someone is going through. Sometimes I must be silent and give them time. So, we just sit. Finally, he takes a long breath.

"Javier?" I reach out and pat his hand.

He looks up. "Yes?"

"Do you remember?" I ask, taking his hand in mine.

His hand trembles as he lays it on my cheek. To me, a week ago it was the pudgy, sticky hand of a seven-year-old. Today, it's warm, dry, and thin. Time has turned his skin into wax paper. We've been across the galaxy on different paths, but we've finally found each other again. His voice shakes. "Petra."

Somehow, in the void of space, we're home again.

"It'll be okay," I sob between my words. "Don't be afraid; I'll protect you."

"How did this happen?" he whispers.

I take the book and set it to the side, facing him. There is too much to say. I can only whisper, "It doesn't matter."

He nods. "What about . . . ?" But he doesn't finish. Javier bows his head. Somehow, he must know Mom and Dad are gone. I'm not ready to say it out loud yet either.

I shake my head. He turns away, staring across the hold toward the entrance. Is he remembering? Remembering our final day with them? Wishing he'd taken the time to feel the softness of Mom's arm? Breathed in the smell of Mom's and Dad's hair and clothes? Of course, he didn't. I didn't either. No one ever thinks this goodbye will be forever.

Javier keeps staring off into the distance. We sit in silence for a long time.

"Javier, do you remember how we had to hurry to the shuttle in Colorado? How when I was putting my coat away you stole my seat next to Dad and wouldn't give it back?"

He glances up at me.

"Do you remember how Dad took us into a separate car for a speech?"

He nods. Dad's pep talk annoyed me at the time. Now his words are suddenly vivid in my mind.

"You've been given an opportunity others would trade anything for," I repeat him exactly. "You have a responsibility to represent our family. To be kind. To work hard. Don't fight."

Javier's gravelly voice continues. "We are Peñas. Everything we do from this moment on will bring great pride or great sadness to our ancestors." He finishes Dad's words.

"Javier," I squeeze his hand and don't let go. "We have to leave the ship. There's no time left. I need you to help me get all of the Zetas on the shuttle."

Are we better off leaving the ship just to escape the Collective? We may die on Sagan. But somehow having Javier with me now makes the decision easier.

His hand starts to tremor and he pulls it from mine. He mumbles quietly, "I know what to do." Then, he smiles.

I wipe tears from my face, but my heart is soaring. Now that he's back, it'll all be okay. But something nags at me—something I've forgotten.

A noise clatters from the far end of the hold near the elevator. Javier jumps up. "Stay here." His eyes beg. He picks up my collection bag with all our belongings and hides it in his room.

"Where are you going?" I ask as he walks toward the elevator.

"Be ready to go." He turns and smiles. "I will go for the other Zetas. I know what to say." He holds his back now as he shuffles more quickly. I wonder what pain he must normally feel. He stumbles a bit but recovers. I want to run to him, but he's too far into the hold before I can react. And he's right. The two of us together would call more attention.

The stale, silent air of the hold buzzes in my ears. A shiver runs up my back. If Nyla finds us trying to escape, both our lives will be over. I do hope he knows what to say if he and the others are seen.

Scuffles echo from behind me like an animal scurrying between the pods and stasis barrels. I turn and sit completely still. There was no one in the labs, and Javier went in the opposite direction. I scan between the empty pods toward where I'd heard the noise. My eyes can't adapt, and I see nothing at first. Then in the center of my vision a small head pokes out from behind the nearest pod.

My breath catches.

Voxy.

He skulks out, hands tucked under his armpits.

I sigh. "How long have you been here?"

"I told you I couldn't sleep, and you didn't finish the happier cuento about the ant," his words echo. "I decided to get the book. But when I snuck in the relic room, it was missing."

I swallow hard.

He continues. "Then I went to your room, but you weren't there. So, I came here and saw . . ."

"I thought reading the book would help Epsilon-5 adjust to the new planet."

He drops his arms to his sides and his shoulders sag. "You are lying to me."

He knows. And at this point, sticking to the lie is riskier than keeping him happy with a story. "If Nyla finds out about this"—I hold up the book—"and the other stories . . ."

"I know," he says. "We will both be in trouble."

"I'd never be able to tell you cuentos again. Should we keep this our secret for now?"

"Just me, you, and Epsilon-5?" He grins, his mannerisms so much like Javier's when he was a kid.

Javier will be back any moment. "I don't think Epsilon-5 will tell," I say.

The corners of Voxy's mouth turn up slightly. "Can you read it one more time?" He points to the book in my hand.

Anyone could walk in and find us. But once we are gone, I can't help Voxy. He will be swallowed by the Collective forever.

And just like they stole this from me and Javier, they will steal it from him.

We have a minute or two. I sit back down, legs crossed. Voxy plops onto my lap just like Javier used to. "Read, read," he squeaks.

"*Dreamers*," I read.

He touches the title's letters. "Green, like tonic for when I'm scared." Voxy turns his head back to me. Then, the smile drops from his face and he turns still as a rabbit, waiting for a rattlesnake to strike.

"Voxy!" Nyla's icy voice goose-bumps up my entire spine.

I shove the book along the floor like a hockey puck so it slides to rest under the nearest pod. I push Voxy up from my lap. "I'm sorry, Chancellor, we were just . . ." I hold Voxy's hand, and we stand and turn to face Nyla together.

My knees wobble. Javier stands next to her, zero expression on his face.

Why would he . . . ?

Javier won't meet my eyes.

"Hello, Zeta-1," Nyla says, stepping toward us. "Or should I call you . . . Petra?"

26

NYLA AND CRICK ESCORT ME TOWARD AN OPEN POD near the decontamination sector. Crick holds my elbow to keep me from running. But he doesn't need to. I am numb. How could I have been so wrong? Javier remembered his book. He remembered me. He touched the butterfly like he always had.

Maybe what Javier is now is more powerful than what he remembers. How much our family loved one another. Maybe the Collective dominates his mind more than the dream of what life would've been on Sagan.

"*We are Peñas. Everything we do from this moment on will bring great pride or great sadness to our ancestors.*"

Nyla faces the pod. The lights in the decontamination room are brighter, the air more sanitized than the rest of the ship. It hums as they activate the machine meant to erase the last of me, the last of Petra Peña. I can't know it won't function properly this time. Nyla will make sure it works. At least when I'm Zeta-1 for real, I'll no longer remember Dad's hopes for us, how Javier betrayed me.

Javier and Voxy stand watching in the doorway.

I teeter to one side and Crick helps me stand. I look up at him.

He turns his eyes back on Nyla. I yank my arm from the coward, and he doesn't fight me. Without Crick to balance me, I'm unsteady on my feet.

Nyla lifts the pod's lid and motions for me to get in.

I have no place to go. If I'm purged, I cease to exist. If they reprogram me, I cease to exist. I clench my jaw and don't budge. It's over either way.

Nyla sighs and lowers her voice. "If you fight, the Collective will be forced to purge Epsilon-5. I am sure you understand why."

I glance over at Javier, who stands with Voxy in the doorway, his hands on Voxy's shoulders. I can't tell if he heard her.

He doesn't even react. Voxy's eyes are wider than when I was telling him about la Llorona. He makes a tiny hiccupped sound. Javier leans over and whispers something in his ear.

I won't let the Collective purge him. Maybe the person I will become—Zeta-1, even if she's not the real me—maybe that person will keep Javier company. I lift one leg over the lip of the pod to step in. My other leg wobbles, and I topple.

I've barely fallen in when Nyla presses a button on the controls and the restraints slither out, lassoing my legs down and cinching my arms to my sides. I lift my head, but Crick sets one of the straps near my cheek and it finds its way over my forehead, locking my head in place. "See you again soon, Zeta-1." He's almost cheerful, no malice in his voice. Like he'll be welcoming an old friend.

Tears drip down the sides of my cheeks. I want to fight, not give up. But it no longer matters. The thing I was fighting for—a life with Javier, a future for the other kids, to be a great storyteller. What kind of storyteller am I if I couldn't even reach my own brother? Lita would be ashamed. I wish they would hurry and get this over with.

Nyla sits on a stool next to the pod and slips on gloves like she's a dental hygienist about to perform a cleaning. "I have never had the opportunity to speak with one of you. A relic, that is," she says. "You are one of the few left who actually experienced what your kind had become. Polluting your own air and rivers and oceans . . . for profit. Starving some so others become bloated. It is for those reasons the Collective exists."

Now, I can say what I want. I don't have to pretend anymore. But I can't speak. And I can't look at her. She's right. Those things did happen for the greed of a few. But most, like my parents, still had hope for something better.

She stops for a moment, staring down at me. "Fascinating."

"Did you really want to have a discussion with me," I ask, "or just hear yourself talk?"

"I speak for all of us, for the Collective."

My eyes shift to Voxy. His mouth is turned down, and I swear I see color in his face. I know what's truly within him, and I want to tell him not to be afraid. That not all cuentos have happy endings. The panic on his face is there for the same reason he wanted the stories so badly. Each story, each person is different. Messy sometimes. But colorful, mismatched, and beautiful.

My chin is trembling, and I can't make it stop. "The Collective won't succeed in the end. You all numb yourselves to erase who we really are. The tonics. The Cogs. But you can't program out love and caring for one another."

She sits back. "You are wrong. We do care. We care greatly for the greater good of a singular Collective. The Collective has made difficult choices over all these units to achieve this point."

"You stole people's lives," I say.

Her face hardens. "Sacrifices have . . . and must be made."

"Sacrifices? We lost our planet! Eleven billion of us! There are only hundreds of you! We lost our homes, our families, our friends." I think of Ben and his brother. "The Monitors were willing to spend their lives on a ship to ensure the rest of us made it to Sagan safely. That was sacrifice!"

Tears fall off my cheeks and drip down my neck.

Lita stands at her front door, smiles, and waves at us the last time we see her. Like it was just another goodbye.

"You have no clue about what sacrifice or bravery mean." My breathing catches. "We weren't perfect, but we still had hope we'd make it across the universe and make our ancestors proud."

"Ancestors?" Nyla laughs and shakes her head. "Remarkable. Misguided, but remarkable."

I realize all of them, created in a lab to be homogenous, can't feel a connection to any ancestors. So many of us on Earth had them not just from one culture, but many.

Crick clears his throat. "Not being tethered to tradition allows us to be logical," he says, and I wonder if he truly believes it.

What the Collective doesn't understand is by honoring the past, our ancestors, our cultures—and remembering our mistakes—we become better.

I saw that love in the wall of wedding photos and birth certificates. Suma's baby book. Nyla, Crick . . . Voxy will never have any of that kind of love.

She leans forward, whispering in my ear. "Your kind, however inferior, was unique. I'll admit, your species contained a certain . . . curiosity." She motions to Crick, and he hands her the familiar box labeled *En Cognito Downloadable Cognizance.* But this time, instead of *Pediatric*, it reads *Adult*. I'm not coming back from this.

Nyla opens the lid. Inside, a much larger, darker Cog sits in a cutout. Nyla puts her cheek next to mine. "Even with your memories of Earth, you proved useful." She sits up and removes the Cog. "We cannot wait to see what you are capable of without the affliction of your flawed past." She sets the Cog in its installer and presses the activator. The Cog glows a deep purple. "Now, Petra Peña, you will live a very long, unburdened life among the Collective."

I cringe, remembering the pinpricks like ant bites, and can't help the side glance at the barrel of stasis gel right next to the pod.

Nyla follows my eyes. "Oh, we will not need that this time. This will not take long."

I try to turn my head to find Javier, but I can only shift my eyes, and I barely see his outline. I have to tell him, one last time while I'm still me. "I love you," I call out.

But if he's in there, he doesn't show it. He does not move or speak. I strain against the restraints as she rests the Cog on the base of my skull. This time, it melts into my neck as soft as a pat of butter. And this time, I grow so tired . . .

I glance in Javier's direction once more as I fall asleep. He's just a blurry form in the periphery of my vision, but he looks so much like Dad.

27

LITA, RÁPIDO, AND I SIT BENEATH THE PIÑON TREE AS Lita brushes the hair off my forehead. The tree's dry needles skitter in the hot breeze across the desert like a flock of birds. Lita's bare feet and the bottom of her white dress are dusty, like she's walked a long way to be with me.

"Do you hear the wind calling, mija?"

A warm gust whistles. "I hear it, Lita."

El Conejo sits just ahead of us, wriggling his nose at me. I glance at the moon. His shadowed form is still not there.

He twitches his ear as if to wave goodbye and hops toward the red mountains.

I might have wanted to follow el Conejo before. But now . . . If this is my last real memory, I want it to be here. With Lita.

"I don't want to leave you." I cling to her soft middle. "What if I never get you back?"

She pushes me up and cups my face in her hand. "I told you once before, you can't lose me." Lita grips her pendant smiling, and tiny wrinkles form around the corners of her eyes. She points toward el Conejo, who grows smaller in the distance. "Go, Petra," she says. "Follow el Conejo."

The mountain glitches a bit. "Lita, they're reprogramming me."

I reach over to squeeze Lita's hand, but she is gone. I panic and stand, circling the tree. Rápido crawls slowly into his burrow under the tree's roots.

I turn to the mountains, where the rabbit is nearly a pinpoint.

This time I sprint. I'm out of breath by the time he scurries into the tiny hole at the red mountain's base.

The wind whistles, but no words form on its breath, no clues to lead me to where I should go.

If this is the end, it should be under our piñon tree, with Rápido somewhere in his burrow beneath.

I'm two steps back to where I came from when, just like before, when guitars and fiddles twang like a distant fiesta. I turn slowly back to the mountain. Then, among the ranchero music,

En una jaula de oro
pendiente del balcón
se hallaba una calandria
cantando su dolor

Even here, in this dream world, I trust my ears more than my eyes. I close my eyes and follow the ballad's words, the story of a sparrow who freed a lark from her cage, only to be betrayed by the lark who flew away. The sparrow remained behind, singing his mournful song of lost love.

Hasta que un gorrioncillo
a su jaula llegó:
"Si usted puede sacarme,
con usted yo me voy."

The twang of the guitar grows louder, and the echo lessens. The music is so loud I feel the vibration in my body.

When I open my eyes, the music and singing are gone.

Instead, flowered cacti not there a moment ago line a path into a ravine, just like a cuento I know. *Los Viejos*? *Blancaflor*? *Itza and Popoca*? Why can't I remember? Their bright-pink flowers glimmer like luzes de Navidad.

I walk and the desert sand gives way to a cobblestone path, its vermillion stones worn and rounded by what looks like millions who must have traveled it before me. So, if millions took this path before, why am I not braver? My feet click . . . clack . . . click . . . clack to where the path ends at a wooden door three meters tall. Twisted iron scrolls run up its center like wisteria vines. One twisted metal vine veers to one side ending in a handle. I reach out. Its dust coats my fingers. The heavy door squeaks open just enough to let me slip through. I suck in my gut and squeeze inside.

The door closes behind me, leaving only the sliver of light under the doorjamb. The passage ahead descends into darkness. I place my arms outward to my sides, my fingers brushing against walls of rock. I take a step and nearly topple down the steep incline. I lean back to keep my balance. As I descend, the fragment of outside light vanishes as I fall into the darkness.

No music. No wind. Is this what dying feels like? No one to hold my hand or guide me.

The Collective has done it. I stop. Why walk on?

As if the darkness hears my question, a light glints in the distance. I continue on, using its glow as my compass until I reach the end of the tunnel. A lantern of golden candlelight flickers over a rocky archway, like the sun over the Sangre de Cristo Mountains at sunset.

I peek through the arch.

In the center of a room, smoke drifts lazily out of the top of a chiminea, leaving the room in a magical haze. I sniff the air. Piñon. As I step inside closer to the flickering blue flames, I scan the space around me. Like spokes on a wheel, rows and rows of wooden shelves surround me. From floor to ceiling the shelves are crammed. I squint to see what is so important el Conejo brought me here. My heart leaps with joy when I realize what they are. The shelves are lined with librex.

I gasp and run my hands over the closest shelf. The entire room buzzes, the ghostly whispers of thousands of storytellers in the bookcases engulfing me.

Lita was right to tell me to follow the rabbit. If I never wake up from this dream, I will be happy. I've found Earth's stories!

But something is wrong. The binding of one librex is hanging askew, like a bird with a broken wing. Many more lie scattered on the floor. Like performances by apparitions, holoscripts play out faintly around the room. The voices of the performers barely whisper. In the next row, more librex lie cracked or shattered into irreparable pieces.

Emerging from one of them, the jittery holographic scene of an old man in a turban speaks to a young boy with tattered clothing. "*Tell your heart that the fear of suffering is worse than the suffering itself.*"

I look through all the rows. Of the thousands of librex, at least a third of them are only partial versions of what they once were. Even here, my stomach lurches.

The image of the man in the turban glitches, and I can

barely hear his final words as he pats the boy on the shoulder. "*No heart has ever suffered when it goes in search of its dreams.*"

I don't know this book, but wish I could have read it.

Nearby, a copy of *A Wizard of Earthsea* rests cracked in half. I've read it at least five times. I could retell it, but nothing like Le Guin. My insides ache seeing it like that, wondering if it can be salvaged. I bend down and pick it up, placing the fragmented treasure gently back on a shelf.

From the shadows, a voice calls out. "Petra?" His shadowy form stands at the end of the stacks. It's not my father, but the voice's familiarity makes me feel at home in an unfamiliar place.

The man doesn't move. Neither do I. I'm not afraid of him. But I can't place how I know him.

He approaches slowly. "Are you finally here?" From the shadows, he steps into the lantern's glow.

I recognize the sandy mess of hair and round glasses. "Ben?" I whisper.

Behind him, a transparent Aboriginal Custodian whispers calmly his Dreamtime story of creation by a fish. His figure grows staticky and his voice garbles.

Ben's eyes glisten with tears. "I'm sorry," he says, staring down at scattered librex. "I tried to save them."

I reach out to touch Ben, then pull my hand back. This is too authentic to be just a dream, so I'm a little nervous for what *this* Ben is.

"Are you real?" I ask.

"Think of me as . . . Earth's last librarian, made to look like . . . someone you trust." He looks around, smiling proudly. "But I can help you find anything. Well, what's left of it. Ben salvaged what he could to the download in your program."

I spin around to see a treasure of Earth's stories recalling his final words. "A *world without story is lost.*" He'd hidden it. Here within me. "Ben was trying . . ."

"I'm a utility program," the Librarian continues, speaking over me as if he has a script he must complete first. "I will adapt as we interact. Ben's download patch worked"—he pushes on the edge of a teetering librex, but in his incomplete form, he can only slide it partway in—"partially, at least. You will need to keep what is left safe now." The Librarian's image shifts on and off like a flickering porch light.

I reach over and push it the rest of the way in, but even as I do, I see my hand fading. Soon I will be Zeta-1, and none of this will matter. The room and all the stories Ben tried to preserve will be lost. With my reprogram, this Ben will be gone soon too.

"Ben knew this was coming," I whisper to myself. "What they did to him, my parents, my little brother. What they are about to do to me."

I turn in a circle, staring around at the fortune of librex cast in a magical haze. "Still, he tried."

"Ben would've been so sorry about your family, Petra," the Librarian says.

I wouldn't have thought grief could find me here in this place. But it's real, and it hits me like a rogue wave.

The Librarian looks up and to the left like he's retrieving something deep within his archived program. "Ben knew he chose wisely." He smiles. "And I will be here when you need me, repairing what I can." The Librarian's brow furrows. "I don't think I can leave, actually."

I look down at my arm. I am growing even hazier. "Ben, I won't be coming back—"

A librex topples off a shelf, and its cover cracks. The ghost of a tattoo-faced man holding a harpoon drifts up from the damaged librex. A pipe in the shape of a tomahawk dangles precariously from his mouth. I don't recognize the character, but I instantly like him.

Ben bends over to pick up the thin librex, and it slips through his fingers. He stares down at it confused. "I'll work on this one later."

What Nyla and the Collective are doing, erasing his home, is not part of the Librarian's program. Fading away to nothing is beyond his understanding. After the Collective has their way, these stories will be gone.

"They're reprogramming me, Ben."

He ignores me. "With these"—he rushes to slide a book back on the shelf, but again, he glitches and his hand passes right through it—"you are bringing stories to a new world." He sounds exactly like Ben. "Priceless."

He's programmed—preservation and hopefulness on repeat. But even if he's just a program, he's right. I could've taken what's here and created new, better stories for our new world. Just the fleeting thought makes my heart soar for what will no longer happen.

And though I'll be gone in any moment, I know in this instant who I am. I am not a scientist. I am not what my parents hoped I'd be. I am what Lita knew I was. I am a storyteller. Just as I let the idea fill me, in the glass of one of the bookcases, I see my reflection. It is dimmer than the Librarian's.

Next to the glass, a small wooden bookshelf in the shape of a nautilus shell holds a curved spiral of librex. I smile as I approach. These librex are perfectly preserved: Adams, Butler, Erdrich, Gaiman, Morrison . . .

I turn to thank Ben for trying. He is staring up at the smoke, now billowing upward, his brow furrowed. "You need to leave now, Petra," he says.

The room, the bookshelves, and the chiminea stutter. I pull *A Wizard of Earthsea* back off the shelf and cradle it in my hands. I sit on the ground next to the chiminea, staring into the flames. "Ben, whether I stay or leave won't make a difference." This is the happiest and safest I have felt in a long time.

Ben's image glitches, but his voice turns urgent. "You ca—ca—can't stay. You n-n-n-need to wake up, Petra."

Piñon smoke and the words of the best characters ever known fill my senses. "I don't want to leave."

Desperation fills the Librarian's voice. "I will be here when you want to come back. You really m-m-must go."

I close my eyes. If I have already been reprogrammed and this is where my mind has ended up, it's heaven. "I've decided to stay," I answer.

Something taps my leg. I crack open my eyes to see the rabbit's furry foot brushing against me. "Wake up," he says.

I ignore him and lie back. I'm done with quests. I stare at the smoke drifting up as whispers surround me. The rabbit speaks again, but as he does, his voice changes. Now it's more powerful and commanding. Lita's voice booms from his mouth. "Petra!"

I open my eyes and the rabbit swirls into a vortex of mist. Out of the haze, Lita stands, her long white dress and loose hair whipping in the wind. A strange glow fills the obsidian in her pendant.

I sit up, smiling. "Lita, you're here."

She stomps on the ground, and the room quakes. "Wake. Up!" she yells. "Now!"

28

I FORCE MY EYES TO CRACK OPEN. JAVIER IS STOOPED over me, holding me up with one arm, while his other arm is curved around the back of my neck. His shaky voice begs. "Please wake up."

The back of my neck burns like a lighter is being held to it, then in an instant, the pain is gone. The *clink-clink-clink* of a metal sphere bounces on a hard surface. Javier's cool, papery-skinned hand cups over the spot.

He stares down at me nervously. It's the same face from so long ago. "*Don't worry, Petra. I will be your eyes for you.*" "Hello. Do you know who you are?" he asks.

My head drops against his chest. A sob sneaks out, and he pats my back like Mom did to him when he had a nightmare.

"I know who I am." I wipe my nose on his shirt and sit up to face him. "Do you know who you are?"

He smiles momentarily, and looks away. "You weren't waking up." Behind him, the purple strip lighting of Pleiades Corporation lines the cockpit. We're in the shuttle. "I thought I had made a huge mistake and you were lost," he says.

Just a moment ago I thought I could spend an eternity in my mind's library. And I thought that'd be heaven. But I'd take this one moment with Javier over that.

"I think I nearly *was* lost," I say. "But it wasn't your fault." I reach up toward the back of my neck. My arm moves like a sloth reaching for a leaf. "I couldn't wake up. I think it was the adult Cog."

"I am so sorry. It was the only way I could think of to help you—" Javier grunts as he lifts me by my armpits into a seat. "I was on my way to get the other Zetas. I ran into Nyla. She asked if I'd seen you near the stasis gel barrels in the hold."

I realize they must have seen me dumping the final vial.

"I had no other choice. I had to pretend—" His voice cuts off in a small cry, just like when he was little. The increasing whir of the shuttle's engine hurts my brain.

Across from us, strapped in their seats and ready for departure, are Suma, Rubio, and Feathers, staring back at me. "You're here," I say smiling.

"What is wrong with Zeta-1?" Feathers asks Javier.

He clears his throat. "Zeta-1's upgraded download from the Collective proved fatiguing. That is all," he says confidently. "With her new intelligence she will lead this group to the final research site."

Suma rubs her eyes. "You are sure that we are to leave now, Epsilon-5?"

"Yes," he answers. "The Collective was specific that this needs to occur sooner than anticipated."

Rubio motions outside. "The winds from the west will be too strong for us to work on the surface now."

Javier places the collection bag containing all our belongings I stole onto the center lab station cubby. "The winds will die down soon. You need to be there at the optimal hour. So, you mustn't waste time with questions."

He faces the three of them. His voice is suddenly stern and rigid like Nyla's. He points to me. "Everyone must listen to Zeta-1's instructions. If not, you will answer to the Collective."

I do my best to sit up taller.

Javier's knees crack as he sits next to me whispering. "The Chancellor will know soon. You know where to go?"

My sluggish mind still recalls Nyla's hologram of the smallest waterfall with the projected target, indicating where they had found the First Arrivers. My head feels like it weighs a thousand pounds. "I think I can get us close before the next wind." I look over at the cockpit, grateful there are chairs for me and Javier, so I don't have to stand while piloting the five of us to the surface.

Javier places his hand on my cheek just like Lita used to. "You are going to have an amazing life."

And because of what Javier has done, he and I still have the chance. "We will, Javier." I smile. Then I glance at Suma with her furrowed brow. "But we should hurry now."

He sighs deeply and wraps his arms around me in a hug. I feel his body shaking. It's the same hug as the time I left for Camp Condor for the week. It's the same hug before he walked into kindergarten on the first day of school. "I'm sorry, Petra. It is the only way."

"Javier? Hurry. Get me to the cockpit. You'll have to help me pilot."

"They could come any time. I have to stay. Please understand," he whispers. Javier stands, his eyes welling with tears. "If this small part of my journey is to give everyone else a chance, then that is what will make our parents and ancestors proud." He turns and shuffles toward the door.

"Javier, what are you doing?" I yell.

He stops at the door and turns. "Goodbye, Petra." His voice shakes. "I love you too." As he steps out, the shuttle door slides shut.

I fumble with the seatbelt. "No, no, no." My body won't cooperate with what I'm telling it to do. I jamb my thumb into the button, but can't push hard enough. "Javier!" I yell. "Stop!"

Through the portal window, I see Javier locking himself in the remote-pilot room on the ship, ensuring Nyla or anyone else can't interfere with us. His face glows red in the flashing light of the remote-pilot function. The vibration of the engine hums through my body.

A wave of swirling nausea churns in my stomach.

The shuttle slips off the dock onto the launch railings with a clunk. With one last push, my belt comes loose. My body crumbles as I fall out of my seat and lunge toward the door, landing at Suma's feet. She stares at me like I have a programming glitch.

I push myself up and stumble to the portal window, pressing my hands against the pane. The inside of the shuttle around me is bathed in the red light. I am powerless to stop it. In the ship's remote-control room, Javier is focused on the panel, but he glances up when I pound on the door. The edges of his mouth sag downward. So do his eyes. He presses something in front of him, and the shuttle spins toward the open sky of the launch portal.

The glow of Sagan's purple-and-blue shimmering atmosphere falls over Javier. He's cradling his *Dreamers* book in one hand now, and the shuttle's control in the other. I watch him helplessly as we continue to spin. The lump filling my throat grows larger and larger until he's out of view.

I stumble back to the cockpit past wide-eyed Rubio, Suma, and Feathers. I thrust the handle toward the docking station, but it won't respond. I hit the neutral switch, but the hum of the engine continues. "No, Javier!" I run back to the window, screaming now. But I know it's too late.

The whine of the engine rises and we launch into the stratosphere. I tumble down the aisle between the center console and the seats.

Feathers unbuckles and hops down to help me. She holds her hand up to stop Rubio when he tries to do the same. When I'm back on my feet, she hurries to buckle herself back in.

She huffs annoyedly at me. "Zeta-1, you are going to be hurt! You are risking all our duties."

I run back to the portal, pounding my hands. The sobs catch in my throat. This is not what we dreamed of. "Why?"

But Javier is growing farther and farther away from me, and I can do nothing to get back to him.

As I watch, a small explosion flashes from the launch port and one shuttle dock rail skews to one side, while the other completely detaches. I can't breathe. He's made sure we can't return.

"What was that?" Feathers calls out.

Thank goodness they are strapped in and can't see. "Nothing," I answer, looking out the portal. "Just thunder from an electrical strike." With the timing of the windstorm, I hope my lie is convincing.

I watch until the ship is no longer visible. I stand at the

cockpit's controls, trying everything I know, but the shuttle doesn't respond. Even if it did, Javier knows I'm not a good enough pilot to steer us safely back in without the rails.

"Zeta-1?" Rubio calls out. "We will have to abort our mission if you are injured."

I ignore him and collapse into the cockpit chair. I can't get back to Javier.

The altimeter calls out, "*Two thousand six hundred meters.*"

Nyla already doubted Javier's worth. His tremor, the mistakes . . . I could have protected him. But now, with what he's done to help us escape, he's sealed his fate.

The last string holding my heart in place is ready to snap.

I stare down onto Sagan, at the trees that look like they belong in the yard of my micro dollhouse village. Javier used to steal my micro dolls when he was mad at me and hide them in the creosote bush. I'd only find them when winter came, and suddenly the bush would be scattered with tiny plastic people deep within its branches.

"*One thousand five hundred meters.*" Even from this distance, the lake's spray is visible skirting off its surface from the gusts. By the location of the mountain range to the east, I know we're nearing the landing site.

That's where I should be walking off the shuttle hand in hand with him. Like his first day at kindergarten. While Mom speaks to his teacher in front of Piñon Elementary, Javier squeezes my hand so hard it hurts. "It just looks scary from here," I say to calm him. "Once you're inside, you'll find kids to play with, a playground to explore. I promise, Javier, you'll love it."

"*Four hundred meters.*" The shuttle rocks back and forth from the wind, and the trees that looked tiny a moment ago are suddenly life-sized. "*Two hundred meters.*"

Glowing, misshapen swarms ripple below like a wave of bees across the turquoise lake. Why didn't I take more time describing the water butterflies to Javier? I try to squint away the image of his old-man, missing-tooth smile when I first told him about them. I could've done more. I glance back at Suma, Rubio, and Feathers. I'll never take shortcuts again.

"*One hundred meters.*" Our descent slows to a crawl, but the shuttle jerks from side to side in the wind gusts.

What choice do I have now? Even if I could find the terra-formers, and they could somehow get us back to the ship, I'll be too late to help him.

"*Ten meters.*" A sick-crow pulsating alarm pierces the air. The ground approaches more quickly than usual.

Just as the shuttle is about to touch down, a squeal like an incoming missile hits us. Feathers and Suma cup their hands over their ears. The gale blows the shuttle forward, and we skid toward the lake. I fly out of my chair and Rubio flings out his long legs, stopping me before I skid past him and into the metal console. The landing gear screeches as we jerk to a stop.

I hear the ramp outside descending. Javier is wasting no time.

The hum of the engine dwindles. Within seconds the ramp door cracks ajar. Hot wind rushes into the shuttle, reminding us of what's outside. Even if he got us to the surface, we're still not safe.

Suddenly, the shuttle's engine winds down into silence. With a *pop,* the reserve lighting flickers on. In one last effort, I hit the shuttle's system switch, but there is no response. I slam my hand on the ramp's retraction button—nothing. I know it's useless anyway. Javier has cut the power supply. He's locked me out of the controls.

I picture the Collective discovering what he's done. I collapse into the chair and sob.

Feathers approaches me. "Zeta-1?"

I cup my hands over my face and take several deep breaths.

"Is there a problem?" Suma asks.

My fingernails pierce my palms. When Nyla finally retrieves the shuttle, it will be to come for us, and by that time she and the Collective will have already punished Javier. If we remain here, I'll have taken away Suma, Feathers, and Rubio's chance for freedom. We can't stay.

I glance at Suma, helmet tucked under her arm.

"Put on your gear," I whisper.

In one final attempt, I press the comm-button in my suit. "Javier?" But there isn't even a momentary sign he hears me. I have no choice. My chin quivers as I turn off the corpomonitor. I will never hear his voice again. I pull on my suit and grab the helmet hanging behind my seat.

Rubio glances at me curiously as he pulls his suit over his clothes. I hurry over, pretending to help. I turn off his corpo-monitor too. I do the same with Feathers. But Suma is already dressed and already too suspicious.

As I'm zipping up my suit, my hand skips over a lump against my chest. I press down and feel Dad's rosary hanging around my neck under my clothes. I look down at my finger. My breath catches. Mom's wedding ring is missing. Nyla must have removed it.

At least Javier knew enough to bring my collection bag. I pull the bag with our valuables out of the cubby and hoist it onto one shoulder, securing its strap around my waist.

By the time I'm done, the others are already waiting by the door leading to the ramp. I join them and ease the door open. Hot wind blows into the shuttle. Water whips off the lake blinding our view.

If the lake is just ahead, I know which direction to head toward the cave.

I raise my voice so they can all hear over the wind. "I know of a shelter until the wind dies down."

A huge elephant-ear leaf the size of a hovercar blows right by the bottom of the ramp. If we'd been standing there, it would have taken all four of us out.

"Why not stay here?" Suma asks, eyes wide.

I glance at the shuttle. The Collective can remotely retrieve it as soon as they get the rails reoriented—and send people after us. I can't let Javier's sacrifice to help us be for nothing. "As

Epsilon-5 said, we aren't to question the Collective. These are the orders, and we are here to serve." I feel guilty manipulating them, but Javier was right. It'll ensure they obey.

Suma sighs and nods dutifully. Even in her fear of the windstorm, she complies.

One by one, Rubio, Suma, and Feathers clomp slowly down the shuttle's ramp. They wait in the shelter of the awning. Strands of Feathers' wispy hair flies in the wind.

I cinch my bag tighter around my waist and head after them.

Even partially blocked by the ship, a mix of sand, water, and wind slaps me across the face. I slip my helmet on and see the others have already done the same. I push down the visor.

A faint voice calls behind me over the shrieking wind. "Zeta-1?"

In front of me, I count the three—Suma, Rubio, Feathers—to make sure they are all there. My mind must still be recalibrating from the Cog removal.

I scrunch my eyes tightly to reset my ears and continue.

"Zeta-1?" the voice calls again, this time louder.

Even in Sagan's warm air, and the heat of the suit, my blood runs cold. I turn around to see the smallest ghost shrimp standing hunch-shouldered at the top of the ramp.

"Voxy?"

29

I MUMBLE UNDER MY BREATH LIKE MOM USED TO. "What were you thinking?"

Feathers, Rubio, and Suma wait five meters ahead in the protection of the ramp's canopy while I race back into the shuttle.

I go down on one knee. "I'm sorry, Voxy, but you need to stay here."

His chin quivers. I remember what it felt like when I was seven and got lost at the Desert Botanical Garden.

"Don't worry. Nyla will see you're gone and find a way to get you back." It's a half-truth. I can't be sure how long it will take for her to get to him. But he's still safer in the shuttle than on the surface with us.

I place my hands on Voxy's shoulders, thinking of what happened to Len. First the nausea, then the blisters forming on his skin. I lean in and speak sternly. "Voxy, you can't exit this shuttle for any reason."

His shoulders sag. "Please don't leave me, Zeta-1."

I pull him into a hug. "Why are you here?"

"I saw what Nyla and the others did to you. I don't want to be like them. If I go back, I will be part of that. Part of the Collective."

The idea of that happening to Voxy makes me shudder.

He bows his head. "And . . . and I want to have cuentos too."

How could I not see this coming? And he's right. He should have all those things. Will the Collective hold his hand when he's scared? Will they tell him stories to calm his nerves?

It's too late for my little brother, but maybe I can give Voxy the childhood Javier never got to have.

"If I stay with you . . . ?" Voxy's timid voice trails off.

I grit my teeth, and a tear falls inside my visor. "If you stay with us, you'd be Voxy," I answer. "Just Voxy. A boy who gets to have his own cuento."

His jaw settles in a stubborn clench. "Then I choose to be Voxy. Voxy who gets to have his own cuento."

I yank an envirosuit off the hook and scramble to dress him.

I turn off the corpomonitor in his suit, ensuring they can't track him either, and place a helmet on his head. I clamp it down and press the airlock. It vacuums tight, protecting him from where we're about to go.

His words are muted like he's speaking into a water bottle. "Will they come for me?"

I place an empty Collection bag over his shoulder. Retrieving him would put the Collective at risk. But I think of all the time Nyla's invested in him. What I think her plans are for him. For us.

"We can't think of that now." I glance in the direction of the waterfalls. We could be there within a day, but we still need our food from the cave. My sigh steams up my visor. "Voxy, are you sure about this? Living on the planet won't be easy. We won't be coming back."

He nods.

"Okay then. Promise to do exactly what I say, and for the time being, you're just here to assist us in sample collection."

The corners of his pale lips turn up, and the helmet nods up and down again. I pull him by the hand down the ramp to join the others.

He skids to a halt and gasps.

I panic and bend down, making sure his visor is closed. I peek in to see Voxy staring wide eyed, a huge smile on his face at the lake. He gapes upward to the spiky mountains, then to the sky.

He lifts both his arms like a magician presenting a trick. "Look at it!"

I realize it's the first time Voxy's seen anything other than the ship's sterile white walls and blue lighting.

"Hello, Voxy," Feathers says, like it's perfectly normal he's here.

Just then, a gust of wind sandblasts the side of the shuttle with tiny rocks.

"Are you sure we shouldn't wait in the shuttle?" Rubio asks.

I think of how Nyla's probably already discovered Voxy missing.

Weaving a cuento for them right now just after losing Javier feels impossible. "The Collective needs us to arrive at the research site as soon as possible," I say, hoping it'll be enough to convince them. Before anyone else can object, I lock elbows with Voxy and the rest follow suit, until we form a human chain.

"Ready?" I take the first step out of the protected cover of the entrance ramp and into an explosion of wind. It's at least forty kilometers per hour, with a few gusts that would send us flying if we weren't linked.

"Oooooooh," Voxy squeals as his foot hits the mossy ground.

In Sagan's twilight, through the haze of dirt and mist, the lake comes into view. When we reach the water's edge, we turn and walk in the direction of the jungle and the cave that lies beyond. Our chain strains with each gust, but we hold tight. Every few seconds I look back to make sure they're all still with me.

Feathers' and Voxy's suits ripple like tarps in a hurricane over their tiny bodies.

The trees at the jungle's edge bend in the exact easterly direction of the wind, explaining their curved trunks.

In twice the time it normally takes, we come to the cave's entrance. The curtain of vines billows in the wind. Inside, gold and green lights skitter over the ground like tiny fairies. The glow reminds me of my mind's library and the lamp beckoning me inside. But here in the real world, it's only Sagan's lightning bugs leading us to shelter.

I pull the vines aside and wave my arm hurriedly for the others to enter. I stare at Suma as she walks by me. The only way to track us now is that one small button inside her suit. If I can disable it, they can only find us on the surface with our heat signature. Our best bet will be to get to the First Arrivers quickly, hiding in caves or the cold lake along the way if they send the shuttle.

In the cramped entrance, Suma, Feathers, Rubio, and I remove our helmets and set them down, catching our breaths. The air is warm and smells of minerals.

Voxy starts to unclamp his helmet.

I lift his visor. "Only inside the shade of the cave. Outside, helmet on." I think instantly of Dad making me wear the helmet in Rockhound Park.

Just like I had, Voxy nods in understanding, but his eyes sag.

Our helmets line the front of the cave wall like shoes lined up in a home's entryway.

For the first time, I walk deeper into the cave. The passageway widens into a larger cavern, and the scattered cave lights merge into a torrent of glowing creatures. This time, I gasp louder than Voxy did a moment ago. The gold and green lights from the scuttling creatures shimmer in an aurora on the cave walls.

Smaller tunnels branch off the main chamber, like a massive glowing version of Lita's fire ant colony sculpture.

Voxy's mouth drops open. Suma and Feathers look mildly impressed. I smile.

I take a few steps back to the entrance and reach up onto the ledge where I stored the bioloaf. I yelp as something furry scurries up my arm and jumps off my shoulder, running out of the cave. Only a mini chinchilla. Then, my stomach plummets.

I grab the edge of a bioloaf box. What's left of it falls off the ledge in pieces. Not a crumb remains. I reach up for another. It's gone.

Pinpricks run up my spine, and my mouth is suddenly dry. We'll need food soon. And we can't spend hours at the lake, out in the open, harvesting enough vines to eat right now. Now we have even less time to find the First Arrivers. I walk back to join the others.

Rubio pokes his finger at a creeping green glow. "Interesting. It's difficult to observe if it's chemiluminescent vertebrate or bioluminescent bacteria." He pulls his atmospheric reader out of his bag. "This may take me a while—"

"Don't get too settled," I speak over the lump in my throat, trying to hold back tears. "We need to move on to the research site once the wind dies down."

Rubio slips his reader back in his pocket, his brow furrowed in disappointment. I want to tell him we can come back another time. Just like Dad promised me about our new tradition of trips to Rockhound State Park. But I know now there are things out of our control. The things we hope for most can't always come true.

We have no food. And if we don't make it to the settlement quickly . . .

Winds howl outside taunting me.

Suma scoffs. "Something does not feel right. Why drop us here only to meet us elsewhere? A suitable landing site for the ship has not been cleared yet."

Voxy faces Suma, hands on his hips authoritatively. "It's all true. The Collective asked me to come help." He winks at me.

My shoulders slump, and I shake my head for him to stop.

Suma bends down to look him in the eye. "What exactly are you here to help the Collective with?"

He puffs out his chest. "I am an Expert in—"

"Voxy, stop. Please," I say.

Suma steps closer to me until we are nearly nose to nose. "I'm going to verify this new directive with the Chancellor before leaving for the new research site." She grabs her bag and walks toward the mouth of the cave.

"Stop!" The shout is much louder than I intended, and everyone jumps. I stand up and pick up my collection bag. "Come with me, Zeta-2." I march past Suma away from the others and out into the cave's cramped entrance. It's now or never.

I wait for her to catch up, biting the inside of my cheek. The wind howls behind me, the vines brushing against the back of my suit. Suma stands in front of me, cave-glow as a backlight, bag over her shoulder. I take a deep breath and reach into my bag, easing out Suma's purple unicorn sweatshirt. I hold it up by the shoulders.

For a long moment Suma stares. Slowly, she tilts her head, brow furrowed. She reaches out, taking it in her hands.

She lifts the sweatshirt to her face and sniffs deeply.

I pull her baby book out of my bag and turn to one of the first pages. With a chime, the 3D image of Suma and her moms projects between us. Suma shifts her gaze to the hologram.

"Do you remember?" I whisper.

She looks at the surrounding rock like she's suddenly noticed where we are. She reaches out to touch the mom who went missing from the holograms halfway through her baby book.

Javier took prodding from our shared memories. But I have no memories of Suma's life to help her, just these images. I point to her in the hologram. "That's you."

"Yeah." She scoffs. "I know it's me."

My heart pounds. Was it that easy? "You know it is you, Zeta-2? Or you know who the girl in this hologram is?"

She remains silent, staring at the image.

I point to the women. "And these are . . ."

"My moms," she whispers.

I turn to the last page. The book chimes, and Suma's mom kissing a holographic Suma, who's rolling her eyes, pops up between us.

"Where is she?" Suma asks.

It's not the time to tell Suma I've seen Preeti Agarwal's empty pod. "I don't know exactly what happened," I say instead.

"Why did you bring us here?" Suma's voice trembles. "I need to find her. I'm going back to the ship." She takes a step toward the door.

"You can't!"

She flinches, and stops.

"If you remember, then you're also aware what the Collective will do to you if they know. Do you remember the first time you came out of stasis and called out for your mom?" I ask.

Suma drops her head and stares down at her sweatshirt.

"I do," I say. "If you go back and they catch you, they'll reprogram you—and I guarantee you'll never come back. They'll make sure of it, and I won't be there to remind you of who you are. What good are you to your mom if you can't even remember her?"

I know how I felt when I was desperate to find my parents. I would have fought the entire Collective myself if it meant I could get to them.

"I understand you want your mom," I say quietly.

I can't tell her the truth now. Her mom's gone. There's nothing to find. And the ship where our parents were last will soon be gone for good. I put my hand on her shoulder, and she pulls away.

"We need to find the people from the fist Pleaides ship, the First Arrivers."

Suma glances up momentarily at the ship's mention.

I continue. "I need your help to get us there."

She stares in the direction of the shuttle. "How long will it take to get there?"

Nyla had said they were within twenty-five kilometers. "If we're lucky, we can make it before the next wind cycle."

Suma stares toward the shifting vines. She quickly pulls her unicorn sweatshirt over her head and slips her baby book into her bag. "Let's go, then."

I let out a sigh. I reach out, and she doesn't even flinch when I turn off the monitor in her suit.

Her chin trembles, and her eyes are full of tears. "I hope when we find my mom, she creates a thermal fission chamber and crams the Chancellor inside." Her eyes narrow. "My mother will split the Collective into a million pieces." She stomps back into the cave. Her back is to me, but I see her raise her hand to wipe her face.

"We do as Zeta-1 says," Suma proclaims to Rubio and Feathers. "The wind has died down enough." She walks past me again and picks up her gear. "We leave now." I know how much she must be hurting, but part of me is happy to finally have someone else who remembers too. There's still some danger from the wind—it's at approximately twenty percent. But I'm not about to argue with her.

I put on my best rigid voice. "Everyone but Voxy, leave your helmets and bags. Everything we need is at the new site." The gear will just weigh us down, and we at least need to try to find them before eking out a life inside caves and eating lake vines. "And like Epsilon-5 and Zeta-2 said, you need to follow my directions, or you will answer to the Collective."

Rubio straightens his clothes and Feathers smooths out her hair, ready to work. They head out along with Suma. Voxy straightens his suit and checks its closures.

"What is wrong with Zeta-2?" Voxy asks.

"Her name is Suma now," I reply. I put my bag with my treasures over my shoulder. "You'll have to learn our real names, Voxy."

He slips his helmet onto his head. "I heard Nyla call you Peeetra."

I snicker. "Pay-truh," I correct.

"Either way, it's a good name," he says. "What about Zetas 3 and 4?" He stares at Feathers and Rubio.

It's not fair for me to assign them a name either. "Not sure yet," I answer.

"So, what's wrong with her?" he repeats. "Suma . . ."

"She's missing her mother," I answer. I think of Voxy's little cell in Nyla's room, how she was grooming him for something more. "You might miss Nyla or Crick someday too, Voxy." I tighten my bag around my waist.

"I don't belong to the Collective anymore."

Something triggers in my memory. I kneel down to him—I have to know.

"Voxy, what . . . what did Epsilon-5 say in your ear? When Nyla and Crick were putting me back in stasis."

Voxy smiles. "He told me not to be afraid, that he had a plan, and that it was not the end of your story."

He clamps the visor shut and walks out between the vines.

I smile ahead at the little runaway who's lived his life isolated on a ship, without ever running or playing, who maybe only laughed when no one was watching, whose favorite color was probably clear.

I follow him outside where the rest are waiting.

"Which direction are they?" Suma asks quietly.

"Waterfalls," I answer.

She nods and stares across the far side of the lake, to the distant icy mountains where the water pours over the plateaus.

Feathers' eyes, on the other hand, are laser-locked on Suma's unicorn sweatshirt, a confused but jealous look on her face.

We walk toward the lake. Without the typhoon of dust and water, the spot where the shuttle *should* be is visible. It's gone.

30

MY EYES BURN, AND MY VISION FOGS OVER. THE SHUTtle disappearing can only mean they've repaired the dock, and Javier has been found out.

And I know. He is gone.

I glance back at the cave. It would be so easy to go back inside, huddle into a ball, and live with my memories of my brother in the safety of those rock walls. What do I have to gain by going forward? Everything I love is behind me. Earth. Lita. My parents. Javier . . .

It's so far to walk without food and water. We may not even make it. We may not find the First Arrivers.

I close my eyes, and Javier's voice fills my mind like he is right here. "*If this small part of my journey is to give everyone else a chance, then that is what will make our parents and ancestors proud.*"

My jagged breathing is muffled in my ears. If there's a chance I can tell the story someday of an old man's bravery to save us, then I will take the risk trying.

"Let's go." I pass Suma, Feathers, and Rubio, pulling Voxy after me. I motion for Suma to remain at the back of the line, sandwiching the three of them between us. "Stay close, everyone," I say.

We duckling-walk in a row along the lake's shore, toward its east side, heading for the smallest waterfall.

Mist churns over the lake as the cold air from the east mixes with the west's fading hot breath. The sky to the southwest burns pink, and every so often there's a break in the mist, leaving a stained-glass reflection on the surface of the lake.

Swarms of water butterflies follow in our shadows as we walk along the lake's shore. From beneath the surface, undulating globes of gold-and-purple spotlights trail us.

Even through his visor I hear Voxy giggling. I look back just in time to see him flap his arms. The water butterflies who've ventured off to observe us scurry back to their flock. It's quiet again for a moment, then the flapping of his rippling suit is followed by his giggles again. Every so often, Feathers joins in. For two hours I listen to giggling and flapping as they entertain themselves with the skittish creatures. Any other time, I'd beg them to stop.

But Nyla and the Collective will be coming soon. This might be his last time to have this kind of fun. If she locates us before we make it to the settlement, who knows how the Collective will punish him.

For the next five or six hours we walk mostly in silence. I don't slow, even though I know they all must be just as tired and thirsty as I am.

At first, I think I'm imagining the rumble. But we round a bend, and the rumble turns to a growl. Ahead, the lake's glassy surface ripples. Suma breaks out of formation, a determined grin on her face as she passes me. I hurry after, the others close behind until we reach the river. White caps of turbulent water ripple on its surface. Directly across the river is a shaded grove of trees running along its edge. Beyond that, the smallest waterfall isn't even a kilometer away. Near the base of the waterfall will be the field. The perfect place for a settlement, and where Nyla's target was projected.

"What do you think?" Suma says.

The winds will be coming back soon, and there isn't a cave or other shelter in sight. We're out of breath, hungry and thirsty. I shake my head. "Let's find a safe place to cross."

"How much longer to the research site?" Feathers asks, her

eyes closed. If I didn't know better, I'd think she fell asleep standing up.

Suma takes a few steps on the sandy shore. "This looks like a good place."

I know she's desperate to get back to her mom, but taking risks when we're so close to being safe isn't the answer. "The current looks too dangerous." I point to a wider crossing with fewer whitecaps a short walk away. "How about—"

The distinct whir of a drone vibrates the air.

Suma's mouth drops open, and we lock eyes.

It's approaching fast. And it's loud. Far too loud.

Voxy clings to my arm. We stare off to a dark pinpoint in the distance, high above the lake from the direction we came. As it moves closer, I see it is not a single drone.

Like a plague of locusts, a swarm of drones is flying toward us.

But these are not harmless collection drones, or rescue ones in search of a missing child. Attached at the base of each one is an aerosol dispenser used for terra-forming. And what makes my heart stop are the auxiliary tanks behind them. They're filled with bright green liquid.

Heat runs over my scalp. I forgot.

The tanks are overkill for just the five of us. The air so still and peaceful moments ago now pulses with their buzz. I think of the vials back in the lab. I never went back to check on them. I've killed us all.

Suma nudges me with her elbow. "What are they?"

I can't answer.

"Impressive," Rubio blurts out.

"Everyone," I yell, my voice shaking, "do not panic."

"Why would we panic?" Feathers waves her arms over her head. "It is just the Collective. But what kind of drones are those?" she asks.

Voxy stands next to me, his rapid breathing muffled through his helmet. He squeezes my hand so hard it hurts.

The drones get even closer, moving south toward us as one tiny triangular unit. There are so many they look like a solid craft.

Suma pushes Feathers hands down and leans in. "Don't call attention to us." Her eyes pierce into Feathers'. I'm glad Suma's on my side.

It's a slim chance, but the cold oxygenated water of the river might be our only chance to survive. Will they even be able to swim? If only we'd brought the helmets. This is my fault.

I grab Voxy's hand and turn to Suma. "I'm the biggest," I say. "I go in first. You anchor us the best you can on the other end."

Suma grabs Feathers' hand. The rest of us follow suit, linking our human chain: Voxy taking Rubio's hand, and Rubio taking Feathers'. "Do not let go of one another!" I shout, wading into the river. The glacial water seeps into my boots, and suddenly I feel like I am back in my pod on the first day on the ship, stasis gel flowing over me. The rush of water tries its best to push my legs out from beneath me.

I look back. One by one, we wade into the water as they

grow even closer, the hum even louder than the river's roar. Halfway across, I look back to see we are all in. Suma's up to her waist and struggling as much as I am. The drones are still too far away, though, for us to be able to hold our breaths yet.

Water splashes into my mouth. With a shove, the river cuts my legs out from under me like a rampaging bulldog. I scramble for a foothold, but the undercurrent's too strong. Voxy clenches my hand tighter, and I get a toe on the river bottom. We centipede down the river until we are nearly to the other side.

My foot catches the bed of the opposite side, and I anchor us down again.

Voxy looks up at me, his eyes filled with tears. Even over the river's roar, his frail words make my heart sag. "This is because of me," he says.

The drones are nearly overhead, their whir deafening. I don't have time to assure him this was going to happen whether or not he'd run away. "Everyone under!" I yell. Voxy's eyes are wide like Javier's when Lita showed us the dead rattler from the chicken coop.

"We'll be okay, Voxy. Don't be afraid, your helmet will give you oxygen."

I grab him. "Ready?"

The kid who's probably never even had a real bath shakes his head no.

I coach him like I would Javier. "One, two . . ."

We go under, and I open my eyes to see if the others are

okay. Beneath the turmoil of the torrent, I see only a dark shadow blocking out the rays of sun piercing the water. We wouldn't notice the shadow of a single drone, but the shadow from the swarm thrusts us into darkness. I hold my breath until the sun's rays brighten the water again. I'm nearly blacking out, but it hasn't been long enough for the aerosol to have dissipated, if the drones detected our heat.

I lift my head to the surface and gasp, panicked I might be breathing in poison. But the drones pass us, continuing south, and there's no green mist above. I pull the others up, and one by one, they raise their heads, coughing and gasping for air. Except for Voxy, who's still safely enclosed in his helmet.

The hundreds of drones either didn't see us, or the Collective doesn't care about us anymore. My gaze follows the lead drone and its trajectory, to where it will end. And I realize—it's exactly where we're going. The lowest waterfall.

I swim toward a large boulder and cling to it with one arm. But my approach is too fast, and I bang my kneecap on its surface. I scream and grab my knee, losing my grip on Voxy. My bag zip-ties tightly around me, and I look to see Voxy's gloved hand holding for dear life to the strap. I let go of my knee to make sure he's secure, and pain hammers my kneecap over and over. I use the bag to swing our chain toward the sandy shore. Suma scrambles up onto dry land. One by one, she pulls Feathers, Rubio, and Voxy ashore until the chain is broken, and I am left alone clinging to the boulder.

Suma pulls on my bag. "Let go, Zeta-1," she yells. "Please."

I open my eyes and realize Suma doesn't even know my real name.

I release the boulder and lunge toward them as the current tries to sweep me away. Suma and Voxy each hold onto part of my bag while Feathers and Rubio anchor them to the shore, until against the river's current, they hoist me onto land.

We all lie on the bank, dripping wet and coughing.

High above, the drones near the ridge of the mountain, where the icy water from the east pours over its ledge.

The drones split into groups, basket-weaving across one another. Bright-green mist spews from their bases with a sickening hiss.

My stomach roils. I helped create that.

The green mist we've brought turns Sagan's orange-and-purple sky a revolting brown. I think of how high the drones are. They're barely visible, far away enough that we are safe, for now.

The grove's massive leaves sway gently in the breeze, beckoning us to hurry inside.

"Are you okay?" Suma asks.

I lie, nodding.

"What do you think they're doing?" she asks, looking at the sky.

I shrug, another lie.

I try to stand up too, and my knee barely cooperates. Voxy holds my hand as I limp with the rest of them to the grove.

High above in the jungle's rooftop, birds—or tiny winged lizards—skitter between the leaves. The ground is a spongy

blanket of moss, and each step feels like stepping on a pillow. Scattered boulders dot the floor of the grove like ripe fruit fallen to the ground.

We find a tree and cluster close together. I can already see my knee swelling beneath my suit.

I glance up at the canopy of elephant-ear leaves. Somehow the shelter of the grove feels like we're hiding under the covers in our beds. But just like hiding under covers, you know if something bad wants to get you, the sheets will offer no real protection.

Suma wrings out her sweatshirt. "What should we do?"

I stare at the murky haze sinking to the planet's surface in the distance, my stomach twisting with dread. Only Voxy has a helmet, and even though it's a ways away, I know the winds could carry it to us soon.

I shake my head. This is not the kind of thing we should have to decide.

We have to at least find the First Arrivers' camp. See if there's anything we can use to help us. I can't imagine Voxy spending most of his life inside a helmet and suit.

Rubio rubs his hands quickly over his arms. "Shouldn't we attempt to contact the Collective?"

Suma narrows her eyes at him. "Epsilon-5 was clear you are to follow Zeta-1's instructions. And if you do not, I will report you to Chancellor Nyla myself."

Rubio swallows hard and leans back out of Suma's line of sight against the tree.

We peer out from under the canopy. Like a murderous legion leaving the site of a massacre, the drones gather back into an organized unit. Once they're a solid, dark mass, they speed off back north.

Suma sidles next to me, speaking out of the side of her mouth. "How long until we leave?"

It's the worst position to be in. We can't go towards the camp until I know the toxin has dissipated. But if we wait too long, the hurricane winds will come back, and the skinny tree trunks and boulders won't be enough shelter.

I can't bring myself to tell Suma about the toxin. Why make her terrified of what will come, if there's nothing we can do to stop it?

"Not long," I answer.

The brown sky begins fading back to burnt orange and bright pink.

We all sit. Rubio is snoring within minutes. Feathers lies on her side to nap. I'd give anything to erase the image of the drones and what I know has happened. Voxy lies on his back, staring through his visor up at the little flying lizards in the canopy.

Suma sits cross-legged against the tree in front of me, the distinct spiral of a silver unicorn horn jutting out from long waves of dark hair. "I'm Suma," she says.

My eyes fill with heat, and tears trickle over like a boiling pot.

I wipe my nose, not even ashamed of how gross it probably is. "I know," I say, realizing I haven't called her directly by her name yet. "My name is Petra."

"Petra," she repeats. "Thank you, Petra."

Her lips quiver and I wonder if, somehow, she already knows the inevitable truth about her mom.

"Zeta-1?" Feathers calls out through chattering teeth. "I'm cold."

"And hungry," Rubio mumbles, half asleep.

I suddenly think I know a tiny bit how parents feel. I stand and walk to the tree line and look at the changing color of the sky.

The field is too far to see.

I hobble to Rubio. "I need to borrow your scope."

He shrugs and pulls it out of his pocket, handing it to me, and closing his eyes again. At the tree line, I focus the scope below the waterfall and scan bit by bit. Small caves smatter along the rock's face behind either side of the falls. I look back across to the open field. The toxin is slowly fading. A field of green, the color of Lita's cactus garden, lies beneath the waterfall. But it's just a grassy field. Beyond the field, just more jungle. There's no settlement like Nyla said there should be. No Pleiades first ship. No people.

What am I missing?

I feel someone next to me and turn to see Suma at my side. I hold out the scope. "Can you try?" I ask.

At that moment, a honeybee lands on Suma's unicorn horn. I'm not sure how she feels about bees, so I shoo it away quickly. Then, I freeze. "It was real," I whisper.

Suma turns her head casually. "Huh?" I remember Mom saying bees are life. Without bees, there's no food, without food,

no humans. Suma shrugs and takes the scope. Within a moment, she goes, "Hmmmm..."

"What?" I ask.

She places the scope to my eye, and points it in the direction of the waterfall and the jungle at its edge, on the distant side of the field. Instead of straw-straight trunks, the elephant-ear trees are braided together, forming a wall like a woven basket. This isn't natural on any planet. How many of them were there, and how long of a head start did the First Arrivers have?

"What do you think it is?" she asks. It has to be the settlement. But there's not a single human in sight.

No matter what happened, we're too late. They're gone.

In the distance from where the drones headed, the praying-mantis ship comes into view.

"Hurry," I say. "Get behind the rocks!" If they decide to fly directly overhead, the rocks won't hide our heat signature, but maybe we have a shot if we hide.

Suma and I rush back into the grove. I grab Voxy and Feathers, and Suma gets Rubio. But the ship stops several kilometers away. Even so far, it looks large enough that its landing gear legs could reach out and pluck us up. The praying mantis hovers in place, not moving any closer.

"Stay where you are until I say!" I call out from our rock. But Voxy and even Feathers are both clinging to me.

I peek out. There's not a single drone with more toxin. No sign of the shuttle leaving the ship to collect us. In the distance, the Pleiades ship's gravity stabilizer starts to hum, louder

and louder. Just like it had when we left Earth, using Sagan's gravity to garner energy. And that's when I know—it's over. Competition eliminated, they're leaving. I feel a small hand grip mine and look down to see Voxy clutching my fingers. I grip his back.

The boosters kick in and the ship catapults into hyperspace. With a rumble, it speeds farther away from Sagan. I wonder if the Collective will return when they've reconfigured their epiderm-filters? Or will they find another Goldilocks planet and never come back? I look down at Voxy, as the only home he's ever known grows smaller in the distance.

"It's okay," I say.

He shrugs. "I know."

We stand and watch as it leaves.

With the ringed planet in the background, the glow of the ship leaving Sagan bends in an oval like a firefly, until the light is gone.

Javier's story ends on that ship. In this ending, he knows I loved him, and he has his book. His story will end as Javier—not as part of the Collective.

And now, with them gone, we're alone. Just the five of us on one huge planet. I've made this choice for all of us. I don't want to think about what it all means. I glance at Suma and tears roll down her cheeks. I realize she must think her mom just left on that ship.

"Suma?" I call, but she doesn't take her eyes off the ship.

"Suma, your mom—they had already—"

"I know." Suma rubs her forearm over her eyes.

I want to give her a hug, but she takes Voxy's and Feathers' hands, and leads them and Rubio farther under the canopy.

I clench my eyes tightly, blocking out the image of the dead bodies we'll find in the First Arrivers camp. If they were even there at all. The toxin should have dissipated, but I don't want to put any of us through that right now. I have to, though. It's the only chance for shelter we've got. I just need a moment.

I reach into my pocket, and a metal spike jams into my thumb. I pull out my silver sun pendant and stare down at it, rubbing a tarnished point. My eyes well with tears and I look up to keep them from spilling over. It feels like only days ago she placed it around my neck. And though Sagan has exponentially more stars, they twinkle the same here as they did in the New Mexican desert, lying on her black-and-red striped blanket, my cheek resting on her chest. Billions of kilometers of space, and more suns and moons than I can count, separate me from home.

I hold up my pendant to the sky, centering the dwarf sun in the middle of the obsidian. The tiny orb glows faintly through the center. I speak quietly, so the others can't hear. "Lita. Are you there?" The words catch in my throat. "I need help."

I wait.

Nothing happens. No magical voice whispers on the wind. No smell of her perfume.

Maybe the sun here is too small, too low, too cold for it to work.

"Zeta-1?" Rubio calls again.

I return the pendant to my pocket and zip it safely inside. I limp back to the tree they're resting under, and sit next to Feathers.

"We'll find food soon," I say with a cheerful smile, knowing when we do, it will be slimy boiled lake vines.

Feathers leans into me, shivering from the wet clothes.

I unzip a compartment of my collection bag. Crumpled inside are Javier's clothes. I pull out his size 7 jeans and Gen-Gyro-Gang hoodie. My chin trembles and I bite on my lip. It doesn't have a unicorn horn, but it's drier than Feathers' envirosuit. I hand it to Feathers, and her eyes widen. A huge smile crosses her face then, and I wonder if Feathers was a member of the GG Gang too, like Javier and every other seven-year-old on Earth.

"They're yours," I say.

"Oh!" She grabs them and darts behind the closest tree. Suma and I grin when we hear how quickly she unzips her suit. A wet thunk follows as it falls to the ground.

A lone gust of wind from the west blows through the tree trunks. It's warm over our wet, goose-bumped skin. Sky lizards are already scurrying into holes inside the trunks, guided by some instinct they've known from a millennium of eight-hour wind cycles.

"Thank you, Zeta-1," Feathers says.

Suma calls softly from behind me. "Her name is Petra."

Feathers faces Suma, hands on her hips. "Zeta-1 is an Expert in all things geo—"

Suma speaks over Feathers, her voice suddenly commanding. "*Petra* is a Storyteller."

A wave of warmth cocoons around me like a hug in Lita's arms.

I close my eyes and suddenly I'm behind Lita's house in the desert. The chirp of the flying lizards here, singing to their friends high above us in the trees, sounds like the coyotes singing back home. I even imagine sweet elephant-ear wood smoke drifting into Sagan's starry sky.

Lita's voice fills my head. "*Set your intention.*" Tears well in my eyes. I let my memories fill me. I am bringing all of them: Mom, Dad, Lita, Javier, and our home. Ben and my crumbling library, deep in my mind. The stories of Lita and my ancestors. I'm bringing them all to this world.

The winds pick up high above, branches billowing in Sagan's warm breeze, just like the New Mexico desert. I look around at Rubio, Feathers, Voxy, and Suma: different colors and sizes. However dissimilar, we feel like an unexpected family.

Feathers sits and wraps her arms around her knees, still shivering. Rubio grabs his growling stomach. Voxy stares at me hopefully like I can fill some void.

At least with the Collective, the four of them had food on the ship. They'd been warm. They had tonics and concoctions to help them sleep. Now, every day will be a struggle. Will life off the ship really be better?

The wind whistles even louder, reminding me we will have

to take cover soon. Through the surrounding trees, it sounds more like a scream. Voxy's voice shakes. "What is that?"

When I was the most frightened I'd ever been in my life, Lita found a way to take my mind off Halley's Comet.

"Oh, that?" I say. "Don't worry. That's just the fire snake." I point to the opposite side of the grove. "He lives on the western side of the planet."

"*Pfft*," Rubio interrupts. "Our life-form studies show this planet has no ophidians."

"*Ssssh*, this is *my* cuento," I say.

Feathers reaches over and pokes Rubio. "Quiet! She's going to tell us a cuento."

I'm taken back like it was only a few days ago. I watch as Lita tosses a piñon log onto the fire.

But this time, I lower my voice and speak slowly. "Había una vez, siglos en el pasado, the fire snake left his mother, planet Earth, to go in search of his father"—I point to the dwarf sun—"who was much larger and more powerful and farther away than Sagan's sun."

"Earth." Feathers whispers, her eyes looking up and to the left. "What is Sagan?"

"*Now* who is interrupting during a cuento?" Rubio chirps out.

I continue, rubbing my hands together in a ball. "The fire snake's father was such a fiery sun." I explode my hands outward in front of them. "His father's greetings burned his eyes when he approached—blinding him!"

Feathers gasps and pushes her back against the tree.

I picture Lita giggling as she watches parts of her story being told on the new planet.

I lower my chin. "Pobrecito. Without his eyes or a single friend to guide him, he returned home, to the love of his mother. Earth, a planet of turquoise blues and emerald greens, immeasurable oceans filled with fish and whales."

I glance at Suma. Her eyes are closed, and she's smiling. A tear falls down one cheek.

I lean in and make my voice raspy and mysterious. "But also creatures yet to be discovered in the seas' depths." I hold up my arms, and their eyes follow. "Mountain ranges so high and remote, no human had ever stepped on their soil. Caves so vast, no living soul had ever marveled at their crystals. His mother, Earth's, ice-capped peaks glimmered gold in the glare of the fire snake's father."

I take a deep breath, thinking of what comes next.

"But on his return, in search for his mother, the fire snake's blind eyes could not see her, and he flew too close and too fast." I close my eyes, and the holographic image Nyla showed at the Collective's party flashes in my mind. I swallow, and know if I'm able to grow old like Lita, this is the spot where I'll ask the others to share stories of the loved ones they lost, when the fire snake flew too close to Earth. I will share stories of my own grandmother. I will share how she put love and life in her food, her home, her tall tales.

"Oh no," Voxy says.

Suma's eyes are still closed, and I can't tell if she's trying to

forget, or to remember. Maybe stories are there to help us do both. I know stories can't always have happy endings. But if there are chances for us to do better, we have to say out loud the parts that hurt the most.

"Instead of the nagual's return being a joyful reunion of the mother and son, it brought death and destruction."

We sit silently. Even though Voxy never knew a soul who perished, his eyes are filled with tears. And I know that these are his stories too. Just like me, someone, somewhere on Earth was his ancestor too.

"A few brave humans left their home on the nagual's mother, Earth. They took very little and left behind so much they loved, in hopes of finding a new home for their children, and their children's children, and all humans to come."

Suma turns and wipes the side of her face.

"The fire snake mourned for the loss of his mother, blaming himself," I say.

"So, what did the fire snake do next? Without a mom?" Rubio asks, leaning forward.

I stall like Lita used to, taking time to give each of them a sly smile. "He had no choice. He followed the only thing that felt like home, the only thing familiar to him. I point to him and Feathers and Voxy. "Humans.

"For hundreds of years, the fire snake trailed the humans on their exodus." I point in the direction of the west. "Staying within a safe distance, for fear he might accidentally harm them too. He dared not get too close. But when they arrived at their new home, and the fire snake with them, he realized he could not live on the dark side of Sagan, to the east, as its ice might extinguish his fiery breath forever."

A warm gust from the west times itself perfectly with my story.

"See?" I say. "He sends his comforting winds to the humans, a promise he will keep a safe distance, but send his breath to keep them warm. A reminder that he's here to protect us, the other children of his mother, Earth."

A stronger gust of wind whistles through the trees. Not a single sky lizard chirps. I bite on my trembling lip. We have to find shelter now. We've come so far. I won't let our story end here. Even if it's just the five of us, I'll share the stories I know from Lita's mother and her mother's mother . . . I will make sure the folklore of my ancestors soak into Sagan's soil. And I will speak the best parts of my mind's magical library into our new world.

As I look at Suma, Rubio, Feathers, and Voxy too, I realize I did find some sort of family in the end. We're lucky. A handful who get to live on two planets. And I know they all deserve to hear the truth now about what's gone wrong. That it's just us left. That all our parents are gone, and hard work lies ahead so that so we can live. I take a deep breath.

Rubio bolts upright, his mouth ajar and eyebrows knitted in a V. "Zeta-1's cuento is true!" he says. "I smell his breath." He breathes in deeply. "Smoke."

"You remember smoke?" I say, before thinking. I realize

how this could go very badly if they all remember home at once.

"Me too," Feathers says.

I wonder if she's just copying him, but then . . .

"It reminds me of burnt marshmallows." Feathers tilts her head.

Suma breathes in deeply. "Petra! Smoke!" She jumps up.

I get to my feet. We walk slowly to the edge of the grove. I take a step out from under the trees so I can scan the river again toward its source.

The twilight is calm but for another gust. I grip my obsidian pendant in my hand—and then I hear it. Lita's voice calling on the wind.

"You will be a great cuentista, Petra."

I look up at the moons to keep tears from pouring down my face. The smallest moon peeks over the shoulder of the larger one. I swear I see the outline of el Conejo on its surface.

Then, I smell it too. If I let myself hope, it will hurt too much. The smoke could be from a fire the First Arrivers started before the toxin was dropped.

But then . . . from the south, and the caves next to the waterfalls. It's only a few notes, but mixed with the soft rush of the wind and the smoke upon it, I hear . . . the strum of a distant guitar, and laughter.

Javier. The toxin in the lab. Could he have done it?

And suddenly I understand exactly what his last words meant.

"If this small part of my journey is to give everyone else a chance,

then that is what will make our parents and ancestors proud." He wasn't just talking about getting us off the ship. He was talking about saving *all* of those who survived the journey from Earth.

The music grows louder.

"What is that?" Rubio asks.

I blink, and the tears spill down my cheeks.

"That, is home."

. . . se acabó el cuento,
se lo llevó el viento
y se fue . . . por las estrellas adentro.

. . . this is the end of the story for me,
the wind carried it off far away into the stars.

ACKNOWLEDGMENTS

I am forever amazed and thankful for the people who support my writing and bring a steady flow of love, encouragement, and happiness into my life.

To my editor, Nick Thomas, for taking a chance on "this different kind of book I'm working on" and letting me flex my writing wings. You not only embraced it, but took those ideas way beyond my strange imagination. You have been a patient guide in helping me learn and navigate the publishing world. We did it again! Look at us!

Thanks to my dear agent, Allison Remcheck, for championing my ideas and believing in me and my stories. And for always asking, "What's next?" with genuine interest and enthusiasm. I am so grateful for your calm guidance and friendship.

Mom and Dad, I'm not sure how I was the fortunate one to end up with you as my parents. I hope I can live up to your example of humor, hard work, and kindness to all. Thank you for encouraging my, ahem . . . imaginative tales.

My husband, Mark. I am so grateful for your support in writing and all the feedback you gave me in creating this book. Thank you for a life filled with laughter.

My children, Elena, Sophia, Bethany, and Max. You are precious to me and inspire me daily in both life and writing. How lucky are we all to have each other!

Thank you to my grandmother, Mary Barba Matney Salgado Higuera. Your colorful stories wove their way through generations. Thank you for a childhood filled with magic, amazing food, and wild stories.

HUGE thanks to my critique group family, The Papercuts: Cindy Roberts, Mark Maciejewski, Maggie Adams, Eli Isenberg, David Colburn, Jason Hine, and Angie Lewis.

I love you all very much! Safe journey, Angie.

Thank you to Irene Vázquez who so early on read Petra's story and helped to make it better. Your editorial expertise was priceless!

To my agency family at Stimola Literary Studio: Rosemary Stimola, Peter Ryan, Allison Hellegers, Erica Rand Silverman, Adriana Stimola, and Nick Croce, and of course, my aforementioned agent, Allison Remcheck.

Thank you to my publishing family Levine Querido for being so supportive of my writing and books. Arthur A. Levine, you amaze me! Thank you for creating a warm and welcoming home for so many. And to the rest of the team: Publicity Manager, Alexandra Hernandez; Marketing Director, Antonio Gonzalez Cerna; and Assistant Editor, Meghan McCullough. You are one hardworking group! Thank you for all you do.

Raxenne Maniquiz. Wow! Thank you for creating what is

quite possibly the most beautiful cover in the history of literature. I wish you could hear the gasps each time I show someone the book. I could not have perceived more magical cover art that pulled the spirit of ancient folklore and futuristic space all in one. It's truly enchanting!

David Bowles. Thank you for your insight and assistance into the technicalities of Mexican folklore and Spanish language. Your brain, hermano!

HUGE thanks to Zoraida Córdova who read the very first infant version of Petra's story. Thank you for not only asking me the tough questions, but giving me tools to understand this character and the world I was placing her in. What a gift to have the opportunity to learn from you!

I would like to give a special thank you to Yuyi Morales for use of the Dreamers excerpt for this book. Your words are beyond beautiful and powerful.

Robert at Rockhound State Park. Thank you for your extreme patience in answering all my questions. You taught me a thing ore two about rocks. You're a gem!

Robert R: Thank you for talking sci-fi, rocket science and space with me, and helping me understand at least a bit how things do and don't work.

To Mandi Andrejka, thank you for catching errors and fixing details. How do you do that?!

The Society of Children's Book Writers and Illustrators (SCBWI): There is no way to extend enough gratitude for all you've given me during this journey. From my writing education, to dear friends, to my husband—you've introduced me to the best things in my life.

Thank you to Richard Oriolo for the brilliant interior design of this book.

To Leslie Cohen and Freesia Blizard in Production at Chronicle, thank you for making this book so beautiful.

And to all storytellers, editors, and those in the art of making books. Thank you for your contributions and hard work creating the most precious thing we take into the future.

ABOUT THE AUTHOR

Donna Barba Higuera grew up dodging dust devils in the oilfields of Central California and now lives in the Pacific Northwest. She has spent her entire life blending folklore with her experiences into stories that fill her imagination. Now she weaves them to write picture books and novels. Donna's first book, *Lupe Wong Won't Dance*, won a PNBA Book Award and a Pura Belpré Honor.

The Last Cuentista is her second novel.

SOME NOTES ON THIS BOOK'S PRODUCTION

The art for the jacket and case was created by Raxenne Maniquiz, who chose elements and a palette inspired by the story. Raxenne first drew sketches on paper, then used Adobe Photoshop for rendering the final artwork. The text and display were set by Richard Oriolo in Celestia Antiqua, a serif designed by US designer Mark van Bronkhorst, evoking the roughness and irregularity of pre-digital printing. The book was printed on FSC™-certified 98gsm Yunshidai Ivory paper and bound in China.

Production was supervised by Leslie Cohen and Freesia Blizard
Book jacket and case designed by Raxenne Maniquiz
Book interiors designed by Richard Oriolo
Edited by Nick Thomas